LIME

A Novel

by
Melda Beaty

ISBN: 1475090714
ISBN-13: 978-1475090710

To my 3 Z's

&

To women everywhere who were victims of domestic violence
but now empowered to never be victims again

Lime

Contemporary Women's Fiction

PROLOGUE

Without Your Permission

AJ's hospital room was frigid for the first day of spring in Chicago. The white walls, curtains, and linen gave it a ghost-like quality. Except for the steady beeps from the machines, it was dead silent. On the telly, Oprah pantomimed an interview with an elderly couple. I swallowed the lump in my throat before pulling back the white drapery that surrounded her. The sight of grayish black melted flesh on one side of her body forced me to bite my lip to silence the sounds of rage and sorrow that escalated inside. Her hospital gown covered most of the burns, but I could see where the flames had attacked her face, arm, hand, leg, and foot. The damaged skin began at her jaw, spread onto her shoulder, and the top of her left breast. Her left arm was nothing but blackened tissue that stopped midway on the back of her hand. Her left thigh and side of her leg were raw, and her foot was ten shades darker than before. AJ was sleeping, but her face made involuntary grimaces like clockwork. The oxygen mask that covered her mouth and nose exaggerated her breath with each exchange of air. I pulled up a chair, grabbed her right hand, and never took my eyes off my best friend.

In the midst of the deafening silence, I could clearly hear AJ's words of wisdom as we stood behind Zora Neale Hurston High thirteen years

ago. "Never let a man put his hands on you without *your* permission."
Those words served me well throughout the years; however, neither one of
us could have fathomed the horrifying day when she'd need to remember
them the most.

CHAPTER 1

Protection

The first time Angela Juanita Henning, aka AJ, came to my rescue was 1991. I was a thirteen-year-old high school freshman who had become the object of all female hatred.

"Who the hell is she?"

"She thinks she's fine, 'cause she's from Europe and got those green eyes and good hair."

"And she thinks she knows it all, too."

I had only been back in the United States for one month and all the girls rejected me before I had a chance to open my mouth. Whenever I did dare to speak, eyes rolled and attitudes were unleashed. They were ready to burn me at the stake for having an accent, green eyes, wavy hair, and for being intelligent. It was only a matter of time before the boys joined in.

James "Asshole" Armstrong was a lanky kid whose basketball palming hands took the liberty of smacking me on my bum with the precision and power of a professional tennis player. The smack echoed over the mechanical ritual of students slamming lockers on their way to fifth period classes. The sound halted every passerby in motion.

At first, James pretended to be my friend. I thought he was cute and welcomed all the flattering attention. I secretly hoped that maybe he would be my first American boyfriend. On the first day of Biology class, he volunteered to be my lab partner since I was the new student. However, everything changed the day I received an A on a lab report and James got a C-. From that moment on, James' mission in life was to harass only me.

The next day in school, the stage was set for James to take hitting practice on my bum yet again. Everything in me said to take a different route, but I knew I would never gain any respect in that school if I took the coward's way out, so I vowed I would just walk in clear view just in case someone had come to their senses from the day before and felt compelled to come to my aid. Never allowing my backside to cross his path, I could already see the same crowd gathering, anticipating another show. It was then I saw his calloused filled hand reach back behind his body like a slingshot, ready for the exact moment of release onto my bum. I shut my eyes tight and sped up, but this time instead of the deafening smack of yesterday, all that was heard was an agonizing "Ahhhhhhhhh!" coming from the ground behind me. The mob paused and when I opened my eyes and turned around, James was on his knees with his head down and his right shoulder and arm twisted so far back behind his body, it looked like he was praying.

AJ, a respected junior, towered over him with her right hand clasped tight on his outstretched arm and her left hand gripping his shoulder blade so hard you could see the blood fill her mahogany knuckles.

James somehow managed to release a falsetto, "Bitch, let me go."

"Now James, you know that's not my name."

And as if on cue, the bell rang, and the security guards approached. AJ dropped James from her damaging grip, stepped over him like spit on a sidewalk, and walked past me without even a glance.

After school, AJ stood cool and collected behind the school, leaning against the gate with some girls I recognized but didn't know. She was talking and dramatizing some event and the girls were doubled over gasping for breath from laughter. I talked myself out of approaching her several times, but I knew I had to thank her, or at least introduce myself. Five minutes turned into ten. I was already late for the informational meeting for track and field. Then one by one the girls began to leave until she stood against the gate all alone. I decided to make my move, but before I could speak, her words halted my steps.

"Hey. Never let a man put his hands on you without *your* permission."

Thirteen years from that very day at that gate, AJ and I have been inseparable.

—⁓—

7:15 AM sharp every morning from that day on the gate, I climbed the steep steps to AJ's second floor flat so AJ and I could take the bus to school together. I can't recall how many times Ms. Henning, a full-figured woman, would answer the door in beige bras, oversized panties, gold house shoes, pink foam curlers, and a Kool Mild Light cigarette dangling from her lips. Ms. Henning was busy getting ready for work at the post office, so putting on clothes just to open the door for me was not part of her daily routine. She was comfortable in her skin and basic attire. Embarrassment was a luxury she could not afford as she dressed for work.

As I took my usual place on the plastic wrapped couch in the living room, Ms. Henning would resume her breakfast of sausages, rice and nicotine at the kitchen table. Her offer was always the same.

"Have some breakfast, Lime?"

"Oh no thank you, I'll eat at school."

AJ would emerge ten minutes later rushing past Ms. Henning with a quick "bye mama." Ms. Henning would always grab her arm and turn her around for a final look over before tapping her finger on her cheek for a kiss.

"Behave yourself, and hey, be aware of your surroundings. I'll call at the usual time."

I was the constant voyeur spying and learning from this womanly community of two that I had adopted as my own. In their home and presence, I felt safe.

AJ and I were two refugees. I was abandoned in Europe and rescued back to United States. AJ and her mum were from Memphis, Tennessee fleeing to Chicago, Illinois on a Greyhound bus in the middle of the night. Ms. Henning had had enough of being Mr. Henning's sparring partner. The day AJ jumped on his back to help her mum, Mr. Henning flung her so hard across the room she hit the back of her head on the kitchen floor. Ms. Henning grabbed for the cast iron skillet on the stove and swung with all her might knocking him out cold. There were still pieces of hot water cornbread in the skillet. They've been protecting each other ever since and now AJ has chosen to protect me.

As AJ's new best friend, I went from being the school oddity to someone you knew not to mess with or else. Despite AJ's popularity and quick wit, we had more in common than what the eye could see. We were both the only child with only one parent. The unconditional love I received from living with my dad made up for Asmeret Amde's negligence, but no matter how hard he tried, it couldn't replace female guidance. So, I spent all my free time with AJ and Ms. Henning learning what girls needed to know. I just wish I could remember the exact moment when AJ and I both stopped learning.

CHAPTER 2

The Honeymoon Phase

Maybe it was when I met Rohan Saxton. The boys in high school were all like James; immature, sex crazed, and dumb. At university, I thought I had hit the jackpot. The guys were tall, handsome, and socially conscious of the world around them, but five minutes into a conversation they would forget my name and start to drool. Five minutes after that, they were inviting me back to their room under the guise of listening to some music or just to chill. And then there was Rohan. He was a slender, suave, dark chocolate senior who carried his trumpet in his backpack wherever he went. There was no question about it; Rohan could make a trumpet talk. He spotted me during one of my daily runs on campus. Rohan didn't approach me; he serenaded me with a song he wrote just for me. *Red Velvet* quickly became our song and according to him described my skin and slightly reddish brown hair.

"My girl, yo 'kin smooth like any little coco butter and yuh sweet like red velvet."

In my mind, he was a good Jamaican boy who wasn't as fascinated with my British accent as other guys, because he had a language of his own.

Patois sat heavy on his lips. When I decided to marry him, the year I graduated from university I figured my half-Jamaican dad would be pleased.

"Why so soon, Lime?"

"It's not soon, dad. I'm twenty and I finished university like I promised, plus he's Jamaican."

"Mi neva even see de mon before." When my dad started speaking Patois, I needed to be careful.

"Trust me dad, please"

I can't honestly say I was ready to get married. I had a job offer as a junior accountant at Boyd & Woods Accounting Firm, one of the largest in the Chicago area. In the entire accounting firm, there were only two women accountants, but Rohan had already left college to travel across the country in a dilapidated van with his best friend Pepper to play lead trumpet in smoky clubs in unheard of towns. He seemed ready to get off the road for a bit and settle down, but Ms. Henning forgot to tell me that it's a fine line between ready and impatience.

"Lime, mi a touch de road for a couple of weeks. Mek sure when mi come back, yuh ave mi food ready an your lovin a wait pon mi."

I knew with that statement he was going to be disappointed. What did I know about marriage at twenty? Let alone how to cook a good meal and we won't even mention good loving, but I conceded. Instead of a big wedding, Rohan only had time for the justice of the peace before the "road" called. AJ was my maiden of honor. Right before we went inside the room where I would become Mrs. Saxton, AJ leaned over to me.

"My car is right outside. You just say the word and we're gone."

"No, I'm okay, just a few butterflies. You know how I get."

"Lime, you know I support whatever you do, but you and I both know when you're lying. Again, my car is right outside."

I did my best to convince AJ that I'd be okay, but I knew she wasn't convinced. When she saw Rohan standing next to the magistrate in a pair of jeans and a tight fitting suit jacket, she eased her keys out of her purse and dangled them in my direction as a last ditch effort.

It wasn't three months after that day that Rohan started working all day and performing or practicing all night. Then the phone calls from Pepper started. There were gigs in New York that he couldn't miss, and if I dared to ask anything about all his travels, he snapped. Rohan only seemed interested in me in public. If his friends were taking their girlfriends or wives to some event, he wanted me there in the clothes he bought for me to wear. In a weird way, I believe his friend's flirting seemed to arouse him. He cared more about their opinions of me than my own. When he came home one day with a flyer from a modeling contest at McCormick Place, it was all about what Pepper said. Pepper said I could win the contest hands down. Pepper said think what we could do with all the money. Pepper said he would even give us the fifty dollar registration fee. ...*Pepper, Pepper, Pepper.* Rohan insisted that I get my dad to take some head shots of me. When the contest turned out to be phony, Rohan was done.

January 1, 2000. Rohan woke me up early in the morning and told me to get dressed. He had just come in from celebrating New Year's Eve in Chicago with his friends. I asked him where we were going, but he didn't answer. He just kept telling me to hurry up and get dressed. When we arrived at my dad's house, I figured maybe he and my dad had planned a New Year's Day breakfast for me, although I knew my dad hated getting up early on days he didn't have to open the studio. Rohan didn't look at me the entire time, although I searched his face for a clue as to what he was up to.

As we waited for my dad to answer the door in the freezing snow, I tried again, "Is dad expecting us?"

Rohan just rang the bell again, as Marley, my dad's chocolate lab, barked louder. My dad was not awake nor was he expecting company. His short, straight, reddish hair was all over his head and his robe was inside out. Rohan was standing in front of me when dad did open the door.

He was in the middle of yawn when he asked, "What's going on?"

With a straight face, Rohan replied, "Mi sai Prince, see hare ere, mi bring are back if yuh."

"What?" Dad and I said in unison.

"She a go be appier with yuh."

I moved to the other side of Rohan and looked at him as if he had two heads. "Rohan, what are you talking about?"

He ignored me and kept addressing my dad. "I check yuh later with are thing before mi touch the road fi the Big Apple tomorrow.

"Rohan, t'hell yuh talkin' 'bout?"

Dad asked in Patois, which meant one thing; he was pissed.

He grabbed my arm and pulled me inside out of the cold. Rohan was unfazed by the outburst and repeated that he would bring my things over later that afternoon.

"Bwoy, yuh got zero seconds to get t'hell off mi porch."

Rohan turned to leave. My dad slammed the door, and I stood there dazed, trying to process what just happened. In less than three minutes, my husband made a decision about my life in front of me without even acknowledging me. I waited for the part when I would awake in a state of panic, but it never happened.

CHAPTER 3

Highway to New Beginnings

It is only the first of June, 2001 and it is so bloody hot. This heat and humidity in Ohio is suffocating. The sun is filling every crevice of my Mazda Protégé. I love the yin and yang of the cool Freon air mixed with the humid breeze of the great outdoors against my skin, and since it is my turn to drive, I have driver's privilege. AJ insists it is a good waste of air conditioning, but after a few minutes of the same mixture against her moist skin, she fell asleep in her seat with her left chin nestled on her collar bone; her hands forgotten by her sides, and her feet crossed at her ankles sticking straight out of the passenger side window. Every time I hit a bump in the road, her feet obstruct the manufacturer's warning that "Objects in the mirror are closer than they appear."

I took the wheel forty-five miles shy of Cleveland, Ohio. We left Chicago at five o'clock in the morning. AJ drove the first leg, almost six hours straight through, because I stayed up all night packing and finalizing things with the modeling agency. In less than eight hours, my life as I've known it in the Windy City will be brand new.

—⁓—

I'll never forget that call from Mrs. Laylah Nassiri. I was sitting in my cubicle at work running my index finger down the center of my head. Ever since I was three, my trademark sign that I am either tired, bored, frustrated, or all three is to run my index finger down the center of my head. Since I was computing stats for our division's annual report, the message was clear. I was bored. I let the phone ring three times before I even looked up. I just didn't want to be bothered. With each ring, I made a game out of it. My finger competed to reach the nape of my neck before the ring ended. After losing three times, I lost interest. Kevin, my co-worker and good friend, gave me the evil eye after the third ring.

I lifted my head to answer the call only to see Faces Modeling Agency on the caller ID. I grabbed the receiver so fast that I said "Hello" into the wrong end of the phone.

"Yes...Is this Lime... Lime Prince?"

I took a deep breath to regain my composure. "Yes, yes, it is."

"Lime, this is Laylah Nassiri, with Faces Modeling Agency in New York. We received your photos and I must say dahling, you are eclectic in every way."

She seemed to be yelling into the phone as if she were talking over a bad connection. It was the first time in my life a woman had ever described me as eclectic, and I wasn't quite sure how to respond, so I chose to listen.

"Dahling, you still there?"

"Uh, yes, I'm still here."

"Well, when your photos arrived in my office I was *très* impressed, to say the least. You seem to be having a love affair with your photographer. By the way, who was your photographer? The inscription on the back of the photos says Apple of My Eye Photography."

For some reason, I didn't think saying 'my dad is a photographer' would go over well, so instead I whispered, "Malcolm."

"Does Malcolm have a last name? I know all the hottest photographers."

"He just calls himself Malcolm."

"Hmm, I think you and Mr. Malcolm have some chemistry going on."
She changed subjects like a New York minute. "Anyhoos, as I was saying,
we are going edgy this year; gone are the days of cute and pretty. America is
ready for unique, daring, and eclectic, and we feel you would be the perfect
poster model. What do you say to that?"

My pause was longer this time.

"You still with me dahling?"

"Yes, I am." She was talking a mile a minute.

"I can see you aren't much of a talker. Not to worry, no one takes pictures
of models talking or pay to hear them give speeches down the runway." She
let out a breathy yet faint chuckle. "So dahling, I'm going to fax you over
some information about our agency, but I'll tell you right now, New York is
ready for you. The million dollar question is are you ready for New York?"

I blurted out, "I'm not sure, but I will think about it," more out of
skepticism than anything rational.

"Oh, so not a talker, but a thinker. Well, don't think too long. We New
Yorkers move fast."

"Okay."

"Oh, another thing before I forget, the green contacts are yesterday.
Although, I must admit they add a mesmerizing *je ne sais quoi*, but dear,
you don't really need them. Like I said, you are mesmerizing enough,
plus—"

I had been defending the color of my eyes since I could talk, but I was
older now and just plain tired of the assumption, so this time I responded
before she could finish her final thought.

"Contacts? Did you say contacts, Mrs. Nassiri? I've never worn contacts a day in my life, and if you can find lime green contacts, I'm suing
someone for false impersonation."

She paused, so I figured the deal was off.

"Hmm, this puts a different spin on things, Ms. Prince. A different spin
indeed. Let's see . . . five-foot-eight, thirty-four, twenty-five, thirty-four,

size four, creamy mocha skin, reddish brown wavy hair, hint of British accent, legs as far as the eye can see, and a thinker with piercing authentic green…I mean lime green eyes. Ms. Prince, when can you come to New York?"

We chatted for another minute and no sooner had I hung up the phone, Kevin spun around, grabbed the back of my chair and in his best flamboyant voice, said "Girlfriend, we are going to New York!"

CHAPTER 4

The Journey

AJ is still enjoying her navigator's nap, so I turn the radio down low and set my phone to vibrate before placing it in the cup holder. Immediately, it begins to hum. By the time I answer it, I miss the call. It read: Missed Call WF. *Shit, that was the third call in less than 24 hours. What could be so pressing?* I'll call on our next stop.

I set the cruise control to seventy-five miles per hour. It is just enough of a breeze to remind me to pay attention and more than enough to tease AJ's skirt. As I speed up to pass another motorist, the breeze just can't take it anymore and with all the force it can muster, huffs and puffs and sneaks a quick peek. It tosses AJ's skirt back far enough to expose the only name brand panties she buys, JC Penney. AJ insists that Victoria's Secret has already been told, "We don't make lingerie for you, big girl." It's not that AJ is a big girl in the "that's enough food for you sense." Her upper body is slender with an athletic build, but the more your eyes travel south the more of AJ there is to see. She's thick with meaty hips, thighs, and calves. I believe the Commodores had AJ and Ms. Henning in mind when they composed their hit song *Brick House.* The Nefertiti tattoo on her inner right thigh that she got on her twenty-first birthday while on spring break in Atlanta, looks startled by the intrusion. As I reach over to restore privacy and order, AJ snorts and rotates her head with the grace of a drunkard. I decide to leave well enough alone.

I beat my palms in sync against the steering wheel to the unorthodox tunes of Zap Mama, and notice that I've devoured my second bag of Trail Mix. Since I've given up smoking, again, Trail Mix is my new guilty pleasure. We are going to have to make another stop soon.

I toss the empty bag aside on top of my cell phone, but the vibrations from the phone again make it topple onto the floor of the car on AJ's side. *Ugh,* I scream in my head. I rip the phone out of the cup holder, and flip it open ready to swear into the receiver, until I see the sweet image of the love of my life and his trusted sidekick, Marley, staring back at me.

"Hi dad." I let out a sigh of relief.

"Hey Apple. How's it going? Where are you all?"

He's been calling me Apple from the moment they first put me in his arms at the hospital, and he would have named me Apple, if Asmeret hadn't interfered in her usual condescending tone. It takes my dad to imitate her.

"Malcolm Edward Prince, Jr., who is going to respect a girl named Apple? Bloody hell, you might as well name her Lime like the color of her eyes."

He said that's when it clicked for him. He named me Lime Norene Prince. Norene in honor of his mum and who I inherited the color of my eyes. Since Asmeret was indifferent to him and me, dad said she waved her hand with a "whatever" motion, turned over in her hospital bed, and Lime was recorded on every document my dad could find.

"Somewhere in Ohio. We still have about seven more hours."

"Wha gwaan? Yuh say yuh gwine check me when unno ah leave." I can hear the anger and concern in his voice.

"Yes, I'm sorry dad. I slept the first few hours. AJ was kind enough to drive the first leg. We're fine dad; no worries. She is sleeping now, but I promise to call you again before we get to New York, okay?"

"Okay now, be sure to call and be careful Apple. I love you."

"I love you more."

AJ snorts and shifts in her seat all at the same time. I turn the volume back up just in time to hear Marie Daulne, the lead singer of Zap Mama, put the final touches on *Sweet Melody*, but no matter how loud I turn the music up, I can't quiet the doubts in my head.

Aside from years of posing in front of a camera for countless pictures for my dad and working in his studio; I knew every part of the camera from the shutter to the lens by the age of four and was developing film in darkrooms by five, but what do I know about modeling? I just don't see what others see when they look at me, or stare in my eyes, or smile when I talk. And what is this fascination with my ethnicity? Truth be told, I've never been comfortable with all the attention when I walk into a room or out having dinner at a restaurant. Asmeret reminded me every chance she got that I wasn't that pretty as she pinched my arms and legs and gripped my mouth shut so I wouldn't scream.

I don't know when society became obsessed with height and no curves. Unlike AJ, I have a hard time embracing any level of bodily comfort. I just can't understand after all of the pinches, why I don't have one blemish on my body recognizable to the human eye. No birthmarks, childhood scrapes, not even a paper cut; nothing that tells stories of a life of an active childhood or a clumsy woman—no physical flaws and no matter how long I search every inch of myself all I see is undamaged skin. Even my skin proves I'm not normal.

"You're not talking to yourself again?" AJ's eyes are still closed.

"Nooooo," I respond like someone caught drinking milk out of a carton. I didn't realize I was thinking out loud.

"To hell you weren't, 'cause I'm asleep." She tightens her face, smacks her lips, and opens her eyes one at a time trying to adjust to the sun's rays. "Where are we anyway?"

"Twenty miles outside of Youngstown."

"We're still in Ohio? Please tell me you didn't park this car and just start driving when I caught you talking to yourself."

"Uh, nooooooo, Ohio is a large state."

With one of her over-exaggerated yawns, she raises her arms over her head to touch the back of her headrest, and lets out a gas mask fart.

"Wow." All at once, I press the electronic buttons down to open the windows. "Not only is it too hot for that, but I think it's illegal in Ohio."

"Well, if you'd been driving a little faster, Ms. Daisy"— in her best Ebonics—"we's be out of Ohio by now and I's could fart alls I wonts to. Pull over at this rest area so I can pay this water bill."

I pull over. I need to stretch, get something to drink, and return this phone call. AJ goes ahead. I stay behind to do my runner's stretch for a few minutes before going in to buy some water from the vending machine. A portly man with sweat on his upper lip and even more sweat under his arms hovers over the vending machine. As I get closer, his eyes track me like radar. First he stares, and then he motions toward me as if his life depends on asking me a question.

"Pardon me."

When I put my money in the machine, his chewing tobacco breath comes closer. "'Scuse me, but I couldn't help but notice ya outside fo' ya come in. You a runnah?" His thick hillbilly accent is almost comical.

"Well, yes and no. I ran a lot of races years ago, but now I just run for pleasure."

"Awww, I can tell. You were stretchin' out there like a real runnah and ya sho' got the body fuh it." He starts to lick his thin, pink lips. "I'm a truck driver. That's my rig over yonder. The shiny silver one."

"Hmmm, it's nice." I ignore his initial comment and make my selection before he opens his sweaty mouth to ask me another trite question.

"Do I hare uh accent?"

Too late.

"You not from round hare, is ya?" His smile reveals a chipped front tooth.

"No, I'm afraid I'm not."

I began to think that AJ had to do more than "pay the water bill," and I wish she'd hurry up, so we can get the bloody hell out of here. As I turn to leave, he puts his fat knobby hand on my shoulder.

"Why ya leavin' so soon, sweetheart?"

AJ's prophetic words "never let a man put his hands on you without your permission," roar into my head like a loud speaker. Just as I turn around to knee him in his sweaty goolies, AJ casually knocks his hand off my shoulder and replaces it with hers.

"No dick needed here; we're just fine."

And to seal the deal, she plants a gentle and slow kiss on my cheek. We walk to the car arm-in-arm with AJ talking to me out the side of her mouth. "Get in the passenger seat." When I get into the car, Mr. Creepy comes outside to watch us and to rub his crotch. The way he smirked revealed more chipped rotting teeth. AJ speeds off and gives him the middle finger out the window.

"You and Fat Bastard were getting pretty chummy." She laughs.

"Whatever. If you hadn't taken all day to relieve yourself—"

"No, ma'am," she said in her classic southern style. "I don't rush dumps. They don't like that."

We both crack up laughing and start imitating the disgusting truck driver. She turns the music on and Zap Mama greets her with their melodious rendition of *Yelling Away*.

"What the hell?" AJ gasps.

"What? It's Zap Mama."

"Yo' Mama?! Girl, open my CD case. I'm so glad I came prepared."

She opens it to the exact spot she wants. Everything is categorized with tabs by her moods: "Get Your Groove On," "Chill Out," "I Need a Drink," "The Rage," "Praise the Lord," "You Don't Know Nothing About That," and "Hell Yeah." She flips straight to "Hell Yeah," and instructs me to play number three. In less than the time it takes to blink, the highway is filled with car shaking bass from Ludacris' *Move Bitch*. AJ gives me a fake elbow shove with the chorus, and says with Ludacris "New . . . York . . . Here . . . We . . . Come." Between Mr. Creepy and laughing with AJ, I forgot all about returning WF's call, but somehow I don't think WF did.

This journey to hit the road to New York City with my best friend is my first step in reclaiming back my life, and pursue what others have insisted since my youth, that I, Lime Prince, could be a Supermodel.

CHAPTER 5

Waterfall

After listening to every disc in the "Hell Yeah" category, AJ gets the urge for some love making music from the "Get Your Groove On" selections. God knows my ear drums need a break. I rub my index finger down the center of my scalp as Luther Vandross cradles me with his silky ballet of *A House is Not a Home.* Just as AJ starts her own version, I turn the volume way up. On this warm night, I am only in the mood for Luther.

As we cross the Ohio/Pennsylvania border, an old Chevy Impala passes us. The woman is sitting so close under the male driver, they almost meld into one. As Luther serenades us, I lean the seat farther back and wonder what makes a woman want to be that close to her man, or to anyone at all.

After Rohan, I just couldn't seem to connect with any man. The few dates I had were always spent answering one annoying question after another about my looks, my parents, and even my favorite sexual positions. Maybe I feel for my dad what that woman in that Impala feels for her man, a tangible sense of comfort.

AJ taps me on the shoulder. "I'm hungry."

"What would you like?" I didn't realize I had dozed off.

She licks and smacks her lips while reciting a list of desired entrees with the intensity of an orgasm. "Mmm, some smothered pork chops, fried catfish, lightly seasoned, fried corn, fried sweet potatoes with a sprinkle of powdered sugar, some mustard and turnips, hot buttered biscuits, and a big piece of punch cake for dessert."

That menu proves that AJ and I are from two different sides of the world. Her lingering southern roots always surface when it comes to food. I much prefer my vegetarian lifestyle.

"One set of clogged arteries coming up." I let the seat back even farther to continue my nap.

"What's up Lime? You're not getting cold feet?"

"Oh, hell no. Chicago has run its course for me." I take a deep breath before exhaling, "Rohan."

The thought of Rohan makes AJ so mad she swerves the car over the dividing line, as she looks at me and shouts, "That nigga!" The car in her blind spot blows its horn even after they speed up. She barely misses hitting it. She regains control again and remembers. "Oh shit, he lives in New York now. You're not afraid, are you?"

"No, but since I've discovered peace of mind without Rohan, I realize that I like it a whole bloody hell of a lot better than Rohan, if you know what I mean. Plus, the thought of him brings up those things from the past that I just want to forget."

"And you have."

"But it hasn't forgotten me. I've gotten five calls since we left Chicago."

"What does she want now?"

"I don't know, but I'm at the point where I would gladly pay her to go away."

"To hell you will. Listen babe, Rohan, strippers, lies, drama, Pepper . . . all of that is in the past. New York is your future now, okay?"

The next song in AJ's "Get Your Groove On" collection comes on and interrupts the tension that was created in the car with the mere mention of Rohan's name. He is one of my main reservations about moving to New York, because he moved there in January, a month before the divorce papers arrived at my dad's house. Rohan was sharing an apartment in Brooklyn with his best friend Pepper.

As *Freak Me* plays, I massage my temples and try to block Rohan, WF, and the night I first heard this song from my mind. Damn, I need a smoke. What was I thinking that night when I agreed to spice things up with Rohan?

—ɯ—

"How is it dat such a pretty gaal is as ugly inna di bed?"

He would repeat these words after each awkward attempt to make love to me. Sex with him was always passionless and unfulfilling, and continued that way until we were rarely having sex at all. Every chance he got, he criticized me for not being more adventurous until that night he took me to the Back Room and brought WF into our lives.

Instead of driving straight home after a night at the movies, somehow our car headed south on I-294. "Me jus waan check dis spot fi a likkle while."

I figured it was some jazz club or something that had to do with his trumpet playing. We exited at Harvey, Illinois about forty minutes south of where we lived, turned down one dark alley after another until we coasted onto a gravel parking lot full of humongous semi-trucks. The electric blue neon sign on the gray building with black tinted windows flashed the Back Room. As we got out of the car and headed inside, I noticed the two OO's in the word "room" weren't alphabets, but neon breasts with exaggerated nipples that flashed on and off. Rohan was grinning from ear to ear as he opened the door to let me in. *What type of jazz club was this?* I wondered.

The nicotine smoke was our official greeter. The plump white woman behind the counter sported a greasy ponytail, a faded Harley Davidson

T-shirt, and black leather pants. She winked at Rohan as she took his $20 for admission. I asked him how they knew each other and he just shrugged his shoulders. He held my hand and led me down a long red corridor with dim red lights. A man on a microphone was shouting above the music as he announced names like Angel, Diamond, Gemini, and Destiny. The music was getting louder and Rohan was running while pulling my arm when the DJ said, "And on stage one, you don't want to miss your chance to get wet by Ms. Waterfall."

We made it just in time to see a woman wearing a thin black bikini thong right below a small navel ring with a long sleeved black halter top. Her black Mardi Gras mask covered her nose, but not her eyes. With her five inch glass heeled stilettos, she switched her hips upon a raised stage. Her muscular body and smooth tan skin were the second things you noticed after a picturesque waterfall tattoo that covered her entire lower back. The running water seemed to pour right into the crack of her bum.

When she pulled out her whip and snapped it in the air, every man in the place, and a few women, rushed to the stage and did whatever she instructed, Rohan included. Rohan pulled a wad of singles out of his pocket and held them in the air three at a time. She slid up and down that gold pole with the leather whip clenched between her teeth stopping and twirling at will. She came down and landed on the stage spread eagle and made her way around to all her salivating fans, giving personal attention to everyone who flashed cash her way.

I kept thinking, what in the world was I doing here and why was I watching some woman grab money from my husband's hand with her breasts? Rohan said something in her ear and she looked over at me and smiled as if he had just disclosed some juicy secret about me.

When Waterfall's time was up, most people returned to their seats with a slight look of disappointment, while others stayed for a less than acrobatic performance by Diamond. We took a seat at a small table with two bar stools and Rohan ordered a few drinks.

"Yuh feel alright?" Rohan asked, looking all around the room instead of looking at me before I could answer.

I lowered my head and voice so no one would hear me. "I had no idea we were going to a strip club."

"A wha di problem? Lots of couples dem go a di strip club to-gedda. They fun, an yuh always a sey mi nah tek yuh nowhere."

Who was he kidding? The Back Room was his idea of fun, not mine, and it was obvious that he frequented the place often. I didn't want to make a scene above the loud music, so I said as calm as I could, "I just feel a bit uncomfortable."

"Cool out, yuh wid mi. Jus try an enjoy—"

"Ready?" It was Waterfall.

She snuck up from behind us and rubbed her hand along Rohan's shoulders as she turned to face us. She wasn't wearing the black mask and her angular features and pearly white teeth made anyone look twice. She was striking, and I dare say, sexy. She looked at me and introduced herself right away.

"Hi, I'm Waterfall, and you are breathtaking."

Her voice was softer than I imagined as she ran her tongue along her top lip, and that is when the metallic ring in the center of her tongue came into full view. I said "Hi" and Rohan leaned over and whispered in my ear that Waterfall wanted to dance for us in the back room.

"What the bloody hell does that mean?" I asked. My annoyance was showing.

"Come and find out," Waterfall answered for him. She grabbed my hand, then Rohans', and led the way.

There were several back rooms with soft, red, high backed leather chairs big enough for two. A linebacker looking black guy with a wireless earpiece stood guard. Waterfall handed him a ticket and he held the red curtains open to let us in. He almost broke his neck following me into the room with his eyes. Before he closed the door, I heard him say

"Lucky bastard" in Rohan's direction. Waterfall escorted me to the chair first, and then Rohan, but once the music began, Rohan moved away from me, and turned his body to face me. I figured maybe Waterfall would be sitting between us, but before I could move down myself, Waterfall was swaying her hips to the beat of the music right in front of me. Every movement of her body was choreographed to some up-tempo beat. It was obvious she had some professional training, but why she chose to waste it on dancing for overzealous drunk blokes in strip clubs remains a mystery to me. After about three minutes, the music stopped and on cue she dropped down into a full Chinese split. I figured the dance was over and began clapping just to be courteous as I stood to get ready to leave.

"Wait dey mon. She 'ave anather song fi sing."

Rohan was just too bloody familiar with this woman and I still couldn't figure out why he had to sit apart from me to watch her dance. I sat back down and some group began to repeat the lyrics "Let me lick you up and down until you say stop." Waterfall's movements became snake like and she was slithering up my legs and right into my cobbler. I closed them on instinct and waited for Rohan to do something. He never took his eyes off Waterfall and the way he was sitting you could clearly see his willy was enjoying the view.

Finally she stood up, untied her halter top, and let her surgically altered breasts out for some air. She turned her back to me; squatted on my lap, and leaned back on me in the time it takes you to blink. She was grinding her hips into my pelvis so hard; I thought for sure a small fire would ignite. I sat there motionless until Waterfall took my hands and placed them on her muscular thighs. Everything in me said to push her off and get out of there, but I knew I would never hear the end of it from Rohan. This just wasn't my idea of fun, nor was I the slightest bit aroused. Waterfall was talented at what she did, and I could see why men fell over themselves to throw money at her, but I wasn't the right audience.

When it was over, she kissed me on the cheek and panted in my ear that she would dance for me anytime and anyplace. All I could muster was a half smile. Rohan kissed her on the cheek and thanked her as he slipped an extra $10 in her hand. For the rest of the night, he followed Waterfall to every stage where she performed. I didn't move from the table unless I had to use the loo.

Rohan came back to the table, puffing on a pipe tobacco cigar. He offered me the cigar. Rohan introduced me to smoking on our wedding night. He convinced me that they would relax me, and that it wasn't really like smoking cigarettes because these cigars came in flavors. The problem was sometimes Rohan's flavors were herbal.

"Mi ah wonder whe yuh de. Tawt dat perhaps yuh and Waterfall guh fe a nudda dance wid out mi." He sucked his bottom lip and raised his eyebrows hoping I would affirm his perverted fantasy.

"Hardly. I went to the loo. Look, Rohan, I would like to go home."

"Dat's why mi nah tek yuh nowhere. It always sometin wid yuh, Lime."

He grabbed his jacket and walked out ahead of me. I hoped that was the end of strip clubs and strippers, but Rohan and his slimy best friend Pepper had other plans. Almost two years later, my pictures arrived on Mrs. Laylah Nassiri's desk at Faces Modeling Agency in New York City, but I didn't expect that fate would also hand me back to Rohan.

CHAPTER 6

There's More to It

"Ooooo, this is my jam." AJ rolls her shoulder blades backward one at a time as she bounces in her seat. "Girl, remember how my mama would play this song right after one of her 'men ain't shit' lectures."

Although, I never knew the name of the song, I never forgot Ms. Henning's talks. Maxine Henning talked to AJ and I like grown women. She would often tell us that a man who truly loves you will "move heaven and earth" for you. Her eyes would light up every time she made that statement followed by a couple of swigs of Corona beer. I knew she was reminiscing about happier times with AJ's dad, before the fighting. She would often drink about three or four beers each time she lectured us on love or sex as if the memories needed a chaser.

"I don't know about the 'men ain't shit' part, but I do remember her talks."

"That's because you practically sat at her feet like Mary did Jesus."

"Well at least someone listened."

"What's that suppose to mean?" AJ shoots me a quizzical look.

"I'm just saying my cobbler went untouched for twenty years."

Whenever Ms. Henning would talk to us about sex, she would compare a woman's vagina to her famous peach cobbler.

"And you think that had something to do with mama's speeches? Chile please, you chose running over sex."

She was right. Running was the only valuable thing I learned from my mum.

AJ let her shoulders relax and shrunk down in the driver's seat a little as her mind reflected on her deceased mum.

"Mama would always wait until she was good and full and just when we were lying on the floor about to watch TV, she had to interrupt us."

AJ puts two fingers together on her right hand and presses the fingertips to her lips pretending to inhale the nicotine from her mum's favorite pack of Kool cigarettes. She let out a slow release of air toward the ceiling of the car just like Ms. Henning used to do careful not to blow all the second-hand smoke directly on us.

In her mum's signature raspy voice, AJ squint her eyes and imitates one of her mum's infamous speeches.

"Look, I know your cobblers get hot and bothered, and these little niggas look good, sound good, and smell good," AJ waves her fingers around still holding the imaginary cigarette, "but the minute you give it up to them is the minute you start giving it up to everyone. Respect doesn't come from sex. It comes from—" I can't help but chime in. "Keeping your dress down and your panties up."

We slap high-fives and laugh so hard, I start choking. I look through my purse for the water bottle I purchased at the vending machine. The text message tone on my phone let me know I had texts all from Waterfall. As I read them, all choking and laughter cease. *U can't avoid me 4ever...'member I was at your house.*" The last one was in all caps *SOMEONE IS GOING TO PAY ME MY MONEY.* I swallow hard and wipe my brow. I truly need a smoke.

"Lime what's up?" AJ can tell something is wrong.

"Now she's threatening me."

"Threatening? Girl, give me that phone." AJ grabs the phone and reads the texts while watching the road. "Call her back right now. She needs to be threatening Rohan's ass not yours."

"She claims they owe her money and since they didn't pay her she wants me to."

"Why is she contacting you now? That happened years ago."

I shrug my shoulders and turn my head toward the window and roll it down. I need to relax the tightness in my chest and lungs with fresh air. Plus I know if I look at AJ, she will see the deceit in my eyes.

Against my better judgment, I kept in touch with Waterfall after that night. Rohan and Pepper promised her $1000 to make some video. Instead of paying her, they both skipped town and gave her my cell phone number instead. In addition to being a stripper, Waterfall is a single mum and in some kind of financial trouble. She was desperate when she agreed to make the video. I guess I felt sorry for her, but I knew AJ would not approve, so I kept my communication with Waterfall from her all this time.

"Well, that's just too damn bad. You don't live in Chicago anymore so she can step off. And if she keeps calling change your number or do like I do when I don't want to be bothered, answer it like you don't speak English."

I want to laugh, but I am not used to this type of stalking and don't quite know how to handle it. Maybe AJ is right. Chicago is my past now and that includes Waterfall and Rohan.

CHAPTER 7

The Strangest Places

AJ pulls up to Cracker Barrel in Bloomsburg, Pennsylvania and announces, "White folks soul food will have to do."

It is seven o'clock in the evening, and the dinner crowd is forming. AJ and I both head straight for the loo. I splash cold water on my face and hair to wake myself up, while AJ squats over the first available toilet. As I stare in the mirror, I can't help but wonder if I've made the right decision leaving everything to follow other people's dreams for me. *Is modeling truly for me? Am I being too naïve? Will it change me? I'm only twenty-three.*

"Is that me or you, babe?" AJ sniffs under her arms.

After driving for almost thirteen hours, through three different states in the blazing sun and muggy night, someone was bound to be a little smelly. I whip my deodorant out of my bag; a habit from my days of running along Chicago's lake front after work with Kevin. I apply a little just to be safe, and then hand it to AJ as an extra measure.

There is a twenty minute wait to be seated, so I decide to step away and call my dad. I haven't spoken to him since he called while we were still in Ohio.

After one ring, he picks up. "Apple?"

"Hi dad. We're in Pennsylvania, about two hundred fifty miles from New York."

"I tried calling." After those texts from Waterfall, I turned my phone off and forgot to turn it back on.

"I'm sorry, dad. I was trying to get some sleep."

"You know I get a little crazy when you don't answer your phone."

I let out a sigh. "I know."

"Wha gwan, Apple?" He has the instincts of a mum, which always makes hiding anything from him impossible.

I take another deep breath. "Nothing, I . . . I just don't know, Dad."

"Know what?"

"What I'm doing." I fight back the tears.

"Then come home. I told you, you are already the most beautiful woman in the world. You don't have to go all the way to New York to prove it."

"That's not why I'm going. I feel like I have to do this, you know for me . . . for all the years I wasted doing what was safe: marriage, that monotonous job, living with you. I just don't feel as if I've ever lived life."

"Then what are you confused about?"

With my tongue, I catch tears from the corners of my mouth before I whisper, "living life."

The hostess announces, "The Hoes, party of two," and I know it's us by the silly grin on AJ's face. I forgot about our restaurant game of giving the hostess some derogatory name and then not answering until they have to say the name out loud at least twice. The hostess is always reluctant and everyone else is embarrassed, but curious as to who has the name, vagina, hoochie, or tonight, hoes. We always give the names with straight faces, and answer with confidence. I wasn't prepared for it this time, but I need the laugh.

I tell dad that I'll be alright and that I'll be sure to call him as soon as we get to New York. His heavy sigh breaks my heart. I shut my phone and hurry to the front before they cancel our seats and to save the hostess from further embarrassment.

"Who was that?"

"My dad."

"Oooo, how *is* your fine ass daddy?"

AJ holds the record for having the longest crush on someone twice her age. She and Ms. Henning always said my dad reminded them of a younger Smokey Robinson. To this day, AJ swears that before this life is over, I will refer to her as step-mum.

"He's concerned as usual about our safety, but otherwise he's fine." I don't feel like rehashing what I am feeling. I just want to eat my doubts away.

"I did some homework on Faces and Mrs. Nassiri. Girlfriend is well connected in New York City and abroad." She grabs my shoulder and says, "I knew there was something special about you from the moment I saved your ass, literally, from James Armstrong."

"Whatever," I respond, unfolding my napkin onto my lap. "I haven't made it yet. We'll see what happens."

"See, that's the problem, Lime, you have to believe that you *have* made it already. Hell, you got this far."

"All I really know how to do is to pose in front of a camera. I don't know how to walk like a model."

AJ waves her hand in the air, from behind the menu, as if shooing away a fly. "Formality."

It doesn't surprise me that AJ has done her own investigating about Faces. It's the "lawyer-to-be" in her. Her LSAT scores got her offers from the top law schools in the country: Harvard, Yale, University of Chicago, Northwestern University, Georgetown, and Stanford. She decided on Northwestern, and in eight weeks, my best friend will be a first year law student, and that much closer to her dream of becoming the first black woman Supreme Court Justice.

As we finish our meals and compare life in Chicago and New York, our waiter interrupts us. "Excuse me ladies, but the gentlemen over there would like to pay for your meals."

AJ doesn't hesitate to accept the offer. "Well alright," without even looking to see who the "gentlemen" are.

"Hold on, AJ," I say, turning to look in their direction. Three state troopers across the room raise their glasses at us and smile.

AJ picks up her half-empty glass of Pepsi and raises it back. She clenches her mouth in a fake smile and reprimands me. "Now what have I told you about turning down a free meal? It's rude."

I raise my glass in their direction as well, clenching my teeth, and talk back to AJ through my fake smile. "'Free' being the operative word, AJ."

"We have to go over there and thank them."

"Oh, no, *we* don't. I'm not accepting that."

"Okay, give the waiter your—" She grabs the menu and starts to compute my total and then gets frustrated.

"Hell, you're the accountant, figure it out and don't forget a tip. I'm going over there to thank them and tell them you said chivalry is dead."

She gets up and sashays over to their table. I sit for a moment, running my index finger down the center of my head. I decide to go to the loo again before we get back on the road. We have about three more hours before we reach Manhattan, and I don't want to have to stop.

When I return, AJ is sitting back at our table with her hand over her mouth, laughing to herself, and shaking her head.

"What's wrong?"

"You ain't gonna believe me."

"Believe what?" I sit back down and try not to sound too uninterested. "They changed their minds?"

"Uh, no, they're still paying, at least for me, but . . . just come over there with me, Lime."

"Why? We need to get going."

"Babe, New York called while you were in the bathroom, and they said they'll still be there whenever you arrive." She grabs my wrist and drags me over to their table.

Like perfect gentlemen, two of them stand up when I arrive, but the other sits there with his back to me and his head down. AJ drags me around to the other side of the table to face the one without any manners. As he lifts his head, my mouth drops. After ten years, I am back in the presence of the man I despise almost as much as Rohan. James Armstrong is not only staring me in the face, but offering to buy my dinner.

AJ breaks the silence by making the introductions. "Lime, this is Officer Ervin Wilson, Officer David Hollins, and none other than *Officer* James Armstrong." By the way AJ said his name, I could tell she'd already "read him his rights."

He stands, grabs my hand, cups his over mine, and looks me in the eyes with the most pitiful look. For a moment, it looks like he is going to propose, but instead he says with conviction, "Lime Prince, I am *so* sorry."

We stay for another hour talking about everything from high school days to our present lives. After high school, James went to Howard University on a basketball scholarship. He had a tryout with the Philadelphia 76'ers and played for one season before he got cut. He got married and has two children, but today he and his wife are separated. Now, he's a state trooper for the state of Pennsylvania.

As AJ entertains his partners, James seems engrossed by me. He keeps apologizing and blaming his high school antics on the fact that he was in love with me, and because he was such an "immature punk" back then, he didn't know how to tell me.

"Thank God you didn't hate me or I might be dead by now." He gets a real kick out of that.

"My partners and I noticed both of you right away when you got out of your car and I told them you looked like someone I dated."

That was a lie.

Officer Wilson is married, but Officer Hollins had his eye on AJ the whole time. AJ tells them we are heading to New York, and that seems to excite James for some reason. I guess in his mind, he thinks that now is his chance to make a better impression on me. I don't have the heart to tell him he is wasting his time, because starting a new relationship and a modeling career is nowhere on my schedule. AJ would have said I was being rude, so instead I let him drool over me, and pay for my meal.

Soon, I give AJ the let's-get-the-hell-out-of-here look. She is having a good time flirting with Officer Hollins. She puts his number in her phone and promises to call. James walks us out to our car, gives me his card, and writes his home and cell phone numbers on the back.

"Feel free to call me anytime, day or night." After a bear hug and a kiss on my hand, he gives us a shorter route to New York that saves us about forty-five minutes. Before I pull off, he salutes AJ with the respect of a private addressing a lieutenant.

"Angela."

AJ gives him a nod as if to say, "I'm watching you." He rubs his right hand under my chin and in his most seductive voice says, "Gorgeous. Absolutely gorgeous," and tells us to be careful.

We both respond "We will," in unison and pull off. We reminisce and joke about James and the irony of life all the way down route seventy-eight, next stop New York City.

CHAPTER 8

The Big Apple

Central Park, Times Square, Rockefeller Center, and delis on every corner. It's our first time in the Big Apple and we are like kids in a candy shop. We arrive late Thursday evening. I'm not scheduled to meet with Mrs. Nassiri until Monday morning, so we decide to spend the weekend being real New York City tourists.

Mrs. Nassiri found me an apartment and even paid the first month's rent. She also offered to help me find a part-time job as a waitress or receptionist until I am doing enough modeling to be able to do it full-time. I saved up quite a bit of money from working as a junior accountant and from living with my dad rent free, to not have to work for at least a year. So, I decline the offer.

We sleep until noon on Friday. We were exhausted from the drive, but AJ wakes up ready to hit the streets. "Let's get this party started," is my wake up call. For two days, we ride the subways from Manhattan to Queens. In Harlem, we dine at Sylvia's, take pictures outside of the Apollo Theater, visit the museums, and see a movie at the Magic Johnson Theater. In Brooklyn, we get $10 manicures and pedicures, and eat at

The Promenade. We shop all day in Soho and see our first Broadway show.

After brunch together on Sunday, I ride the subway with AJ to LaGuardia Airport. The half-empty trains only intensify the unspoken energy between us. At this moment, words are poor tools to describe what we are thinking and what our hearts are accepting. I stay by her side until her boarding number is called.

"Well, babe, this is it."

My eyes fill with water. I am excited about a new life, yet inside I am terrified being here without her presence and protection. She erased the loneliness after Rohan and even when we were married. I don't want or need any more loneliness in my life.

"Yup, this is it." My voice is barely audible.

She wipes one of my tears away, "Now you know how we do. I'm just a phone call and a plane ride away." I nod and wipe the other tear away. She stretches out her arms and says in her southern way, "Now give mama some suga."

We kiss on the cheek, and I hug her as if my life depends on it. Before, I let her go, I whisper in her ear, "Thank you for everything." She smiles and winks at me, grabs her carry on, and heads down the long corridor to board her plane. I stare out the window until the airplane carrying my best friend disappears into the clear blue sky.

On the subway ride back, I stroll down the aisle and take a seat in the rear of the train in case I feel another urge to cry. I doze off, thinking about all the good in my life and what I am leaving behind, and the only things I can really think of are my dad and AJ.

When I awake two stops before mine, I am staring into the face of a total stranger. A wide-eyed black man wearing too much clothing for a hot June day is holding a magazine pointing in my direction. He stares at me as if he were counting the minutes until I awake. As soon as my eyes meet his, he stands up and falls against the seats from the shaky movements of the train as he makes his way over to me. He plops down right across from me and leans forward. The heat and aroma of his breath make me lean back.

"I don't normally do this, but is this you?"

He shows me a picture of a half-naked model cupping her breast, wearing a pair of Donna Karan panties. The model has a milky complexion, and although we have the similar hair texture, length and shape, she can easily pass for a white woman.

I was warned New Yorkers can be hostile if provoked, so I respond as politely as I can "No, I'm sorry it's not me."

"Oh, 'cause I couldn't really tell, 'cause you were sleeping, but now that I look at you, shit, she don't have your eyes." I look away. "I mean you fine as hell." Now his voice was louder than the sound of the moving train and his breath was even more pungent than before. "I ain't never seen no one with green eyes like yours." The other passengers don't even look in our direction.

I stand as the train approaches my stop and also to get away from him. I say thank you, and as I exit the train, he yells at the top of his lungs, "Yo, can I get yo number?" I pretend not to hear him, and wonder where is AJ when I need her.

It is only four o'clock in the afternoon when I return to the apartment, and the sun's heat is subsiding. I need to think and running is always how I do my best thinking. I decide to head for Central Park. I change into a tank top and a pair of running shorts, lace up my Mizuno's, grab my CD player and Ms. Jill Scott, and head uptown. There are walkers and runners, women pushing strollers with smiling babies and sleeping babies, people reading on park benches, teenage boys playing hack-n-sack on the grass, and couples stretched out side-by-side or under each other on a blanket. The park is alive. I find a tree to begin my stretches. I put my headphones on my ears, press play, and Ms. Jill and I run six miles through a bustling and picturesque Central Park.

I can't believe that a couple of days ago, I was packing up my life and now I am running through one of the most famous parks in the United States. My life has been a series of solo transitions, so why should this move to New York be any different? Jill Scott understands as she reassures me that, *One is the Magic Number* in my ears. As I pass another runner looking down at his watch, I realize I am supposed to call my dad.

CHAPTER 9

Boss Lady

My first meeting with Mrs. Nassiri is first thing Monday morning. I have no idea what to wear, what to expect, or what she looks like. After forty-five minutes trying on different outfits, I settle on a handmade Native American summer dress that I bought at Lake Geneva on my over-due honeymoon, since Rohan was in LA performing the day after we got married. The powder blue dress with a kaleidoscope array of beige, mint green and yellow colors makes me feel good. I choose a cute pair of beige open toe sandals with a wide, wooden heel. Since, I'm wearing my hair in a short bob these days that stops at the tip of my earlobes; I don't have to spend a lot of time styling it. My maternal grandmother, Grandmother Genet, gave me some Ethiopian jewelry the day I left England to return to the United States. The colors in the Imperial Coins Bloodstone necklace, bracelet and earrings, compliment the colors in my dress. I feel her spirit with them on and recite a small prayer for her before I head out the door.

I take the express train to Mrs. Nassiri's office located on Lexington Avenue in the heart of New York's business district. Although it is still early June, and the weather is a balmy eighty-eight degrees, black, blue, and brown are still the colors of the day. Men and women march down Lexington Avenue in high powered designer suits, stilettos, and matching briefcases. The pace of the crowd moves so fast, I have to step off the sidewalk to find the building before I became a permanent piece of it by the moving herd.

Faces Modeling Agency is on the eighteenth floor. The ride in the elevator is a bit uncomfortable, but as soon as I enter, one man from the back of the crowded elevator shouts, "Push 18 for the lady." More well-dressed white men in suits and briefcases peer at me out of the corners of their eyes while white women strain to lift the corners of their mouths, in a half smile, in my direction.

It's like everyone is exiting one floor at a time. When eighteen finally lights up, I look at my phone and notice I'm ten minutes early. The receptionist informs me that Mrs. Nassiri is running behind and offers me coffee while I wait. My palate hasn't quite acquired the taste of coffee in the United States. My grandparents own Addis Ababa Grocery Store/Café in Brixton, so in addition to feasting on Doro Wat, Shiro, Injera bread, tropical fruits, fresh vegetables, and *Dobo Kolo,* nothing went better with those delicacies than Ethiopian Harrar Coffee or spiced teas. I just ask for the next best thing; my favorite flavor of Ginger Peach tea.

The office is bright with cobalt blue plush carpeting and silver signage everywhere. The walls are covered with life like pictures of the models Faces represent. I recognize Elle McPherson, Iman, and my Ethiopian kinsman, Liya Kebede right away. My mum's sisters always said I was going to be the next Liya Kebede. Somehow that comparison never motivated me, because at that time I had no knowledge of the modeling world or any inclination to be one. I wonder what they'd say if they were here with me now.

Everyone in the office walks past me without even a nod in my direction. It is a different scene from the "all-eyes-on-me" ride in the elevator. I skim through a few fashion magazines and drank my tea in silence. Soon nature calls. I ask the receptionist for directions to the loo. As I am just about to squat, two women come in snickering and talking to each other as they go into their respective stalls.

"Did you see the one out front in the lobby?"

"Oh yeah, pretty."

"Yeah, must be Laylah's. You know she's partial to them."

"Yeah, I know. She got Liya Kebede right?"

"Right. Well, you know Laylah's Persian, so I guess she feels some kind of *sisterhood* with them."

They both laugh and exit the stalls together. I wait until I hear complete silence before I come out. I wash my hands, and refresh my lipstick. It was Hurston High School all over again, but this time jealous teenage girls are Faces' modeling agents.

"Ms. Prince, Mrs. Nassiri is in her office now." The receptionist escorts me back to her office.

The receptionist knocks on the open door and Mrs. Nassiri reaches her left arm around her right shoulder and waves us in without turning around. I walk in without the receptionist and stand waiting for an invitation to be seated. She is standing with her back to the door, looking out her window while talking on a wireless headset. Her office is like a hotel suite. Everything is brown Italian leather. There is a mini couch, wet bar, and four gigantic windows that overlook Manhattan. Her brown jacket is thrown across her desk and I can see the Diane von Furstenberg tag. Her hair is jet black and straight, and hangs down well past her shoulders.

On her window ledge are two pictures in large glass frames. One captures a distinguished looking gentleman and a young girl about ten years old. They are all on a sailboat, wearing sailor caps. Another picture is of a beauty contest. I assume it is a younger Mrs. Nassiri with a red sash around her that reads "Ms. Iran." She is waving with one hand while holding a bouquet of red roses in her other hand. Her tiara is sitting off her head and she is surrounded by other contestants.

On her headset, she calls someone "dahling" and tells them to be patient. "We'll see you within the hour." When she turns around, she raises her thick eyebrows and as if satisfied, her expression relaxes. She motions for me to have a seat.

You can tell that she was a knockout back in the day just like in the picture. Her face is still fresh except for one or two crow's feet at her temples. Her eyes are dark like coal and her lips are full. She wasn't a petite woman anymore. The years seem to have added a few flattering pounds, but her attire packages it well. Her nails are perfectly manicured with French tips and her princess cut wedding ring has its own area code. Mrs. Nassiri is still gorgeous.

"Welcome to New York, Lime."

"Thank you. It's nice to finally meet you, Mrs. Nassiri."

"Call me Laylah. And why is that?"

Her question throws me. "Well, we've been talking on the phone for awhile so it's nice to put a face with a voice." I feel uncomfortable, and a bit flushed.

"Did you think we weren't going to meet?"

"No, not at all. It's just nice to finally meet."

"Yes, it is, dear. Yes, it is. Did you find the apartment satisfactory?"

I think about my answer before I respond in case she is setting me up for something. "It is cozy and convenient to everything, thank you."

"Good. Well, let's get started, dahling. People are waiting on you."

She begins talking a mile a minute again about the agency, explaining go-sees, photographers, and how my life is going to be one audition/open call after another.

"I've been in this business for over 15 years and only been wrong about a girl once, and depending on how fast you catch on will determine how fast you will rise to the top. With that said, I hope you have tough skin dahling, and take direction well, because although you are mesmerizing, only about one percent of 'mesmerizing faces,' become Supermodels. If you follow my lead, and do as I say, I'll keep my almost flawless record." She takes her first breath. "We have your first photo shoot in a half hour. It's with one of *the* best photographers around a personal friend of mine, Yanni, and I already know he's going to love you. We need to create your portfolio. This is no time to be camera shy, dahling, but after looking at the pictures you submitted, I don't think that you are. Any questions?"

Laylah talks so much and so fast, I am never quite sure when she was finished, so I hesitate before I respond to make sure. "No...no questions."

Just then, I think about the conversation I overheard in the loo and wonder if I should tell Laylah about it, or just ignore it altogether. The fact that women make snide comments about me is nothing new, but I can't help but wonder if Faces is going to be another Hurston High. As I shake my head to dismiss the thought, Laylah senses that something is wrong.

"Lime? Speak now or forever hold your peace."

Too late.

"Well, it's not really a question, just a comment."

"I'm listening."

"I overheard a conversation while I was in the loo right before meeting with you. Two women were discussing me, and you, for that matter. They said that I must be 'one of yours and that you are partial to *them*.'"

She sits back in her chair, peers into my face, and begins tapping her fingers, one at a time, on her desk, and then, as if she has figured it out, she presses the intercom button on her phone and the receptionist answers.

"Yes, Mrs. Nassiri."

"Ah, yes, Elmira, please tell Cindy and Alicia to meet me in my office now."

Laylah's entire demeanor goes from excited to evil in zero seconds. Her temples are bulging and the once subtle crow's feet around her eyes are now more defined. My heart is racing. *Is she going to make me confront them or ask me to point them out like suspects in a line up?* Instead of retracting my statement, I just face forward and try not to show too much emotion. I want Laylah to also respect me. Cindy and Alicia arrive together.

"Yes, Laylah, you wanted to see us?" They say unsuspecting.

"Right, give your accounts to Elmira and clean out your desks. And the next time you want to gossip about what I do and who I do it for, make sure you don't have that conversation in a bathroom stall."

I glance over my shoulder for a quick second and they both look at each other dumbfounded, and back out of the office with their mouths wide open. Once Laylah exhales the tightness in her chest, she looks at me sideways, and asks, "Any more *comments?*"

CHAPTER 10

Adonis

Laylah makes cell phone call after cell phone call during the ride over to the photo shoot. It's amazing what you can learn about a person from eavesdropping on their phone conversations. In twenty minutes, Laylah handles business, schedules and reschedules meetings, and directs her driver, all while on the phone. According to AJ, Laylah doesn't own Faces Modeling Agency, but she is the CEO and is solely responsible for signing Elle McPherson, Liya Kebede, and Giselle Bundchen. She has also launched the careers of several Supermodels overseas. In a nutshell, Laylah is the breadwinner for Faces and everyone in the modeling world knows her and respects her.

When we arrive at the spacious studio, I feel like I am back at Apple of My Eye Photography with my dad, except for the elaborate fluorescent and strobe lights, shutters, backdrops, tents, and people bustling everywhere. Although, dad has similar equipment, it is usually just the two of us doing all the work. Laylah tiptoes behind a muscle backed, dark haired guy sporting a full ponytail that hovers just above the nape of his neck. He and another guy are leaning over a light box examining some negatives with a loupe. Laylah puts her right hand over his eyes. Without as much as a twitch or pause, he says, "You're late."

"Ah dahling, you know New York traffic is a bear. Be nice. I have something for you."

She motions for me to come over. He scrutinizes the negatives for another fifteen seconds, before he says, "She better be good."

Laylah pauses and hands me to him like an unexpected Christmas present. "No dahling, she's mesmerizing."

He lifts his head and turns around and our eyes lock onto each other. A camera dangles around his neck over a tight black T-shirt that hugs a protruding six pack with the words, "Point and Shoot," in white letters. His skin is pure olive and his eyes are the color of brown sugar. I am witnessing Greek mythology in the making. Adonis has nothing on him. He takes a deep breath and crosses his arms over his chest while still looking only at me and talking to Laylah, "You sure can pick them."

"Yanni, meet Lime Prince, the next face of Faces."

He folds his lips inward and nods. The thing is, guys like Yanni are always looking at me like I am lunch, but it is something about the way he looks at me that suggests maybe a nice romantic dinner on the veranda and flowers the next day. The look is pleasant and his face, although chiseled like it is carved from marble, is non-threatening. He is smooth, and my sexual radar is signaling for the first time in a long time. I stand there for a few moments devouring this Greek god with my eyes, before he takes my hand and leads me to a dressing room with an abundance of closets full of clothes and shoes for every occasion. There are two women in the room who stand at attention when Yanni and Laylah enter. Laylah interacts with them like old friends.

"Pat, Sarah, dahlings. I need you both to work your magic."

Pat is the wardrobe stylist and Sarah is the hair and makeup artist. Yanni explains to them that I am here to create my portfolio and that we would start with a body shot. He beams at me and I don't hesitate to beam back. As soon as he leaves to set up the shot, Laylah, Pat, and Sarah poke, prod, and pass me around like a rag doll.

Sarah washes and conditions my face, paints, cuts, files, and massages my nails and toes, and arches and waxes my eyebrows to heights unknown. Her experiments with my hair are less than desirable, but I don't dare challenge. I figure she is the hair stylist and knows what she is doing. I try on swim suit after swim suit: bikinis, thongs, crop tops with swim bottoms, suits that are held together with a string, sarongs; you name it, I try it on. This is the first time that I ever completely dressed and undressed in front of women, or total strangers. Even when I was with AJ and Ms. Henning, I did most of my wardrobe changes in private. At one point, I stand in the middle of the room naked as a robin, as I wait for them to decide which outfit I should try on. Neither Laylah, Pat, or Sarah notice or seem to care that I am naked, let alone uncomfortable. I keep putting my hands over my cobbler and my breasts while thinking that AJ would be the perfect double for me right now.

Laylah hates every one of the outfits. She keeps telling Pat that she wants not too edgy and not too commercial. I notice a unique mixture of pink and chocolate on the floor. It is a two-piece pink and chocolate swimsuit; the bikini top has one pink cup and one chocolate cup and it ties around the neck. The same colors are evenly striped on the bottom. I love it. Pat and Sarah think it will work, but Laylah has doubts. When I slip on a pair of brown stilettos and tower over all three of them, the muscles in my legs and calves do an involuntary flex. All the years of running have toned my body and stomach in a way crunches and weights never could. All of a sudden, my four pack seems to come to life as I stand there breathing in and out in front of everyone. Laylah begins to see the possibilities. As I walk out to take my place in front of the camera, I can feel the heat from everyone's eyes. I walk at a slow pace in case Laylah is judging if I can walk like a model or not.

Yanni is measuring the light with a light meter and stops in his tracks as soon as I step onto the canvas.

"Ready?"

I take a deep breath and nod, "Ready."

Yanni takes shot after shot and I obey each photo command without hesitation. All of a sudden, Laylah interrupts and pulls Yanni aside. They whisper in a corner, look back over their shoulders at me, and whisper some more. As long as the camera is clicking, I feel fine, but the minute it stops, I feel like a display mannequin. Yanni calls his assistant over, and the next thing I see is a five foot step ladder headed my way. The photo is transformed into an aerial view of me on my back with my legs crossed at the ankles, knees up, and my back arched high. I peer into that camera as if it is only Yanni's face and beautiful body suspended over me.

For the high fashion shot, Laylah and Pat choose a backless silver number with rhinestones and rhinestone hoop earrings. They even make my shoes and toes sparkle. Sarah slicks my hair back and paints my face with highlights of silver. Yanni, with Laylah's approval, wants an outdoor shot of me leaning against a building with an expression that says I am waiting on someone special. As long as Yanni is taking the pictures, I would have stood on my head if he wanted me to. He makes it easy, which allows me to shine.

Our last shot is my beauty shot. In a black, fitted ribbed turtleneck, True Religion Jeans, and my hair pinned up without a strand out of place, Yanni gets up close and personal with me and I fill those shots with the many faces of Lime. What emerges in the end is a tender, yet bold face upstaged by lime ovals and soft cinnamon skin. In all the years I posed in front of camera after camera, this is the first time I truly feel beautiful. After a dozen or so more shots, different poses, and wardrobe changes from sporty to professional, I have my first professional portfolio.

Laylah is pleased and Yanni is interested. When I finish dressing, I find the two of them discussing me.

"So, what do you think?" Laylah asks Yanni as she puts her hand in the center of his back.

"She is breathtaking and very comfortable with the camera. This was one of the easiest photo shoots yet. She worked it."

"Yeah, I have a sure feeling about her, and you know I've only been wrong once. Now we have to see if she can walk." Laylah pauses. "What's going on, dahling? You got that twinkle in your eyes."

"Nothing for you to be concerned about."

"I just got her today, at least let me mold her before you start sniffing. You know what happened the last time."

I interrupt. "Laylah?"

"Lime, dahling, you must be exhausted. Let's make our way back to the office, shall we?"

Yanni grabs my hand, "Lime, it was a pleasure to shoot you. Believe me when I say every photographer in the world will want to photograph you, 'cause you make our jobs easy. You're born for the camera."

He kisses my hand, gives me his card, and asks me to call him whenever I like. I tell him that I will and before I can thank him, Laylah is pushing me out the door.

As hot and bothered as Yanni makes me feel, tonight all I want to do is to take a warm bath and go to bed. Laylah is right. I am exhausted from the photo shoot and from her talking me to death back at her office. Just as I step out of the tub, my cell phone rings. I don't recognize the number, but it is a New York area code, so I figure it is probably Laylah calling from another number.

"Hello, Lime. This is Yanni." He has me on speaker phone.

"Yanni," I say, closing my robe as if he can see through the phone. "How are you? How did you get my number?" Although I am surprised by the call, I can't help but smile.

"Call it photographer's privilege. Should I have not called?"

"Oh, no, I was just curious," I try to sound apologetic by the line of questioning.

"Well, that makes two of us." He lets out a slow, sexy laugh. "Wondering if you were busy tonight?"

"Tonight? Well, no, but—"

"Good. Would you like to see New York at night?"

"What does that entail?"

"Actually, a friend of mine owns an art gallery and he's having an exhibit tonight, so it entails some art, wine, hors d'oeuvres, and me."

I am really tired, but I figure it might be nice to hang out with a sexy man for once. The gallery is nothing more than a huge loft on a rooftop. There are two guys in the corner playing the bongos over low, jazzy music. Everyone is busy studying the paintings and talking low with a glass of wine or champagne in their hands. Yanni seems to know everyone and keeps introducing me as "*the* new face of Faces." I don't think he uses my real name once the entire evening.

The featured artist is a woman name Nan-C and her exhibit is "Desire." She is a short black woman from Atlanta with locs down her back. She is dressed in mud cloth garments and her locs are adorned with numerous cowry shells. Each painting has a different shade of red as a background and some object that symbolizes her impression of desire. There are bloody lips, half-bitten fruit, female hands clawing on a male's back, and people painted from the waist down with zippers and shirts halfway open. Yanni introduces us. She thanks me for coming and comments on how my features would make for a great portrait. Yanni agrees. As I compliment her locs, I can't help but think about the time Rohan decided that I should grow locs like him. I knew the texture of my hair wouldn't allow it, but he thought it would be fun if we both had them. After three months of limp twists all over my head, he said they looked like wet noodles and ordered me to take them out.

After about two hours of introductions, looking at the same paintings, and two glasses of champagne, I can't stop yawning. I feel like I'm going to pass out if I don't get some sleep. Yanni catches on and we soon leave.

When we arrive at my apartment, he asks if he could use my loo and make sure I am in safe and sound. I agree. As he walks, I can't help but notice how perfect his jeans hug his bum. I shake my head out of my trance, and kick off my shoes. It is muggy in the studio flat, so I begin opening the windows one by one. Yanni calls my name. I turn around, and as if someone has given me a slight nudge, I fall back against the window. Yanni is standing in my living room as naked as the day he entered this world.

"Why so startled?" he asks walking towards me.

"Uh, Yanni, what are you doing?" I move sideways toward my kitchen, in case I need something in my hand.

"I'm just getting comfortable. Why don't you do the same?"

"You want *me* to get naked?" I say each word with a bit of sarcasm.

"Lime, don't play games. It was obvious when we met that there was a sexual energy between us."

I put my hand over my mouth, and say, "What was obvious was that we were attracted to each other. That's it, Yanni."

"Really? Well, I don't believe you."

He is standing in my personal space and his body heat is warming me all over. He puts his hands on each side of me gripping the countertop. I'm trapped. He brings his lips close to my left ear and puts his tongue in it. I open my mouth, but no sound comes out.

"Do you want me to stop?" and before I can answer his willy is poking my zipper.

I think about how long it has been since I've been this close to a man, and a handsome man at that. Every nerve on my body is standing at attention and my mind and body are in a serious brawl.

Yanni takes my hand like he did this morning at his studio and leads me to my bed. My eyes fixate on his round bum. This man is sinewy from his head to toe. My body lands a knockout punch on my senses and the referee is giving it a three second count. Yanni sits down on the edge of my bed and leans back on his elbows. He gives me the "what-are-you-waiting-for" look and I feel my senses regain consciousness and stand right before the referee declares my body the winner.

"You're not expecting me to . . ." I can't even say it, much less do it.

"What's the problem?" He grabs his willy with his hand and starts stroking it.

"The problem is I don't go around sucking men's willies." No more being polite. I'm pissed.

"Good to know." He smirks.

"Yanni, put your clothes on and please leave."

"What? Why are you acting like a bitch?"

He sits straight up. All of a sudden, it is no longer Lime Prince standing before him. I become AJ and Ms. Henning all in one and now we were all standing before Mr. Hard On.

"Excuse me—'a bitch'? Get the bloody hell out of my house Yanni before you see a real bitch."

He jumps up and gets in my personal space again and shouts, "You models are all alike, either sluts or teases."

He goes back into the loo and grabs his clothes and puts them on without realizing he has his shirt on inside out, and forgot to zip his jeans. As he walks out the door he turns and says, "You're going to learn real quick, sweetie, that it takes more than a beautiful face and body to make it in this business." He imitates my accent. "So I suggest you *start* sucking men's willies. Just ask Laylah."

I slam the door in his face. What the hell did he mean, "Ask Laylah?" Why did I think that Yanni was different? He is just another man who refuses to make love to my mind before making love to my body. I get ready for bed, and call AJ. Her phone goes straight to voice mail, so I leave a long message about the entire day. I knew she'd have some choice words about how to handle Yanni in the future. Knowing her, she might ask for his phone number so she can call and curse him out herself. I debate whether to tell Laylah about the Yanni fiasco. They seem so chummy that it might cause more trouble than it is worth. For all I know, she and Yanni might have set up the entire evening to see if I have the goolies to handle men like Yanni in this business. Whatever, I don't need her protection from men like him, but I wonder if Yanni will tell her first and what he will say.

CHAPTER 11

Go-See Battle

Within a week of meeting Laylah and creating my portfolio, I am learning my way all over New York from one go-see, or model audition, to another. Laylah said the designers and casting directors judge you as soon as you walk in the door. She coaches me on the "do's and don'ts" of go-see etiquette via the phone on her way to a meeting.

"Introduce yourself and don't socialize with the other girls. You're not there to make friends and no one likes a chatterbox. Always be polite no matter how rude they are. Don't volunteer information and know when to be quiet and just listen. Make sure you have pen and paper when they select you so you'll have the correct name and address and always, no matter what, say thank you. If they ask your age or year of birth just put something down in the mid-range. Don't you even think about negotiating anything—refer everyone to me and make sure you tell them that you're with Faces. And Lime, I want you to eat, sleep, and pee with your portfolio. Don't even think about going to an audition without it. I watched you walk at the photo shoot and dahling we definitely have work to do, but I'm going to get you out there now. Time is money." She hangs up without even saying goodbye or wishing me good luck.

Laylah schedules two go-sees for my first day. The first is an open call for a catalog. When AJ and I arrived in New York, she made me buy my first pair of designer shoes by someone named Jimmy Choo. They sat in the box until today. I chose a red and orange silk knee length spaghetti strapped summer dress that matches my new reddish brown designer shoes to a T. I figure if the walking doesn't convince them this dress and my pictures will.

I arrive at the hotel a few minutes early only to find that fifty other girls had the same idea, and there were at least thirty more waiting in line to register, portfolios in hand. As I wait in line at the door to fill out the data form, I notice the girl next to me wrote Faces down as her agency. She looks to be about nineteen years old, with a short, blond asymmetrical hair cut over her left eye. The eye you can see is powder blue. After I get my form, I decide to sit next to her to fill it out since we have Faces in common.

In my most polite voice, I ask "So you're with Faces, too? Did Laylah send you?"

She doesn't answer at first so I figure maybe she isn't sure if I am talking to her. I lean closer and talk a little louder because I know my accent can be soft at times.

"Pardon me, but I couldn't help but notice that you are represented by Faces. So am I. My name is Lime."

She throws her head back in frustration and with the powered blue eye that isn't covered by her 1980's hair cut; she squints at me while giving me a quick look over.

"Look, I'm trying to fill out my registration form. I suggest you do the same."

She gets up from her chair, walks to the other side of the room and continues writing without looking back in my direction even once.

I swallow the ball of pride in my throat, glance around the room to see if anyone noticed, and begin filling out the form. I don't look back up until I'm done and sure everyone who may have heard our embarrassing exchange has forgotten about it. Laylah's right; I'm not here to make friends or conversation. When I'm done, I hand the form back to the assistant, place my number on my clothing, and wait like everyone else in complete silence until it is my turn.

It is almost eleven o'clock before my number is called. I almost doze off when I hear "Seventy-three. Number seventy-three."

I jump up, grab my briefcase, and follow the young woman inside a small room with bright lights and large windows. Two men and one woman, with sunglasses on her head, sit behind a long wooden table, with notebooks in front of each of them. The assistant tells me to wait until I am called. The balding man in the middle makes eye contact with me first. A brief introduction reveals that he is the photographer and the other man and woman are in charge of the catalog's layout and artistic design. They are too busy reviewing my data sheet and pictures to even take a good look at me.

The photographer speaks first. "Lime Prince, that's a unique name. Faces, huh? Okay, walk."

I treat his command like any other occasion and put one foot in front of the other, with my arms almost glued to my sides, no bounce, or strut in my stride. After a few steps, my feet send an immediate signal to my brain that these are brand new Jimmy Choos'. They stop me a few feet before my approach.

The woman with sunglasses on her head interrupts everything, and blurts out, "Laylah knows this is a catalog shoot, not an ad for Benetton. Too exotic, and we won't even comment on the walk." She tosses my pictures aside like junk mail.

"Sorry, sweetie. Pretty pictures, but no." The photographer closes my folder and grabs the next one from a pile and starts going through it before I can process what happened.

I look at the other gentleman to see if he has an opinion, but he is too busy looking at the next girl's data form and pictures as well. I thank them for their time, all twenty seconds of it, grab my things and walk out. The assistant calls "seventy-four" in my ear, and Ms. Asymmetric walks past me so fast her shoulder bumps up against mine, almost knocking my briefcase to the floor. I pause for a moment, thinking she might turn around and apologize, but she keeps going without even a glance. I reposition my briefcase, and walk out as fast as I can. As soon as I am out of view, I slip off the shoes and put on my second pair of feet my Mizuno running shoes. The relief is instant. I keep telling myself "Tough skin. It's only the first one."

The next go-see isn't until one thirty back in Manhattan. I am starving and decide to grab a quick bite before heading uptown. The next one is for a magazine swimsuit ad. It looks like rain when I leave the restaurant so I stop in the drugstore on the corner to get an umbrella, just in case. I figure ten minutes early is too late in go-see time, so I hail a cab at twelve thirty. The cab driver does more talking than driving and after a few residential streets, he seems to be taking the scenic route. It starts to drizzle five minutes into the ride and ten minutes later it is pouring. I look at my cell phone and it reads 1:10 PM. I perch in the middle of the back seat leaning forward, trying to see where we are through the raggedy windshield wipers. Just as I am about to call Laylah and ask for the correct directions, he turns the corner onto East Broadway, and comes to a standstill. The rain is coming down even harder and Broadway is a parking lot. I ask him how far it is to the building, and he points and says about three blocks that way, but after another five minutes and he still hasn't moved an inch. I throw $25 on the front seat, grab my briefcase, and jump out. My running instincts kick into high gear, but not my memory. *Shit.* I forgot the umbrella. When I turn around to go back and get it, he is already turning onto another street. It's 1:20 P.M. now. I sprint as fast as I can, dodging in and out of the crowded New York streets.

When I arrive at the dance studio where the go-see is being held, my clothes feel ten pounds heavier and my hair is flat and lifeless on my head. The colors of my makeup are starting to blend. My dress is sticking to my wet skin, and to top it off the air conditioner is on full blast. I have less than five minutes to sign in, change my clothes, and try to salvage myself before the go-see begins. My eyes do a frantic search down the hallway of the studio for the registration desk. The guy at the desk hands me the registration forms, collects my portfolio, making sure I don't touch him or drip any water on his pristine white counter. After I fill out the forms, I ask him for the nearest loo. He points around the corner with his ballpoint pen without even looking up.

I must be the last person, because this time my data form has "Group 25 Final" printed at the top in bold red, underlined three times. There are almost as many girls in the loo putting on makeup, styling their hair, or just hanging out, as there are in the long hallway. I slip into the first stall I see and begin to undress and reassemble myself right there in the stall. I'm so glad I packed an extra dress. I take out my compact mirror and makeup bag and try to restore some order to my flushed face and flat hair. When I'm done, I take two deep breaths, open the door and slip back out unnoticed.

There are more girls than couches and chairs, so for the next few hours, my bum makes friends with the carpeted floor. I am just happy not to have to stand in those heels any longer than I have to. I just want to get through this audition and get back to my flat and forget this day ever happened. Almost three hours later, the assistant yells "Group 25." Four other girls and I walk into the all-white room with mirrors. It is a short walk to the room, but the two designers, and photographer sit on a raised platform, almost in the next room. I guess they really want to see our walk. I think about the Ebony Fashion Fair show I saw last summer with AJ, and do my best to emulate some of their moves. One by one, we are instructed to walk to the white X on the floor.

The first girl gets halfway before they tell her to stop and with a non-chalant tone say "You can go." The second girl makes it a bit farther. After a few whispers, they tell her to wait around. I try to pay attention to everyone's walk as my feet throb. Girl number three is a bit shorter than the rest of us, but her appearance from her hair to her French manicured toenails is flawless. She puts her hand on her hip and floats down the middle of the hardwood floor, but she too only gets halfway before someone blurts out that she was still only 5'5" with heels. "You can go now."

It is finally my turn. With every step, my feet slap the floor with a loud thud as I try to crisscross them like the models from the show, and girl number two. I squeeze my toes so tight that at one point my big toe starts to cramp, which makes me stumble a bit. *Where is that damn X?* I am not sure what to do with my arms, so I put them both on my narrow hips. I wait for someone to stop me dead in my awkward tracks, but no one says a word. They just let me continue. As I get closer, I can see everyone's raised brows and blank looks. It takes a minute before someone speaks, which makes me think that despite my hellish cab ride, an unplanned rain shower, and that poor excuse of a runway walk, that maybe they see potential. I stop right on the X and flash an exaggerated grin at each of them.

"If you could walk like you look and work that camera, we could all retire, but until then, you're wasting our time."

For a second, I don't know what to do, so I give a gracious nod, but right before I turn around to start my walk of shame, one of the designers asks me to turn around for a second. I do a slow turn in case he wants to see my physique from the rear, but midway through he stops me. "Just as I thought. Honey, next time, don't get dressed in the dark."

I look down and that's when I notice it. In my haste and embarrassment, I put my dress on inside out. The tag and lining are as clear as day. I force another exaggerated grin and thank them for their time. In the three hours that I waited to be called, not one girl in the room bothered to pull me aside or say in passing that my dress was on backward or that I might want to look in the mirror again.

Outside, I do a frantic search in my bag for my smokes. *Come on... where are you?* I always keep one or two at the bottom of my bag or purse for emergencies. Although, I swore off of them after Rohan left, right now, trail mix isn't going to do. I just need a couple puffs to take off the edge. I find a bent one covered with lint and wrappers. I don't give a damn as long as the flavor is intact. After a long drag of the vanilla tobacco, the day seems to melt away. Maybe Asmeret is right, maybe I'm not that pretty or talented at all.

CHAPTER 12

You Betta Work

Modeling classes bore me to death. Six weeks of walking, sashaying, turning, posing, swinging, and walking some more in three to four inch heels is not my idea of fun. Running shoes are more of a natural extension of my feet. I am starting to wonder if my inability to walk will be my downfall and my one way ticket back to Chicago.

Laylah is still sending me out to go-sees. I get a few "holds" for some catalog and magazine spreads, but I am always the third or fourth or no choice. My walking is improving some, but as long as the auditions aren't for fashion show auditions only, I halfway have a chance. I can tell Laylah is getting impatient. She isn't going to let my awkwardness in heels stand between her and the money I can bring Faces or the money she's already spent on me. I can tell she is ready for some kind of return on her investment. When I arrive at class one evening, the instructor informs me that I have been dropped from the class.

"Dropped?" I ask puzzled.

This is only week three. I figure the instructor has given up on me, although she told me just the day that I was improving slightly. She tells me to call my agent and she will explain. Before I can dial Laylah's number, she is calling me.

"I'm coming to pick you in five minutes."

I have no clue what is happening and Laylah's message doesn't aid my understanding. Her driver arrives outside of the studio exactly five minutes later.

I stand outside the rear door waiting for Laylah to roll down the window. "Laylah, Ms. Miller said I've been dropped from the class."

"You were. Get in."

"Okay, why?"

"Look, dahling, I don't have time to wait while you learn how to do what runway models are born to do. So, we're speeding this process up. I got you the person who put the WA in walk. If he can't teach you how to work that runway, then nobody can."

"So, who is he?"

The tinted partition glass starts to roll down and a peculiar face comes into full view, and says, "Boo." I jump and grab Laylah's arm and my heart at the same time. Laylah and the mystery guest laugh for the rest of the ride.

His name is QT; born Quincy Tatum. Everyone who is anyone in the modeling world not only knows QT, but he probably taught them how to walk, or as he calls it, "prance." He was a dancer with Alvin Ailey for years before he started launching the careers of Supermodels like Naomi, Tyra, Kate, Alek, and many more. He is a tall, slim man with short twists and eyes that seemed to pop out of his head when he is trying to make a point. When he steps out of the car and walks up the flight of stairs to Laylah's home, I know his services are guaranteed. QT is wearing four inch emerald green pumps and never misses a step. They fit him like his own feet and he keeps them on for the rest of the evening.

While Laylah gets us some bottled water, QT circles around me like prey, examining me from head to toe. I follow him with my eyes, careful not to stare. When Laylah returns, she asks him what he thinks. He steps back and puts his right hand over his chin and places his left hand on his left hip. He takes one last look. "You were right chile. She is stunning and since green *is* my favorite color, and my Manolos' match her eyes, I think it's doable."

Laylah shoves a pair of four inch stilettos in his hand, and says, "Well, you have five days to work your magic, dahling. Fashion Week is in six weeks so let's get started."

QT is a perfectionist and for the next five days, he expects nothing less than perfection from me. Everything that he asks of me, he demonstrates with ease. He walks straight lines in his heels, blindfolded, shoulders straight, head up, hips swinging, and can do three quick turns in the time it takes you to sneeze. He has a runway in his loft equipped with flashing lights and a high tech sound system. We walk to everything from Bach to Wu-Tang Clan.

The first two days, I try to impress him with everything that I learned in modeling class, and he can tell.

"Uh, suga, stop walking like you have an encyclopedia on yo head. You got to move those hips. Now I know you ain't *all* black, but someone in your family is, and that means rhythm." He claps his hands twice in the air and shouts "Give it to me."

I walk so much that by the end of the night, I am beat and my feet are numb. QT makes me wear heels every day and everywhere I go, and threaten that he will know if I don't.

"I'm like God honey, omnipresent."

On day three and four, QT makes me meet him at an indoor track. For some reason, I figure he'd be dressed in gym attire. Instead he wears a mint green sweat suit with matching pumps and is oblivious to all the stares. When he sees me first he starts waving in my direction while shouting my name in first soprano, "Lime, over here." I pick up my pace to avoid him bringing any more attention to us.

"Look familiar? Well, the way I figure it, you are comfortable in this environment; a track, running, you know what I mean? So we need to make you as comfortable on the runway as you are here, and how do we do that, Ms. Lime? We practice here."

"Here?"

As he points to the track, he says, "Yes, here, but here is here," and points to my head. "Visualize it."

As he wraps his arm around my waist, my hips pulled into his, and our feet toe-to-toe, we swing and turn around that track way past closing hours. The janitor threatens to call the police if we don't leave. For the first time since my arrival in New York, I feel like I am getting closer to the goal, and that coming to New York may not be a mistake after all.

When I arrive at QT's home the last day of our training, he opens the door in complete silence. I figure maybe he's had a bad day or since it was our last day he didn't want to spend it talking. I take my position on the stage and wait for the music to start.

QT takes a seat at the front of the stage and instead of his usual, "Let's go girl," he just pops his eyes out at me to let me know he is waiting. I close my eyes for a half a second before I begin so I can visualize a quick run through Central Park, and then I take off. QT sits lifeless, but his eyes stay on me. I just keep looking down, do my turns, and prance back. Each time, QT keeps changing seats. He moves from sitting at the front of the stage, to the left side, and then to the right, or he sits farther back. I'm not sure why he is playing musical chairs, so I continue to walk just in case he is trying to throw me off. Then in the middle of a turn, he stops the music and speaks for the first time all afternoon.

"Ms. Lime, *what* are you doing?"

"What do you mean? I'm walking."

"Yes, a blind man can see that, but you're not blind, so why the hell don't you see me?"

"Pardon me?"

"Eye contact, suga. When you walk that walk and make that turn you got to burn their retinas with those emeralds in your eyes. That's what they coming to see. The Supermodel with the killer eyes working those clothes."

He makes me take a seat at the foot of the stage as he demonstrates. When he stops in front of me, he focuses his eyes straight ahead and then in my direction and for a moment I feel violated. He looks through me in a playful kind of way, and for a second, I imagine that he is flirting with me until he turns around and switches all the way back. I quickly come to my senses.

Before our time is over, he puts on one of his favorite songs, "You Make Me Feel (Mighty Real)" by Sylvester. It is my turn to take the stage. He takes his seat at the front of the stage, and I can see his lips move in a silent prayer that all his efforts on me for the last five days aren't in vain. I am comatose with exhaustion, but I want to pass this final exam with flying colors. The music reminds me of Friday nights on the radio in Chicago and seems to energize my tired body. I close my eyes again, but instead of visualizing myself running, for some odd reason an image of my mum comes into clear view. I imagine her sitting next to QT with her usual smirk doubting me, but this time I don't want to cry and lock myself in my room. I want to walk right up to her and swing my hips right in her twisted face. I take off down that runway poised, confident, head up, and eyes in full view. Right before I take that turn, Sylvester hits a note that runs up my spine, and I look at QT like I have something that he wants for his pleasure and his pleasure alone.

As I sashay back, I hear him holler, "FIERCE!"

CHAPTER 13

Fifteen Seconds of Fame

After my five day walking boot camp with QT, I nail my next few go-sees with confidence. Laylah even sends me back to some previous ones just to prove a point and to keep her reputation intact. They can't believe the transformation and start calling me back and booking me for more shoots and shows than Laylah can schedule.

You can feel the tension in the air with the other models. Some make ignorant comments in my presence in dressing rooms and even after auditions. The most common one is that I am Laylah's new pet. It's that secondary school competition I abhor and refuse to acknowledge; otherwise, I might have told them a thing or two, but I know the moment I stoop to their level is the moment my reputation is ruined and my chance of getting booked for future gigs will be in serious jeopardy. Plus, I'm sure Laylah will fire me just as quick as she dismissed those two agents the first time we met.

My big break comes at a magazine shoot for Ralph Lauren. He called Laylah himself to request me. The shoot is for *GQ* Magazine at the Four Seasons Hotel, one of New York's most luxurious hotels in Manhattan's shopping and business district. It is the debut of Mr. Lauren's new blue line pinstriped suits. He decides to deviate from the norm of having some exotic European male model advertise them. He wants androgyny this time and he thinks I would be the perfect model.

The crew at the shoot almost outnumbers the number of hotel guests. People are buzzing around everywhere, including around me. Laylah rearranged her entire day to be here. "I leave nothing to chance, dahling." I soon learn in agent to client language that means, "You're not screwing this one up."

The photographer is Jung, a hot new Korean photographer, who is getting rave reviews for his clever and unorthodox poses. His claim to fame came from his years at *Korea Vogue*. Laylah is talking his ear off like old friends as soon as she sets foot on the premises.

At the go-see earlier, I tried on a few of Mr. Lauren's suits, but this one is tailored just for my specifications. When the stylist brings the deep cobalt blue suit with gray pinstripes into the room, I can't help but wonder how a woman can help sell tailor made suits for men in a men's magazine. It all seems so counterproductive. After my makeup is applied, the stylist dresses me like it is my first day of school. Everything is meticulous from assembling the buttoning of the vest to the fastening of the cufflinks. Then she brings in a pair of dark blue, leather, square toed Albin Wingtip Polo shoes in a woman's size ten. As they place them on my feet, I feel a sense of nostalgia like I did as a child when I slipped my pint sized feet in my dad's shoes and tripped all around the house.

The hair stylist does one final check to make sure my wavy hair doesn't even think about moving from its slick backed position. He even makes perfect curly side burns on the sides of my face. Then, as if putting the final touches on a work of art, he places a dark blue fedora hat on my head with the steadiness of a cake decorator. Afterwards, he runs his fingers along the rim of the brim until it tilts down midway over my right eye.

The set is the lobby of the hotel. A bench is placed right in the middle of two off white marble pillars. Laylah is squinting and smiling at me at the same time as I make my grand entrance. Right before the shoot begins, the wardrobe stylist hands me a long Cuban cigar. Little do they know how this cigar helps to calm my nerves. They don't want me to just look the part of an androgynous woman, but to act the part, too.

For six long hours, I pose standing, leaning, lighting the cigar, blowing smoke, holding the cigar between my front teeth, one leg on the bench with one leg off, legs open wide while my hands rest on my thighs, staring into the camera, and staring away from the camera. My facial expressions and posture try to capture the male demeanor the best it can. When we are done, I feel a sense of real accomplishment. I've done my first professional photo shoot in New York for a real magazine and designer.

Laylah calls me the following week brimming with excitement. "Multiple, dahling."

"Multiple?" I have no clue what she is talking about.

"Ralph wants to use your photos from the shoot, not just for *GQ* but for multiple ads. You're on your way, Lime."

"That's great news, Laylah. Thanks." Now I'm excited, too.

"The ad should be out in two months. In the meantime, don't rest on your laurels. We still have more auditions to do, although I'm sure after Ralph, they're going to start inviting you to audition, but we have to get some fashion shows in first. We weren't quite ready for Fashion Week, but we will come February. Much work to do."

In my eight weeks in New York, I quickly learn that Olympus Fashion Week is part of the fashion world vocabulary. Only the most successful models headline the event at Bryant Park. I know I'm not even close to being a headliner, but the possibility of being in the show is both frightening and intriguing.

When the ad came out, I woke up extra early before the corner newspaper stand even opened. I don't want to take the chance of them running out. The ad is on the second page of the magazine. I stop right in the middle of the New York hustle and bustle and just stare at myself. I can't believe it. There I am, posing in a man's suit for one of the world's most famous designers for a major magazine. *GQ* chose the pose of me sitting on the marble bench with my legs open and a semi-profile shot with the cigar dangling out of the side of my mouth. The ad reads, "Everyone looks manly in a Ralph Lauren."

I call my dad and then AJ and scream into the phone that the ad is out and to be sure to get a copy. Dad says he's going to buy ten copies. AJ promises to run to the nearest drugstore and get a copy too. I want to stop everyone who passes by to tell them the good news and show them my picture, but their faces tell me that they can care less and have much more pressing business. My "fifteen seconds of fame" are over in no time before I am back running from one audition to another.

CHAPTER 14

Ashes

I have another nine o'clock in the morning go-see in Lower Manhattan. These designers requested me, so Laylah calls me bright and early Tuesday morning, September 11th, to make sure I know where I am going and that I am not a second late. I lay back down right after Laylah's call and wake up twenty minutes later, which leaves me twenty minutes to shower, brush my teeth, dress, and get out the door. I decide to just jump in a cab and be there in less than the time it takes to get to the subway.

For some reason, it's taking a little longer than usual to hail a cab, which is unusual for a weekday morning in New York City. I tell the driver I am running behind and need to be at my destination no later than 8:45 A.M. sharp. It's eight thirty now and this time I know my way around a little bit better so there is no way it should take him more than fifteen minutes to pull up to the front door of the mid-town Manhattan hotel. *Whomp*. As he races through the New York streets, something shakes the cab with a thunderous bolt. He probably hit a giant pothole trying to meet my time request.

I grab the door handle with both hands to keep from falling over as he yells "Shit, what was that?"

I move forward to see what's happening and all I can see are parked cars all in the middle of the street. The cab driver slams on the brakes and looks up into the sky. "What's going on?" I ask, but he just ignores me and keeps stretching his neck to see. I move to the back window and search the sky too for some kind of answer. What is just a scene of blue sky and white clouds changes, in an instant, to an ominous black sky with gray, smoke filled clouds.

Whomp. Our car rocks again. New Yorkers are screaming, running, and falling over each other everywhere. I'm not sure which is safer, being in the cab or out on the street trying to make some sort of escape. The cab driver is reluctant to leave his cab and I am beyond confused by the sudden mayhem. *What in the world is happening?* I go back to the window. Now even more people are running and back peddling while gazing up at the sky. The look of horror on their faces makes my heart stop. When I turn my face upward out the window, snow like ash pours from heaven, and in a New York minute the streets of Manhattan are dusty white. I have my answer, stay in the cab.

The cab driver starts reciting what sounds like a religious prayer. He seems to know something that I don't and since he isn't talking, I decide to roll down the window and find out if this is indeed the end. The dust and debris are so thick I have to cover my mouth and nose. A man covering a woman with his jacket runs past the cab and I scream out to them, "Sir, what's going on?"

"The Towers are coming down! You better get out of here!"

The distress on their faces tells me they are serious, and as long as we stay in the vicinity of the Towers our fates are in serious jeopardy.

The cab driver screams that his nephew works in the South Tower, and with that realization, we both exit the cab. He takes off toward the Towers, and I stand frozen, watching white, ash covered zombies, once ordinary citizens, hurrying on their way to work, run around in hysterics. It is the day the world changed and I stand by myself in the street witnessing one of the most tragic events in our nation's history.

—⚏—

Dad wants me to come home, but even if I could, there are no planes leaving New York. After an attack like that, I feel much safer on the ground than in the air. I stay glued to the television for updates and insight into who would do such a thing. It becomes an obsession after awhile. I don't hear from Laylah for days, and all go-sees, appointments, and photo shoots temporarily cease.

I am all alone in New York City in the midst of an attack on the city and all I can think of is the way Asmeret scolded me when I was six. I was crying hysterically on the plane ride to England, because I missed my dad, and from the pain of her twisting my arm in a futile attempt to stop me from crying.

"Lime, just grow up. Your father is not here to coddle you. You are just going to have to learn how to take care of yourself."

I can't help but think that by now she had heard that I am living in New York and that everyone in the world, whether they owned a telly or not, knows about the devastation that has rocked the city. Regardless, she makes no attempts to learn of my fate. As I sit in my small flat, with chaos all around me, her words haunt me.

"You are just going to have to learn how to take care of yourself."

CHAPTER 15

Cornbread Fed

The high pitched ring of my phone displays another unknown New York number. I know it isn't Laylah and I pray it isn't Yanni. I haven't befriended any of the other models, but the anonymous calls are coming at least two times a week. The few times I do answer, the person on the other end never responds. First, I think maybe Waterfall has moved to New York in a desperate attempt to find me. As crazy as that idea sounds, I know it has been months since her last call or text. I hope that means she settled things with Rohan and Pepper, but I can't help but wonder if it could it be Rohan calling? If so, what the hell could he want? I decide not to answer.

Months after September 11th and New York still seems to be at a standstill. For the first time in the history of our friendship, AJ and I go from talking every day, sometimes two to three times a day, to once a month. The culprit is her first year of law school. Although my schedule is full of ten hour photo shoots, go-sees, interviews, and more photo shoots, it still doesn't seem to compare to the demands put on a first year law student. AJ finishes her first quarter with a 3.8. According to her, it was her "anal ass" Property One professor who ruined her chances for a 4.0.

I couldn't make it home for Christmas. I landed a couple fashion shows in New York. Despite the tragedy, designers don't seem to care about time off with family. AJ decided to go home to Tennessee for Christmas and the New Year. I haven't seen her since she drove with me to New York in June and now it is January. The year 2002 ushered in and was already moving too fast.

While in South Beach, Miami, attending a benefit for Versace, I have some down time before my flight back to New York, so I decide to give AJ a call. The phone rings four times before she answers.

"Happy New Year, babe?" She's yelling above the sounds of traffic.

"Happy New Year to you too, stranger. What are you doing?"

"Saying goodbye to someone."

Her seductive laugh suggests that this *someone* is significant. I say "uh-huh," in anticipation of knowing who "someone" is.

"Lime, there is this guy in my Criminal Law class this quarter and Lord have mercy."

I can see her shaking her head from side to side with every word.

"Tell me more." I'm getting excited for her.

"Wait, what time is it?"

"Seven thirty my time."

"Oh, okay, six thirty my time. I have a study group in thirty minutes."

"Then start talking."

"Well, his name is Jim Bryant, but he goes by Jimmy, and we just finished having dinner together. Mmmmm. He's a former NFL football player. Get this, with the Chicago Bears. He's originally from DC, but went to school in Tennessee, that's right, my home state. He played tight end and broke all type of school records. Got drafted by the Bears, but got cut after a season because of a back injury. Decided to go back to DC to work and figure out his life, but he always wanted to be a lawyer; a Sports and Entertainment lawyer. So, he took the LSAT and got accepted to Northwestern and his fine ass is in my Criminal Law class this quarter."

"So he was an athlete who majored in more than athletics, huh?"

"Oh yeah. He was valedictorian of his high school class and majored in Engineering at UT Knoxville."

"Really?

"Yeah, but don't let the books fool you, he's straight hood. He loves hip-hop like me, playing bid whist like me, having a little libation once in awhile like me, and just having a good time, like me. He's kind of like Tupac and Cornel West all rolled into one."

She claps her hands and smacks her lips at the same time.

"Well, how does he look?"

"I said 'fine ass,' didn't I?"

"Yes, and whereas that description works well for a rap song, I need more details."

She begins to talk slow and soft as if he is standing right beside her. "My goodness, Lime, he's delicious. Brown skinned sexy bald head, mustache, goatee, and pretty white teeth. He's a big, stocky, solid brother. One of those cornbread fed dudes; you know, pot liquor instead of milk in his bottle. Oh, and the best part, he rides a motorcycle, and you know I'm a rider."

She lets out a deep laugh and I can't help but think about Ms. Henning and how much they sound and even laugh alike.

We both start cooing and laughing together. I'm happy for her. As long as I've known AJ, she's only had one serious boyfriend, Antwan Petty. They met in college during her sophomore year. He was a basketball player and the relationship was rocky from the beginning. He had a quick temper and used to yell at AJ a lot, especially after losing a basketball game. One day in her dorm room, in the middle of an argument, he threw her candy jar at her telly. AJ's rationale was always the same, "He can fuss, cuss, and throw things all he wants, but the minute he puts his hands on me he better sleep with one eye open." I was always afraid that it was only a matter of time before he did just that. A couple months later, he cheated on her with some white cheerleader. Since then AJ has flirted with more men than the law allows and gone on numerous dates, but has had no real love interest worth mentioning until now.

AJ notices the time and asks about me before she has to go. "How are you doing, babe?"

"Tired and busy."

For a second, I contemplate telling her about the anonymous phone calls, but I don't want to spoil her moment. I'm sure she will tell me not to answer my phone.

"Well hang in there and I'll call you before the month is out."

She sends a kiss through the phone and I send one back. Now that Jimmy is in the picture, I have a feeling I might be hearing from her a lot less often.

CHAPTER 16

Money and Friends

"How was Miami?"

Laylah, like the New Year, is in full swing. She calls as soon as I return.

"Alright, I guess. I really didn't do a lot."

"Appearances dahling. It's what Supermodels do."

She snickers as if she knows something I don't. The truth is I was bored in Miami. Everyone who was anyone in the fashion world was there, but it all seemed so pretentious for my taste.

"Well, we are all trying to make up for lost time after Sept. 11th. I heard the shows in December went well, but now we need to get your face back out there for the world to see. It's camera time, dahling."

Soon my days are filled with one photo shoot after another. Whenever a magazine or catalog uses your pictures in multiple ways it means big money and I am finally able to move out of the studio flat. Even though the flat was small, I had grown accustomed to it, but Laylah insists, "Think Supermodel and start living like one."

I'm not exactly sure what that means, so I decide on a loft in Central Park West. I don't want to be too far from Central Park, which has become my own private track. Although traveling by plane out of New York is arduous, duty calls. I'm on planes so much that I can count the number of nights on one hand that I've spent in my loft since purchasing it, but it fits my personality. The exposed brick, high ceilings, winding staircase, sun roofs, modern appliances, and open areas, allow me to create a world of my own.

The first thing I do is fill it with the artwork of others and some of my own. I designate an entire wall to my black-and-white photos, and uniqueness of the places that I've lived. My pictures capture Chicago's L train, theater marquees, Buckingham Fountain, Navy Pier, Sears Tower, signature restaurants, the Art Museum, Wrigley Field, and Lake Michigan. The other half of my wall juxtaposes Brixton/London trademarks with pictures of my grandparents' café, Big Ben, double-decker buses, Buckingham Palace, Brixton Market, the Old Cooltan Building, Coldharbour Lane, St. Matthew's Church, and Brockwell Park. Chicago and Brixton exist in photographic harmony on my walls.

Dad gave me my very own life sized framed picture of the two of us when I was only a year old. It is the picture that hangs proudly in his studio of me raised high in the air above his head, complete with spit bubbles and a head full of brown wavy hair. It greets me each time I walk through my door. The rest of the walls display the works of my favorite artists: Max Sansing, Frank Morrison, Paul Goodnight, Margaret Burroughs, and Ethiopian's own Merikokeb Berhanu. In smaller frames and in more secluded places in my loft, are pictures of my dad and me riding our bikes along the lake front, eating dinner together, my dad and Marley, me and AJ sightseeing in New York, and even a picture of Asmeret on a chilly October day in Chicago 1976.

She is dressed in her signature green, yellow, and red running attire in honor of the Ethiopian flag. She ran a 2:10:47 on that day, a new record. The cameras captured her every move and my dad was right there. At the time, he was doing freelance photography for the *Chicago Sun-Times*. The picture he took appeared on the front page the next day. With his keen photographic eye, he was able to capture more than a runner breaking tape, but got up close and personal with her intricacies. Her defining high cheekbones, cooper skin, almond shaped eyes, and featherlike hair became love at first sight for my dad. She looks content, soft, and striking. It is my favorite picture of her, and also my only picture of her. These pictures are more than fond memories; they help to chase away the loneliness that I've endured since coming to New York.

Even though I am making more money now, it just doesn't compare to having my family and friends close by. So, I do the next best thing, I spend my money on them. I convince dad to get some new digital equipment for the studio and take a trip home back home to Jamaica. All AJ wants is free trips to New York to visit me and a chance to accompany me to some foreign place when our schedules allow.

I send some money to my grandparents in Brixton. Although the café is providing for their immediate needs, they are older now and I know they can't work forever. I even surprise Kevin, my former co-worker, with two tickets to New Zealand. He always talked about saving up enough money so he could go hiking there someday. He called me, crying, and promising that in his next life he is going to propose to me and make beautiful babies together.

I, on the other hand, have few needs that money can buy. Instead, I decide to put my accounting background to work and make sure I have the proper investments for a rainy day, because as Ms. Henning always said "Good looks don't pay the bills." I know my looks, fame, and money won't last always, and it will never buy me any true friends.

—∞—

It's February and that means one thing to Laylah, Olympus Fashion Week in Bryant Park. I will be modeling for world class designer Tom Ford.

Laylah is in heaven and doing her best to become my new best friend, until I meet Deidre Divine. Dee-Dee, as she is called, has been hired by Maier Modeling & Management to be the hair and makeup stylist for all the models in the show. I remember some of the models commenting on how Maier spares no expense, hiring no one but the best in the business, and Deidre Divine and her staff are the most sought after hair and makeup artists in New York.

When she arrives two hours before the show, everyone pauses, sits back, and watches her work. I'm not sure what to expect. I conjure up an image of an older white woman, who looks every bit of twenty-five, with flawless skin and a jazzy haircut, or a younger white woman who looks like she just stepped out of a *Cover Girl* advertisement. To my surprise, Deidre Divine is none of the above. Dee-Dee Divine is a hip, twenty-eight-year-old black woman from New Jersey with the full Jersey accent to prove it. She comes complete with round lips, curvaceous curves, short blond hair that illuminates her caramel skin, and a silver eyebrow pierce above her left eye.

Her crew, as diverse as the United Nations, has his and her own distinct style and flair. Their black smocks and black leather makeup bags with the company name, *You Look Divine*, inscribed in purple letters on the front, make them look more like doctors than makeup artists. On the back of their smocks is the Spanish word, *Belleza*, written in eloquent purple letters. They walk into the dressing room, survey the place, and then, along with Dee-Dee, take charge. After all the assignments are made, Dee-Dee gravitates over to me.

"Hello, I'm Dee-Dee," Her distinct Jersey voice fills my ears.

"Very nice to meet you. I'm Lime."

"Oh, yes, I know. We all know. You're the hottest model to come along in a long time."

I roll my eyes, "I don't know about all that."

"Well, trust me, you are."

She squints at me as if she were trying to put my face into focus. I squint back, almost on reflex.

"Oh, girl, I'm sorry. I've seen your face in ads, but now that I'm looking at you, I'm a believer. Your eyes are actually lime colored, and your accent is wonderful, British?"

"Thank you, and yes, it is." I look away.

Then, as if she comes to her senses, her voice takes on a more professional tone. "All right, let's get to work."

In a few short hours, every model in the room is transformed from looking like we just rolled out of bed to glamour queens.

Although it is a mad house, Dee-Dee and I talk every chance we get. She is the first stylist who seems comfortable and creative with the wavy texture of my hair and realizes that less is more when it came to makeup. Talking to Dee-Dee helps to calm my nerves a little. So much is riding on my first Olympus Fashion Week runway appearance. Backstage is full of models, cameras, stylists, producers, assistants, reporters, and even some celebrities. Someone is always yelling and calling out random directions. Dee-Dee holds up my first outfit and stands there waiting for me to undress. I ease off the high chair and reach for the dress as if it is a time bomb I am assigned to diffuse.

"No sweetie, I put this on you."

Once again, I have no choice but to get over my anxiety of being naked in front of others. I take a quick look around the room for any available closet or small space, because that is where Asmeret used to make me dress and undress. There is no private room just for me and regardless if I am the "hottest" model or not, we are all the same at these shows. As I undo my robe, the temperature in the room seems to rise. I wipe the moisture off my neck and clear my throat a couple times. Dee-Dee says "today" before she takes my robe off and unfastens my bra.

I am supposed to model three outfits for my first Olympus Week audience. The top magazine fashion editors, department store buyers, designers, and celebrities are all there. I am first in the second scene. The white, knee length dress with wide off the shoulder straps, hangs loosely on my upper frame, but conforms like an hour glass on my hips. The white puffy purse with big black buttons and short snakeskin straps give me something to do with my hands. My black, open-toed leather sandals have a reasonable two inch heel. Dee-Dee makes me bend my head over and with her long fingers shakes my hair so it is looser all over my head.

The stage flashes black and white to the sounds of Pat Benatar's *Love is a Battlefield*. Right before my cue, the stage goes completely black and then a dazzling white. The model behind me is standing so close the air coming from her nostrils seems to dry the beads of sweat that are beginning to saturate my neck. All of a sudden, I feel warm and flush. The tightness in my throat has its grip on my heart. The production assistant lowers her head piece and asks me what I am waiting on. I want to move but my feet feel like cinder blocks. As the murmuring of the crowd grows louder, someone pushes the model behind me past me, shoving me out the way. For a minute, all I can see is the blond asymmetric girl from my first go-see looking over her shoulder jeering at me as she takes my first place spot. One model after another parade past me and then I see Dee-Dee approaching and down I go.

"Lime? You okay?" All eyes are on me waiting for my response. "You want some water?"

I nod yes as I slowly raise myself from the floor. One of the male models helps me to a chair. Dee-Dee instructs someone to get me some water and her bag. As I drink, she retouches my makeup that is wet from perspiration.

"Are you sick?"

I take a few deep breaths before I whisper. "No, I...I just need a moment."

Just then one of Tom Ford's people interrupts. "Lime, what's wrong?"

He kneels down so that he can be eye level with me.

"Just got a little warm and lightheaded that's all." I take another swallow of water.

He moves his face closer to mine and seems to search my eyes for something. Then he stands up and folds his arms across his chest. "Are you able to go on?

"Yes. I'm fine now." I say between deep breaths.

After forcing a fake smile, he turns to leave and barks at one of the production assistants. Dee-Dee quickly finishes and tells me to take my time. "Girl, they don't give a damn if you are half dead."

Instead of being first, I am now the last model to go on. I have to "bring it" in order to make up for lost time. I take a short, deep breath, shut my eyes, and do what QT told me to do, visualize myself leading some race or taking a leisure run in open country, then "get out there and walk all over them bitches." The images and his buck eyes give my legs fuel. As cameras flash and the music plays, I strut on that runway with a sway in my hips and a renewed sparkle in my eyes. It is difficult to see actual faces with the blinding white lights and flashes of hundreds of cameras, so I keep my attention straight ahead, and make my T-cross turn with ease. I slow up when I'm done to take it all in and that's when one of the directors shouts "Move it!" in my face. This is no time or place for accolades.

After the final walk with Tom himself, there is a big party for the models and the designers in the grand ballroom above the show, but even before the party, one reporter after another pushes over each other to talk to me and some of the other models. One reporter from *Vanity Fair* called me ". . . fashion's new hopeful." I remember to keep my comments brief and modest as Laylah instructed, otherwise she said I'll look up one day and see my face and slanted comments on the cover of some tabloid in the midst of a shameful scandal. So many people are coming up to me that I get a bit overwhelmed and slip away to an empty corner to change, compose myself, and breathe.

At the party, I can't believe I am face-to-face and in the same room with actors, Supermodels, top designers and musicians, like Janet Jackson, Mary J. Blige, Halle Berry, Sting, Sean Puffy Combs, Leonardo DiCaprio, George Clooney, Jay-Z, Colin Farrell, Eve, Missy Elliott, Justin Timberlake, and many more. I want to call AJ right in the middle of that room and scream in her ear with details of who just walked past me, commented on my performance, or smiled in my direction. I can't wait to get home and call her.

The room is filled to capacity and the champagne is flowing. As I hold my glass out for the waiter to fill it up again, I feel something on the back of my ear. Before I can turn around, I hear "boo." It's QT in his loyal green. Someone forgot to tell him that it is February in New York. His money green Michael Kors surplus shorts and green mules are not to be outdone by the short sleeve Polo shirt and matching hooded cashmere cardigan tied neatly across his chest. In QT's world, it is whatever season he wants it to be. The final touch is the green glitter that hangs on his short twists like morning dew.

"Ms. Lime, Ms. Lime, Ms. Lime." He does three snaps in the air in a half circle.

I turn around and give him a big hug. "I'm so glad you came."

"Well, suga, I didn't, but I'm sure every other man out there did."

He lets out a piercing yell and puts his arm through mine and walks me around the room showing me off like his prized protégé. QT knows everyone and everyone knows QT. I was meeting and greeting and saying "Thank you," all night. All of a sudden, the DJ plays something that QT recognizes and he drops down in front of me, does a bounce or two, and springs back up like a diving board. Before I realize it, I am being made to dance. After ten minutes on the dance floor and two glasses of champagne, my feet, body, and head tell me to sit the hell down. I make my escape while QT is gyrating with his back to me. I don't think he even notices I left the dance floor.

Dee-Dee and one of her stylists are sitting on a couch, mingling with some of the other models. The other stylist is Dee-Dee's cousin, Vera. She helped Dee-Dee start *You Look Divine*, and handles all the accounting for the company. She's not only a hair and makeup artist, but she knows numbers, and has a background in accounting like me. I plop down next to Dee-Dee.

"He wore you out, huh?"

"Oh, my goodness, he's nuts."

"Yeah, Mr. QT will be out there until they turn the lights up, and then he'll probably find the light switch and turn them back down." We both laugh.

QT finally makes his way over to us and jumps on the armrest of the couch, and lands with his legs crossed and his right mule dangling from his foot.

"Uh, Ms. Lime, you left me out there by myself."

"Did you just notice?" Even QT has to laugh at that one.

He pats his face and neck with his green silk handkerchief and cuts his eyes at Dee-Dee. "So, I see you've met *the* Deidre Divine, Ms. Belleza?" He snaps his fingers in the air again.

"Yes, she was my makeup and hair stylist for the show."

QT looks at Dee-Dee again and makes a sly smile. "Of course she was."

Dee-Dee cuts her eyes back at him and they both start chuckling as if they'd just shared an inside joke.

"Well, you're in the hands of the *diva* herself." He stands to leave, but turns his head over his left shoulder and says, "Dee-Dee, suga, handle with care."

I stay a tad bit longer to talk with Dee-Dee and Vera some more after QT made his grand exit. I discover that Vera and Dee-Dee's fathers were brothers. Their family is originally from Cuba. Just as my mum chose her career over her family, Dee-Dee's mum and dad chose drugs over Dee-Dee. Their drug of choice was heroine and it was also the cause of their senseless death when Dee-Dee was just three months old. Dee-Dee's mum left her on their grandmother's front door, in Jersey, and never returned. By the end of the night, we seem to connect like old friends. At one point, we are grabbing each other's arms from laughing to the point of tears, but by one thirty in the morning, I am beat.

As soon as the limo driver lets me out in front of my loft, I call AJ.

"Hullo?"

For a moment I thought I'd called the Smoker's Hotline.

"AJ, I'm not even going to ask you if you're asleep. I have to tell you about the show and who I met tonight."

"Wait, hold on." She makes me wait for about thirty seconds. "Okay, now who is this?"

"Real funny. AJ, I not only met the folks we used to watch on the telly, and listen to on the radio, but I talked to some of them."

"Like who?"

"Like Halle Berry, Sting, Colin Farrell, Sean Puffy Combs, Jay-Z—"

"Did you say Jay-Z?" She's whispering again and trying to control her excitement at the same time.

"Yes, and he even asked me if I'd be interested in starring in one of his upcoming videos."

"And . . ."

"Now you know that's not my style. I can't dance and I don't even watch rap videos, let alone want to star in one."

"So you told him your best friend would be interested, right?"

AJ thinks Jay-Z is one of the sexiest men ever and is number two on her Top 10 list of "fine ass black men." My dad still remains number one.

"Right. Anyway, I did my best to keep it cool since everyone else seemed to be used to the famous crowd. QT was introducing me to everyone and singing my praises. The entire show was a huge success, and the clothes were hot too, but I almost ruined everything right before my first scene. It was so awkward AJ, but I managed to get it together with the help of the coolest makeup and hair stylist in New York. Her name is Deidre Divine, but she goes by Dee-Dee." I notice AJ isn't saying a word, not even an "uh-huh," or "what?" I figure she fell asleep.

"AJ?"

"Yes."

"Are you asleep?"

"Not anymore. I hear you."

"Then what are you doing?"

"Listening to you."

"Then what did I just say about the fire?"

"You said that—"

Now I know she isn't listening, so I cut her off.

"AJ, what are you doing?" Then it dawns on me. "Is Jimmy there?"

"Yes, but he's in the other room sleeping."

"Where are you?"

"On the couch, talking to you."

"Why didn't you just tell me he was there when I called?"

"Because I wanted to talk to you."

"Babe, it's late, we can talk tomorrow."

"You sure?"

"Yes, I'm sure."

"Okay, I'm glad your show went great, and I'm proud of you, even though I told you if you ever met Jay-Z you are suppose to give him my name, number, address, and measurements, but I'll forgive you this time. Mwah."

She gives me a quiet kiss over the phone, and I give her one back. I roll over and put my phone on the charger. AJ is the first person I thought to call, but it is too late; plus, she and Jimmy are getting closer and it isn't unreasonable that he might spend the night. I have to get used to the idea of sharing my best friend. I stare at the ceiling, recapping the entire night in my mind, and think about my best friend's new relationship. I wonder when AJ will call me and I'll be too preoccupied to talk because some wonderful, delicious man is holding me tight. I fall asleep wondering.

CHAPTER 17

Place of No Return

I finish my last shoot for the day for the cover of *Essence* magazine. They are featuring black women of the Diaspora. I am going to appear on the cover and the centerfold picture. For me, an opportunity to be featured on *Essence*'s cover outweighs any opportunity to be in *Vogue, Elle, Vanity Fair,* or any of the others. With *Essence* I feel like I'm finally gaining some acceptance with other black women. Laylah doesn't seem to care who hires me as long as they were paying and have a large enough circulation.

After the shoot, Dee-Dee and I are starving, and decide to grab a bite at Justin's in Midtown. My cell phone rings just as we are leaving and Laylah's picture appears on the screen. She hates the picture, because I took it while she was eating a bagel with avocado cream cheese oozing out of the sides.

"Lime . . . Dolce & Gabbana."

"Dolce & Gabbana what?" Laylah has this annoying habit of saying one or two words and then expects me to infer the rest.

"Dolce & Gabbana are having a closed call for their summer line, and I got a call today."

"What did they say?"

"They said that they want you, dahling, but they don't want the cold feet."

For a second, I am clueless as to what Laylah is talking about then I remember. "Oh so they heard."

"Dahling, everyone heard and I spent an hour on the phone convincing them that it was just Fashion Week jitters and you will be better than fine for their show and any show hereafter, right?"

"Right. I'm fine Laylah. Like you said 'Fashion Week jitters.'"

"Well, they saw how you stole the show when you finally got it together and that is why you need to start packing your bags, my dear, because you leave for London on Sunday."

I'm no longer hungry. Dee-Dee motions the "I'm hungry" sign from across the room by rubbing her belly and pretending to chew with her mouth. Since she agreed to wait to eat until after my shoot, I thought I should at least accompany her even if eating for me has been replaced with uneasy thoughts of returning to the place I spent seven of the loneliest years of my life.

"A portabella mushroom for your thoughts." Dee-Dee, a fellow vegetarian, senses my mood change.

I let out a sigh. "I leave for London on Sunday. Dolce & Gabbana."

Damn, now I'm playing Laylah's word game, too.

"And the problem is? You lived there, right?"

"Brixton, but I haven't seen my family since I left ten years ago."

"Damn girl, that's a lot of missed presents."

"If only it were that simple."

I know my apprehension is about more than missed presents, my adolescence, marriage and divorce, or even a word of advice when I moved to New York. My issues, like Asmeret's career and her selfishness, run much deeper.

"So, if you don't mind me asking, why has it been so long since you've been back to England?"

I put my fork down and finish chewing the Arugula salad I forced into my mouth right before she asked the question. Dee-Dee and I are cool now, so I don't mind sharing the long saga with her. I start from the beginning when my parents were married and had me and then take her down memory lane with me as I describe Asmeret's Olympic career, their six year marriage, the decision to leave me in England, and my decision to return home to Chicago to live with my dad. I purposely leave out the dark details about Asmeret's parenting. Some things are better left in the past.

"...although my new family was kind and loving and did their very best to make me feel included, something was always missing. In a room full of family, I was all alone, parentless, and empty. After seven years, my grandparents were getting older and although Grandfather Dawit's cancer was in remission, you could see the fatigue on their faces. Through the years, I saw my dad whenever I could. He was more established in his photography business by then and had more time to spend with me, so he and I decided that I could come back and live with him, in America, since I was a teenager, a lot more self-sufficient and about to enter secondary school—"

Dee-Dee makes a time out symbol with her hands and points to the loo. I didn't realize that I've been talking for almost an hour. When she leaves, I call my dad to give him the news.

"Hey, Apple."

"Hey, Dad, what are you doing?"

"Marley and I just got back from our walk. Now I'm about to cook some dinner."

"Sounds good. Guess where I'm headed on Sunday?"

"Where?"

"London." No answer. "Dad, did you hear me?"

"How do you feel about that?"

I blow out, throw my head back and say to the track lighting, "Weird. Ten years, dad. Ten years and all I have to show for it are a few letters I wrote with no response. You know I could go and do the show and not even contact them."

"That's not right Apple, and plus, you are a Supermodel now. They're sure to find out. I know your mother's absence for all those years don't make sense to you, but doing the right thing makes perfect sense."

I concede and lift my head up to see Dee-Dee walking back toward our table, surrounded by a small crowd following behind her. They seem so happy for some reason and when they don't leave when she takes her seat, I realize they are waiting for me to get off the phone. Dee-Dee gives me the "you-know-how-this-goes" look with her eyes as she gulps down her second glass of wine. I force a smile and tell dad I'll call him back tomorrow.

The women turn out to be the "Sisters Over 40 Book Club," who meet at different restaurants in New York once a month to discuss their chosen books. Since there were only ten of them, I agree to sign their napkins, address books, slips of paper, whatever they can find, and smile for their cell phone cameras. They are sweet ladies who keep telling me how proud they are of me and wish God's continuous blessings on my career. One woman tells me her teenage son has one of my pictures in his school locker, so I address a personal message just for him in her book. Although I have a lot on my mind, I don't mind the interruption.

As I say goodbye to them, Dee-Dee's phone vibrates and she asks me to hold on a second. I pick up my spoon and try to finish my soup, but the film on top tells me that it is cold. Dee-Dee's excitement is evident, but she seems to talk in code for the rest of the conversation. I push my soup aside, let out a slow yawn, and lean my left elbow on the table as I run my index finger down the center of my head. I think about the day I first arrived in Brixton and met Asmeret's family for the first time.

—ɯ—

Our arrival in Brixton was in the midst of the Brixton Riots from 1982-1989. Tensions were high and blacks in Brixton weren't happy. It wasn't the ideal time to move to Brixton. Asmeret hadn't been back in almost ten years. She left without her parent's blessing to pursue her running career instead of becoming a doctor like they had hoped. And on top of that, she married a non-Ethiopian man. When we arrived at the airport, Grandmother Genet, Asmeret's sisters, Miriam and Fenayte, their husbands, and all their children were there. Everyone was so attractive. Fair, copper toned, flawless skin, feather like dark brown hair, high cheekbones, and almond eyes filled London Heathrow Airport. It was an Amde family reunion minus the patriarch Grandfather Dawit.

Grandmother Genet was the first person to walk up to us. She took slow deliberate steps as if she were unsure of the journey. Asmeret took a few steps toward her with me in front as her peace offering. Grandmother Genet stood in front of both of us, silent for what seemed like eternity. Then she cupped Asmeret's face in her strong brown hands and said in Amharic, "My precious daughter." Their eyes filled with tears. I stood there looking up at them both as they embraced, wondering if she even noticed me.

Grandmother Genet reached down and placed my face in her gentle hands as she had with Asmeret, and said, "Hello, granddaughter. I have missed you," and smiled as far as east is from west. The next thing I knew, I was submerged by Ethiopian love.

—⁂—

"All right, 'bye, baby," Dee-Dee said into the phone, with a Cheshire cat grin. She closes her phone, looks at me, and without missing a beat rejoins our conversation. "So how long did you live there again?"

I've only known Dee-Dee for a few months, but in that time, I've never seen her with anyone or heard her talk about a man in her life, so I'm extra curious to know who was on the other end of that phone.

"Uh, Dee-Dee, not my business, but whoever that was made you light up like a Christmas tree."

"Oh, girl, whatever, just a friend."

"So, why all the code words?"

"What code words? I just didn't want everyone to hear my conversation. You know how I hate when folks talk all loud on their cell phones in public places."

"But that doesn't explain why your *friend* has you glowing right now."

"Let's just say it is a *good* friend and leave it at that, Ms. Lime."

"All right, Ms. Dee-Dee. I hope I get to meet this *friend* one day."

We change the subject and talk about Dee-Dee's upcoming hair shows until the restaurant closes.

CHAPTER 18

What a Difference a Summer Makes

I can't believe I'm back in London again, but this time for the Dolce & Gabbana European Fashion Show. After my conversation with dad and a sleepless night, I decided to call my grandparents about my visit. I am only going to be in town for the show, but the option to extend my time is up to me, so I decide to spend the next day in Brixton.

Dee-Dee couldn't make the show with me. She is in Paris for another show she booked months before. I asked dad to come, but he thought it would be awkward, and AJ is in Indianapolis interning for the Indiana Civil Liberties Union for the summer. As fate would have it, I made this sojourn alone.

A glass stage surrounded by colorful water greets everyone who walks into the venue. It is like walking on a sea of pastels. It is my very first time modeling a bathing suit on the runway. They rub me down with all types of oils that make my entire body shine, and sprinkle me with pink glitter everywhere. I am assigned a hot pink triangle halter bikini with silver rings connecting the cups on the side of my hips. It is a sexy number. To top it off, I wear a pair of cap toe suede pumps with four inch silver heels.

As the cameras flash, and the Black Eyed Peas perform, I add an extra bounce in my step. It is a fun evening and I have never been in a show with so many sexy male models. It is testosterone heaven, and their six packs and bulging biceps kind of make me tingle. However, at the after party, the way they dance on top of each other means only one thing. I have nothing they want.

This party has more celebrities than Fashion Week in New York, but I'm a bit calmer now and able to interact with them without almost wetting my panties. Since I don't have Dee-Dee or QT there to talk to all night; I socialize with a few of the other models in the show. I find Alek Wek and some other models huddled together in what seems like a serious conversation. I stand close by and decide to join the semi-circle, having overheard Alek talk about her efforts to raise awareness about the refugee situation in Sudan. A middle-aged white man, dressed in black, wearing black, horned rimmed glasses with disheveled hair, clears his throat louder than the music playing. His thick sideburns and a tiny piece of hair right below the center of his bottom lip puts him in the over fifty Beatnik club from head to toe. All three of us turn around to face him, but for some reason when Alek realizes who he is, she excuses herself from the group. He touches my elbow, asks the others if he can steal me away for a moment, and leads me to a nearby couch.

He leans over and shouts in my ear, "Two words, brilliant and bold."

His British accent blends with the tobacco on his breath.

Not sure if he has the right person or not, so I look at him and raise my eyebrows. "Okay."

He can tell I am clueless as to who he is and what he's talking about, but I pretend to be interested. He sets his glass of wine on the table and stretches out his hand to kiss mine.

"Blak. Erick Blak, and your performance tonight was brilliant and bold."

I have heard some of the other models, and Dee-Dee, mention a new designer with some wild shows and even wilder designs named Blak.

"My fall show is in September in Johannesburg and I want and need you in it. Who's your agent?"

"Laylah Nassiri with—"

He cuts me off. "Faces. Ah, yes, Mrs. Nassiri. Well, have you seen my designs?"

"A few," I lie.

"No worries, I'll talk to Laylah soon. You're British, no?"

"Yes and no. My family lives here, and I lived here for awhile when I was younger."

"What part, dear?"

I mumble, "Brixton."

He nods and smiles before saying, "Charming."

I fake a smile back and wonder why I am ashamed to acknowledge my South London roots. A bald headed, slender gentleman, also dressed in black, comes over and whispers in Erick's ear. He looks puzzled, apologizes for having to leave so abruptly, kisses my hand again and says he will see me in September.

It is approaching midnight and I remember my grandparents like to open the café by seven o'clock. I want to get there early so I will have enough time with them before my return flight back to New York tomorrow night. The two glasses of Merlot are going through me fast, so I head for the nearest loo. I am stopped at least three times by all sorts of people who either want to chat or just to say hello. As I am about to push on the loo door, a young looking man comes running in my direction.

"Excuse me, Ms. Prince?" He is breathing hard.

I take my hand off the door and turn to face him. "Yes?"

"Please excuse the inconvenience, but it looked like you were leaving at first and I've wanted to talk to you all night." He runs his hand along his tie, takes a deep breath, and extends his hand. "I'm Dennis Roberts the marketing director for Pepsi's L.A. division in the United States. We would love to talk to you about a future product endorsement."

He begins going into some of the details as small drops are trickling into my underwear. I cross my right leg in front of my left.

I politely cut him off. "Mr. Roberts, is it? Sounds promising; however, if I don't get into this loo soon, I'm afraid we will both be standing in a small puddle. Please contact Laylah Nassiri at Faces Modeling in New York as soon as you can, and she'll arrange everything, okay?"

He thanks me about three times before handing me his card. I turn around and open the first door I see. After a few steps, I see what looks like three urinals out my peripheral. *Crap*, I say to myself, *I'm in the men's loo.* As I turn to make a quick exit before someone sees me, I hear a woman laughing. *What is a woman doing in here?* The laughter is coming from the larger stall at the end, reserved for the handicapped. I decide to see if she is okay, although laughter is seldom an indication of a problem, but my curiosity is peeked.

I notice the stall door is ajar and I can hear the low murmurs of a male voice as well. *What in the world is going on?* I quietly grab the handle and peek inside. A blond haired, shirtless woman is straddled on top of a man as he sits on the toilet. They appear to be kissing, but when she throws her head back, it is obvious they aren't kissing; his face is buried in her large bosom. As she giggles some more, he runs his face across her breasts from right to left, making a loud snorting sound. A gentleman walks in and stops in his tracks when he sees me. I freeze like a deer in headlights and let the door go hard. The noise and force of the door closing makes it bounce back open toward me and all of our eyes lock onto each other. Almost a year later, my eyes meet with Yanni's again. He isn't the least bit surprised and with his white powdered covered mouth and nose chuckles, "Lime, come join us." I hurry out of there so fast; I almost knock the gentleman at the door down. In all the chaos, I forgot to pee and head straight for my hotel room.

—m—

When I arrive at the Addis Ababa Grocery Store/Café, the same copper bell with dangling chimes on the other side of the door announce my arrival like it did so many years ago. I can tell they have remodeled it since I left. It has a fresh paint job. There is soft music playing through elevated speakers, and the signage in the windows is electric now. A handful of patrons are eating and/or having a beverage while reading the paper. What hasn't changed is the feel and spirit of Ethiopia. Ethiopian artifacts and artwork are proudly displayed on walls. There is even a glass stand with handmade scarves, jewelry, and clothing for sale. Above the kitchen door are pictures of the Amde family. When I look closer I see a newspaper clipping from the *London Daily Star* with a picture of me. It is right next to the family pictures. I get teary eyed as I look around for someone I recognize. I ring the bell on the counter and tap my fingers with nervous energy. My Aunt Fenayte comes out wiping her hands on her apron.

"Yes, may I help—?"

Her voice trails off when she realizes that it is her niece standing before her ten years later. She puts both of her hands over her mouth and shakes her head from side to side in disbelief. We both stand there trying to hold back the tears. We hold each other in tight grips. Then she takes a step backwards, holds both my hands out in front of me, and just stares at me from head to toe. She calls her husband, Uncle Tesfai, from the kitchen and as soon as he sees me, he picks me up and twirls me around, and starts yelling at the other patrons. "Everyone, this is our niece, Lime Prince, the Supermodel."

I am embarrassed by the scene and try to deflect some of the attention by leading them back to the counter. Aunt Fenayte seems to get more beautiful with age. Her face is smooth and tight and her hair is longer and healthier than before. Uncle Tesfai is still slender and handsome as ever. They both look like the pillars of health.

Over a cup of Harrar coffee and Yemarina Yewotet Dabo, Ethiopian spiced honey bread, she fills me in on the last ten years in the Amde family.

She makes a point to tell me that Asmeret moved to Spain with some mystery man about five years ago. She stopped running after winning the bronze in the '96 Summer Olympics in Atlanta, Georgia. Since then she's done some runners' commercials throughout Europe. On the ride to see my grandparents, I observe the new, cosmopolitan Brixton. The market on Electric Avenue is vibrant with diversity, and Coldharbour Lane is now home to bars, restaurants, and new construction everywhere you look. We ride by my former school, Sudbourne Primary School. As we drive along, I can't help but think about the fact that Asmeret had been in the United States six years ago for the Atlanta Summer Olympics and not once had she made any attempts to contact me. I don't even know why I am so disappointed; I know not to expect her to.

As we turn onto my grandparents' street, I take a deep breath and let out a slow exhale as the car comes to a stop. On reflex, I reach for my purse for my smokes, but remember that I packed them in my suitcase. I need something to do with my hands and nerves. Everything looks just as I remember. Inside, the smells from Grandmother Genet's cooking mixed with resin incense permeates the house, which is silent except for the predictable tick-tock of the large grandfather clock along the wall. Aunt Fenayte calls their names, but when they don't answer we go to the back of the house to find them. Grandmother Genet is on her knees in a gray summer dress, dark shades, and a wide straw hat. She is busy planting and watering her garden of fruits and vegetables. I visualize all the summers I knelt down beside her to help. We would put our hands in the cool, moist soil, and sing spiritual songs together.

Grandfather Dawit is reading the paper underneath the shade. He is even smaller than I remember. His oak African walking stick leans against his chair. Aunt Fenayte calls them again and they both look up in our direction. Unlike the scene at the airport, when I first arrived in England, this time I am walking to them. Grandmother Genet steadies herself, removes her hat, and moves her shades down to the tip of her nose to squint in my direction. She says something to my grandfather in Amharic and he puts the paper down on his lap. For the first time in a very long time, I look into my grandmother's glaucoma smoky gray eyes.

She wipes her hands on her dress before wiping my tears away, and says, "Hello, granddaughter, I've missed you." They are the words I long to hear and put a larger than life smile on my face. I walk over to my grandfather and kneel down beside his chair. I kiss his forehead and thank God for this moment.

Before I leave, Grandmother Genet sits me down alone. She holds my face like she used to do when I first came to live with them and cried for my dad almost every night.

"Granddaughter, I want you to know that we got all your letters, cards, and pictures you sent us over the years. I keep them in a safe place." She grabs my hands, and the warmth from her hands seems to melt mine. "We are so very proud of you. You always were a beautiful girl and now you are a beautiful woman and we thank God for the time we had with you." Her tone drops. "We are getting older now and may not have another ten years, but no matter what, never forget that your grandfather and I love you very much and you always have a home here."

We hug and rock each other until Uncle Tesfai asks me if I'm ready to go.

Grandfather Dawit doesn't say much during my visit, but as I'm leaving, I find him sitting by the door. He takes his time to stand up on his own while gripping his stick. He stretches his arms out to me and presses me against his wide chest. I feel his hand stuff something into my pocket.

"Just in case."

I thank him and tell him that I love him very much.

On the ride back to the airport, I sit in silence in the back seat, as Uncle Tesfai drives with his youngest son in the passenger seat. I lay my head back and think about how afraid I was to come back and how coming back was the best thing I could have done. Just then, I remember that my grandfather gave me something. I reach my right hand into my pocket and pull out the British currency. It is twenty pounds, about the equivalent of fifteen U.S. dollars. I chuckle to myself and realize what my grandfather was trying to tell me: No matter how successful you are in life, you never know when it can all be taken away and you are left with nothing but twenty pounds.

CHAPTER 19

Truth be Told

Laylah has left three messages on my cell phone and it's not even 10:00 AM. I knew it was about Erick Blak. Whenever there is an opportunity to book me for some big gig, she tracks me down like a bill collector. I keep scrolling down my list and see AJ's number and another New York number on my missed calls list. Even though, I am curious about the mystery number, I just tell myself that it can't be that important if they don't bother to leave a voice message. Plus, I am more interested to talk to AJ.

AJ ended her first year of law school with a 4.0. Her involvement with Jimmy is getting hotter and heavier. He spent his summer in Chicago, interning with the Chicago Bulls in their legal department, while AJ was in Indianapolis. They spent every weekend together and at the end of the summer, right before classes begin, they are planning to take a trip to Cancun, Mexico. AJ asks if I want to come and bring some fine Hollywood actor or have Jimmy hook me up with one of the Chicago Bulls players. As tempting as all of those choices are, I just don't have the time for a trip to Cancun in a few weeks.

I have only seen pictures of Jimmy on email. AJ always looks ecstatic in every photo, standing beside him with her head on his chest or hugging him around his thick neck, and although he is handsome, he only half smiles in every picture. I always comment to AJ about it, but her explanation is always the same.

"Jimmy says only punks grin in pictures."

According to her, his expression makes him look even sexier. In AJ's eyes, Jimmy Bryant can do no wrong.

My phone rings again. It is Laylah again.

"Dahling, where have you been? I've been calling you for days. I thought something might have happened to you."

I roll my eyes and wait for her to get to the point. It's not that I don't like Laylah. I just know my welfare is only a concern if it affects Faces' finances.

"Not at all. I just needed some down time."

"Good. Well, I would ask you to come to the office, but I'm on my way to L.A. tonight. I have so much to tell you, dahling. First off, Dolce and Gabbana called me again and they want you back. Second, the magazines are calling my cell phone left and right to feature you, and get this, Tiffany & Company wants you to be the face of their new line of diamonds. I scheduled a photo shoot for you in two months, just in time for their Christmas marketing. And lastly—" She didn't come up for air. "Erick Blak, the rave new designer in all of Europe and soon here in the U.S., called me from London. He's willing to spare no expense to have you in his show. Ever been to South Africa? Well in September, you will." She finally pauses, then asks, "You still there, dahling?"

"Yes, Laylah. I'm still here."

"Okay, like I said, I'll be in L.A. for two days. I'm the keynote speaker at a conference for some modeling agents, CEOs, or something like that. If it's an emergency, you know how to contact me, otherwise, call Elmira."

She never says goodbye, so I keep listening. Then she blurts out, "Dahling, I heard about the fiasco with Yanni, and I think it was just a huge misunderstanding."

"Misunderstanding?"

At first I'm not sure what fiasco she is referring to, the one at my flat or the one in the loo in London. I wait for her to tell me.

"Yes, these photographers assume that they can have their way with every new model in the business. Yanni is truly a sweetheart and wouldn't hurt a fly. It was just a misunderstanding."

I'm not sure where Laylah is going with this so I just play it cool, but I'm anxious to know what Yanni told her.

"Did Yanni say it was a misunderstanding?"

Since I know only AJ and Dee-Dee know about that night, it had to be Yanni who mentioned it to her.

"No, he said you invited him up to your place and kicked him out when things got too hot."

"That's what he told you?"

"Yes dahling, but it's no big deal. I wanted you to know that I understand, and that your paths could cross again and I'm surprised they haven't by now, since he is one of the top photographers in New York."

"Hmm. Well, I definitely understood *his* misunderstanding. Yanni's a liar, Laylah, and he knows what really happened that night and not to worry about 'our paths crossing again.' I handled him that night and I'm sure I can do it again."

"Lime, there is no need to get all bent out of shape. These kinds of run ins happen all the time, and speaking of running I have to go. I'll call you first thing when I return."

I hang up pissed the bloody hell off. I decide to call Dee-Dee this time. She knows about the Yanni episode, plus and I haven't talked to her since before the Dolce-Gabbana show. Dee-Dee is so happy to hear from me. She has an appointment in an hour, so we decide to meet at my place later that evening to catch up. My phone beeps as I hang up from Dee-Dee. It's AJ.

"Hey, did I catch you in the middle of a shoot?"

"No, I'm home for once."

"Uh-oh, what's going on?" AJ can hear the disgust in my voice right away.

"Just got off the phone with Laylah and she tried to justify Yanni's behavior that night when I lived in the model's flat."

"Justify how?"

"Something about it being a big misunderstanding although Yanni lied about what happened.

I told her it was no misunderstanding and Yanni was a liar. She wanted to warn me that our paths could cross again."

"And . . ."

"Exactly."

"Girl, Yanni is crazy, not stupid. He better not even try to do anything when he sees you again or I'll slap a law school lawsuit on his ass so fast."

"I'm not worried about it. Anyway, you didn't call about that. What's going on?"

"Well, I was in Chicago this weekend. Jimmy and I went to see *Lord of the Rings*, and guess who I see walking up the aisle looking for a seat?"

"Who?"

"Your fine ass daddy and some woman who I started to beat down for being with my man." She laughs.

"What?" I can't believe it.

"Yeah, they shared popcorn and everything and he was holding her around her waist and helped her with her jacket."

The entire time I lived with my dad when I was a teenager, he never brought any woman to the house or even stayed out all night. I always tried to find eligible women for him among my friends' single mums, because they were always asking. My track coach was in love with my dad and would always spend more time talking to him than coaching us during a track meet. I remember they talked on the phone a few times, but I don't remember them ever going out on a date. When I came back to live with him after my divorce, he spent most of his time at the studio, church, or with me. The idea of dating always seemed to make him uncomfortable. I knew my dad wanted to be with someone, but he refused to settle for just anyone. I also knew that deep down he was still in love with Asmeret.

"Did he see you?"

"No, they sat a few rows in front of us. Jimmy and I like to sit in the back of the theater so we can fondle each other." AJ starts laughing again.

"I'm sure. Well, I have no idea who this woman could be. He hasn't mentioned anyone to me at all."

"Maybe they just met. She was very attractive, and as much as it pains me to say it, they made a cute couple."

"Hmmm . . . Well, okay."

"All right, it's almost quitting time. I'm really enjoying this internship and I might have found an area that I could pursue after law school."

"Good." My mind is elsewhere, and AJ can tell.

"Okay babe. Let me run. I'm meeting some of the attorneys for Happy Hour." She makes a kissing sound into the phone, and I do the same. I call dad like a parent about to scold their child for lying to them.

"Hello Apple."

"Hey, dad, what are you doing?"

"Driving to a wedding rehearsal dinner to take some pictures. What are you doing?"

"At my loft for once." I pause. "Dad, what did you do over the weekend?"

"Ah, nothing much, why?"

I cut to the chase. "Did you go to the movies with someone?"

"You can see all that from New York?" He starts to laugh.

Her name is Lona Carroll and they met at church. She's a registered nurse and a widow with two adult sons. They've been seeing each other for three months now. I wonder why Dad didn't tell me about her. I feel left out and betrayed that AJ found out before me. He says whenever we talk it is always about what is going on with me and that he gets so caught up with my life that he never gets around to mentioning it. I feel bad that I spend so much time talking about me every time we speak, and that I need to listen to him more.

According to dad, they are having a good time together going to movies, having dinner, and even bike riding on the weekends. I can almost hear him smiling as he describes how wonderful she was. He says she knows all about me, and how he hopes that we'll meet one day soon. Instead of telling him about my upcoming show in South Africa, and boring photo shoots, I just let him talk for once.

—ᴍᴍ—

It is six in the evening when I hang up with my dad, and the August sun is hibernating. Since Dee-Dee isn't coming over for another two hours, I decide to take a quick run through Central Park to process all the news I heard today from Laylah and dad. I have to wear hats and shades now in order to run in peace. The last time I ran without them a small crowd started running behind me. I finally had to confront them so they wouldn't follow me home. Laylah tells me to take some body guards with me, but I never run late at night, and I don't know too many body guards who can keep up with me, plus running is my solitude, my solo affair. As usual, I lace up my Mizunos, grab my CD player, and another one of my neo-soul divas, Ms. Erkyah Badu, and set off for a seven miler.

Dee-Dee is actually waiting for me in the lobby when I return. Her last appointment cancelled so she came over early since I sounded so upset on the phone. She brought some tofu pad Thai and schezwan vegetables. It is just what I need after an exhilarating run. Dee-Dee works on serving the food, while I jump in the shower. We sit on my couch in yoga positions, eating Thai food with decorative chopsticks.

"So what did Laylah say again?"

"She had the nerve to say the situation at my flat with Yanni last year was a misunderstanding, as if she were his lawyer pleading his case." Dee-Dee shakes her head. "I just don't get Laylah. Yanni said something to me before I shut the door in his face that night I didn't tell you before." Dee-Dee puts her chop sticks down. "After his so-called advice about 'learning to suck willies' he told me to 'just ask Laylah.'"

"Humphf" Dee-Dee snorts, rolling more noodles on her chop sticks and then stuffing them in her mouth.

"What do you think he meant by that?"

"Just what he said. Laylah sucked her way to the top of Faces."

"What?!" I'm shocked.

"Everyone knows, including Yanni. Listen, the man who owns Faces is a rich old white man who discovered Laylah when she tried to break into the modeling world. He's twenty years her senior, but that didn't stop him from hitting on her. Eventually, they were being seen everywhere. It was like Anna Nicole Smith and that decrepit old man she married. As long as he was spending the money, Laylah was getting noticed. I guess his wife just accepted the relationship since they're still married today. Well, when he decided to retire, was around the time Laylah's modeling career was going sour. She just wasn't in demand. The world wasn't ready for Persian models and her attitude sucked. The old man gave the agency over to his only son, who was more interested in sleeping with the models, racing cars, and snorting cocaine. After two years, the company was almost bankrupt, which is when Laylah offered to run things for him and the rest is history."

"So are they still messing around?"

"Oh, I don't know about that, but she's been with her share of others from photographers to designers. Mrs. Nassiri gets around."

"What about her husband?"

"Girl, he's just a trophy husband who actually was a stay-at-home dad for years. Now, I think he's an administrator at NYU or something."

"Wow, I didn't know."

"And why would you? You are Laylah's prize right now so no one's gonna speak ill of her in your presence."

For a moment I'm a little offended by Dee-Dee's comment, because it sounds like Laylah owns me, but I soon realize that it is just Dee-Dee talking and she doesn't mean any harm by the reference.

"Well, Laylah is just my agent, not my God."

"Amen, sister." We slap high fives. "So what else is on your mind?"

"What do you mean?"

"You only run now-a-days when something is bothering you." Dee-Dee is getting to know me well.

"Oh, it's just everyone around me is finding love and happy about it. AJ, my best friend, fondles her boyfriend in the back of movie theaters and my dad has been seeing a woman from his church for three months and I just found out about it today."

"I don't get it, Lime. You're a gorgeous woman both inside and out and could have the pick of the litter. I see how men get whiplash looking at you, and I've heard others talk about you. Are you just not interested in men?"

I put my plate down and my hands over my face in frustration.

"My life doesn't allow for love right now Dee-Dee. Don't get me wrong, I'm not complaining. I know this is a dream for most, but there is no time for intimacy. I see those same guys and hear the same rumors, but no one seems sincere. Remember the movie director who was only interested in phone sex, and then there was that new actor who I was supposed to accompany to the Oscars? Well, he didn't call me until the day of and I had to meet him there. When the photographers were taking more pictures of me than him, he got an attitude and was standoffish the entire night. I didn't hear from him again for months. By then, I'd forgotten his name."

Dee-Dee put her plate down, scooted closer to me, and put her arm around my shoulders. "In due time."

"I guess. Speaking of love, what about the guy who called you that night at Justin's?"

She looks confused. "Oh girl that ended weeks ago. We were going in opposite directions." She changes the subject right away as she picks up her plate again. "Did you hear back from Erick Blak?"

"He called Laylah and insisted that I be in his show."

"Well, he's 'the man' right now, and an opportunity to be in his show will be icing on your modeling cake." She winks at me.

"Please come with me. I could use a familiar face."

"September?"

"Yes."

"I'll find a way to be there."

We make some tea, listen to music, and talk about her trip to Paris until the wee hours of the night.

CHAPTER 20

Diamonds Are a Girl's Best Friend

In light of my show in South Africa in late September, the Tiffany shoot gets moved up from early October to the end of this month. They want time to do a huge marketing campaign. It is their debut of a new line of colorful diamonds. They want enough time for my face and their diamonds to appear in every major magazine and billboard in every major city.

Laylah calls to tell me the news about the change. She also tiptoes around the subject of who might be at the shoot. I refuse to play games with her, so I remain silent until she gets tired of talking to herself.

"By the way, Tiffany has hired Yanni as the photographer." I hadn't seen him since the fiasco in London. "Will you be okay, dahling?"

"Why wouldn't I be okay?" I snap.

After I hang up, I fight the butterflies in my stomach and just kept telling myself to remain calm. Yanni means nothing to me and there is no reason for me to be afraid of seeing him again.

When I arrive, the Tiffany executives are so accommodating. There is fresh fruit, juices, and bottled water in the dressing room. Dee-Dee arrives five minutes after I do and apparently starving, because she eats over half of the fruit as soon as she arrives.

There is a knock at the door and Yanni, his assistant, and Paul Pennington, Tiffany's head of marketing, enters. Yanni is wearing shades. I figure it is to avoid direct eye contact with me, or maybe to disguise his high.

"Hello, ladies. So very nice to meet you, Ms. Prince and . . .?"

Dee-Dee swallows the strawberry she just popped in her mouth. "Deidre Divine. I'm Ms. Prince's makeup artist."

She wipes her hands on her jeans before extending her hand to Mr. Pennington.

"Wonderful. Very nice to meet you as well, Ms. Divine. Do you both know Yanni, the photographer for this campaign?" We all nod. "Ms. Prince, I'm not sure what you were told about this campaign, but this is our baby. We have some of the rarest and most beautiful colorful diamonds in the world and we can't think of anyone more qualified to debut them for us than someone just as beautiful." Yanni fidgets. "We want your look and your amazing eyes to breathe life into our jewels. So, this shoot will focus on those two things: your eyes and our diamonds. Yanni can explain further."

Yanni clears his throat. "Well, the mini diamonds will be placed all around your eyes in a half circle, starting with your eyebrows and curving down just below your eyes. Your neck and shoulders will be bare—"

"How does that sound?" Mr. Pennington interjects.

"Creative. Let's get started."

"Great. We'll give you and Ms. Divine some time to prepare and we can get started in a few. When Ms. Divine is finished with your makeup, someone from our staff will come in and place the diamonds on you."

Everyone leaves and Yanni looks over his shoulder at me before closing the door. I act as if I don't even see him.

"The nerve of him." I clench my fists.

"Girl, he's not even worth it. Now let's get this show on the road."

She pops another strawberry in her mouth. Dee-Dee can't wait to see the final product. She makes my face glow, and dusts my face, neck, shoulders, and head with a shimmering powder. The woman who will place the diamonds on my face arrives clutching a silver briefcase. She is all business and makes me sign a form confirming how many diamonds I'm wearing and how many are to be returned after the shoot. Using a kind of facial glue, she places each one on me with surgeon like precision. After the glue dries, the amalgamation of colors resembles fireworks. The backdrop for the shoot is pure white, with soft white feathers all around. I sit in a white leather recliner and wear an off-the-shoulder winter white sweater.

Yanni takes several shots of my eyes conveying different messages. As he shoots, he calls out different expressions in a fever like pitch. "Surprise... Curiosity...Pensive...Confident...Sensual...Playful...Innocent...Content . . ." After six hours, my face and eyes are spent. The executives like them all, but seem to like the "confident and sensual" expressions the best for their audience and diamonds. After all the diamonds are returned and Dee-Dee and I are ready to go, Yanni stops me on the way out.

"Uh, Lime." His voice was low. I ask Dee-Dee to give me a second. "I want to apologize for the incident at your apartment last year and the incident in London. Shit happens sometimes and, uh, you know."

"No, I don't know, Yanni, especially when you lie and tell Laylah I invited you up to my flat and kicked you out when things got too hot and heavy, and as far as London is concerned, I was in the wrong loo and could care less about what you choose to put up your nose."

He starts to laugh. "Yeah, well, that's how I remember things happening."

"Well, you know that's *not* how things happened. That cocaine must be erasing your—"

He grabs my arm and digs his fingers in so deep that my fingers start to go numb. "Keep your voice down." His voice is angry and deliberate.

Before he can say anything else, as if on reflex, I raise my right arm up high above my head and bring it down on the side of his chiseled face with an open palm that spins his head in the opposite direction. The sound from the slap bounces off his face onto the wall, then the ceiling, then the floor, and lands with a piercing echo that rings in everyone's ears. Yanni lets go of my arm and grabs his face while poking his tongue along the wall of his throbbing cheek.

I'm not sure what to do, but I know Yanni just put his hands on me without my permission, and Dee-Dee, as well as a few Tiffany employees, is my witness. Dee-Dee starts running towards me. Her eyes are open wide like saucers.

After a few seconds, Yanni looks at me and says "You've fucked up now."

I turn toward Dee-Dee, who is holding my things, and give her a look that says "let's get the bloody hell out of here." She and I storm out the door. I make sure that this time there are no more *misunderstandings*.

Laylah's call early the next morning means only one thing, news travels fast.

"Yes, Laylah." I answer very poised.

"Uh, Lime, tell me you didn't slap Yanni at the Tiffany photo shoot. Tell me I received a prank call by someone pretending to be Paul Pennington and they must have the well mannered, very professional, and humble Lime Prince mixed up with someone else."

I let out a heavy sigh into the phone.

"Lime, dahling; why in the *hell* did you slap Yanni?"

I start from the beginning, then back in London, to the moment he physically assaulted me at the Tiffany's shoot. She is quiet for awhile and asks why I didn't tell her sooner about London.

"What for, Laylah? Yanni is a grown man. He can snort all the cocaine he wants."

"Well, I could have at least had a talk with him about it before the Tiffany shoot." Laylah lets out an even heavier sigh. "Remember when we first met in my office and I told you that I had an almost flawless record in my sixteen years in this business? The model in question not only went around slapping people, but cursing them out as well. She showed up late to photo sessions and missed a Paris Fashion Week, because of her all night drinking binges. She was a mess, dahling, and although her body was svelte and her look was fierce, it was only a matter of time before her true self came forth. She even tried to attack me in my office the day I decided to terminate my contract with her. The police had her in handcuffs before I could finish dialing nine-one-one. My point is temper temper, dahling. Yes, Yanni was wrong, but slapping him in public was not a point in your favor either."

I listen to Laylah, but I wonder what she would have done if Yanni had gripped her arm so tight that it left a slight bruise.

"What did Tiffany's say?"

"I assured them that that was not like you, and there must have been some mis—I mean, there must have been some logical reason for the altercation. It also helped that some of Tiffany's staff witnessed the entire episode. As long as I can keep the media from getting a hold of what happened, it should all blow over. I have yet to hear from Yanni, but Tiffany still wants to go ahead as planned."

When I hang up with Laylah, I want to go home to Chicago. I want to sleep in my old room, cuddle up with my dog, and eat my dad's famous peas and rice with plantains. Things just seem to be spinning out of control and what I fear most about this fantasy world is becoming reality.

CHAPTER 21

Everything Must Change

The summer is over before it begins. It is already Labor Day and Erick Blak's show is only three weeks away. I feel like I worked the summer away, except for the couple days of photo shoots in the Caribbean. It was my first opportunity to spend a few days relaxing and enjoying the beach, but it is never long enough before work calls again.

I relax on my couch for a second before the phone starts to ring. It's Laylah.

"Yes, Laylah."

"Demi Moore." I look at the phone and wonder what the bloody hell Laylah smokes sometimes.

"This is Lime, Laylah," It is hard not to be sarcastic.

"Did you ever see *G.I. Jane*, dahling?"

"D.I. who?"

"*G.I. Jane* with Demi Moore."

"Can't say that I have. Why?"

"Well, I want you to buy it and then tell me what you think about her hair style."

"Buy a movie? When do I have time to watch movies, Laylah?"

She takes a deep breath before saying, "Erick Blak's people called again and the show is going to be extra fab. You're going to share the stage with Claudia, Alessandra, Tyra, and Liya. It's going to be the best show of this year. I wouldn't miss it for the world."

All I hear is "sharing the stage with Liya Kebede." I've been modeling for over a year now and this is the first time I will share the same stage with her. I'm nervous and excited all at the same time and the show is still three weeks away. Laylah continues.

"Despite the ones I named, Erick is most interested in you, and he really wants to showcase you in his designs. He says your look and walk will help put his designs on the map."

"So what does this have to do with Demi Moore and P.I. Rain?"

"It's *G.I. Jane*, dahling, and I'm glad you asked. Erick thinks, and I agree, that the look you need for this show is shaved."

"Shaved? What does that mean?" I figure it is some hip modeling term I don't know.

"Shaved, as in your hair."

"Pardon me?" I know I just didn't hear Laylah tell me to shave my head.

"Erick wants you to shave your head for the show. It's only hair, Lime."

Now, I *am* convinced that Laylah is smoking something. I pause for a few seconds, lest I cuss her out. "Well, you can tell Erick that it is *my* hair and the answer is no."

"Lime, don't be so hasty. Did you hear what I said about this being *the* show of the year and Erick wants you to be the main attraction? You, not Tyra, not Alessandra, not Liya, you. You're going to pass up this opportunity because of an issue with your hair?"

"So, why isn't he asking them to shave their heads? What does that have to do with modeling clothes?"

"It's part of the look, Lime." For a minute, Laylah sounds as if she is addressing her daughter. Her tone is much more condescending and direct.

"Look, the choice is totally up to you, but as your agent, I strongly encourage you to consider it. In this business, and life, we all have to do things we don't like and what you're being asked to do is not the worst thing you can do in life. It's just a change to the outside appearance, not to Lime the person." Her tone softens a bit.

I pause for a moment before I respond. "I need time to think about it."

"Please do dahling, but I need to know your answer by Wednesday." And she hangs up.

It's already Monday. I call AJ and to my surprise she answers. She just got back from Cancun this morning.

"Hey, how was Cancun?"

"It was fine until the end. Jimmy got sick. He ate some ice and that Mexican bug got his ass. Girl, he was shitting and sweating all night. I've been at the hospital with him since we got back. As soon as he started describing the symptoms, the doctor knew we'd been to Mexico. He's at home now, resting. I've been over there all day. Hopefully, he'll feel well enough to attend classes tomorrow."

"I'm sorry to hear that. How about you?"

"No way. I made sure none of that water touched me. I started to boycott showering. So how're you?"

"I was fine until Laylah called."

"Ooookay . . ."

"She wants me to shave my head."

"What?!"

"Yeah, can you believe it? She said all the top Supermodels will be in Erick Blak's show, but he wants to highlight me and one way to do that is by having me shave my head."

"What does that have to do with the price of eggs?"

"Exactly. I don't know what to believe with Laylah. She's so money hungry and I'm sure this is part of some self-serving scheme. I said I wasn't shaving my head. Then she had the nerve to say it was only hair and that it wasn't the worst thing I could do in this business, and something about it not changing who I am."

AJ is silent. Then she says something that I wasn't expecting. "Well babe, she may have a point. You said this Erick guy is unconventional and although Laylah *is* a money hungry heifer who seems to have slept her way to the top, so far she has made things happen for you, positive things. So, you cut your hair for this show and it grows back a few months later. You're still Lime."

"Then what is she going to ask me to do next? Walk down the runway naked?"

"And if she does you say 'hell no.' Never compromise your values and who you are, Lime, but you and I both know that you are more than a haircut."

This time I'm silent. "Well, I still need to think on it, but thanks."

"For what?"

"For being such a great friend."

"Always babe, always."

We conclude with our phone kisses and I lay back on the couch, staring up at the ceiling. I've heard rumors back in Chicago about models and actors doing compromising and even unscrupulous things just to make it to the top, like those pictures of Vanessa Williams in *Playboy*, but it is just hair; another physical feature that prevents others from getting to know the true me. The more I think about it, the idea of freeing me from worries over my hair's style and maintenance is becoming more and more appealing. Before I fall off to sleep, I decide to call Dee-Dee in the morning to set an appointment for my new hairdo.

—∞—

I try calling Dee-Dee for a week. I leave voice messages on her cell and at her office. I sent a couple text messages, but she hasn't returned any of them. It is so unlike her not to tell me when she's traveling and when she'll return. I'm starting to get concerned. Laylah calls me first thing Wednesday morning to find out my decision. Before I tell her what she wants to hear, I asked her if this will affect future modeling opportunities for me. She assures me that they will only increase and might even set a modeling trend.

She ends the conversation with, "Dahling, no need to worry yourself about your modeling career. That's what I'm here for."

Somehow, I knew Laylah had told Erick that I would shave my head long before I agreed to it.

Two weeks before the show and I still haven't heard from Dee-Dee. I keep telling myself that if I don't hear from her by tomorrow, I'll call the entire deal off, but each day I give it another day. My phone starts to vibrate while on break at a catalog shoot. It's a text message from Dee-Dee.

In Jersey. Nana is sick. Call me 2nite. Dee.

Dee-Dee's grandmother is ninety years old and a diabetic. Dee-Dee mentioned that she was forgetting to take her insulin. When Dee-Dee talked about hiring a nurse to come over to regulate her insulin for her, her grandmother refused. When I call Dee-Dee, she tells me that the last time she talked to her grandmother she didn't sound well, so Dee-Dee drove to Jersey at two o'clock in the morning over the Labor Day weekend. She found her grandmother almost paralyzed on the kitchen floor with her two cats by her side. She had lost consciousness from hypoglycemia. As Dee-Dee tells me the story, I can hear the fear in her voice. She said she got my messages, and agrees to still shave my head; however, I have to come to Newark.

I arrive in Newark early Sunday morning. Dee-Dee bought her grandmother a modest, yet spacious three bedroom house. It has a huge front porch with a big white rocking chair and flowers all along the railings. The hired nurse answers the door, because Dee-Dee is upstairs with her grandmother. I wait in the family room. Her grandmother keeps everything so neat and organized. There are pictures everywhere, and bright colors and fabrics from her Cuban homeland. I see baby pictures, graduation pictures, and pictures of Belleza Salon, pictures of Cuba, and a worn looking photo of her grandmother and three young boys. I figure one of them was Dee-Dee's father.

A somber voice from behind me whispers, "Now that you've seen my baby pictures, I'll have to kill you."

I turn around and smile. "How are you?"

"Tired and scared."

Her puffy eyes and no makeup confirm what she is feeling. It is the first time I've ever seen Dee-Dee with no makeup on. It takes me a minute to get used to the natural Dee-Dee. I hug her and rub her back.

"All right, you ready?" She musters a smile.

It is unseasonably warm for early September, so we decide to go out on her grandmother's deck. There is a shiny BBQ grill that looks like it has never been used and a patio table with four chairs under a wide marigold umbrella in a corner of the deck. Dee-Dee pours some sun brewed iced tea for us. I sit down in one of the chairs, kick off my shoes, cross my feet at the ankles in the chair next to me, and close my eyes. As she drapes one of her smocks over me, all I can hear are the sounds of Dee-Dee changing the blades, snapping them into place, and birds flying overhead. As the clippers hum, Dee-Dee places her hand on my right shoulder and says "Ready?" I give a slow nod of my head and exhale. "Ready."

Within seconds, I can feel hair falling all around my ears and face. It feels heavy and thick. I think about all the styles I've tried in the past, like the press and curl phase. While at AJ's house, Ms. Henning would place an old straightening comb on the fire and stand over AJ waiting for it to get nice and hot. I sat at the kitchen table, for moral support, watching AJ grimace with her head bent over as far as it would go. Each time, Ms. Henning would let the comb get too close to AJ's neck and ears. When it was over, AJ's hair smelled like fried sulfur oil, but it was as straight as a die.

I convinced Ms. Henning to straighten my hair a couple of times. I was always amazed at how long my hair was after she straightened it all out, but the waves always found their way back within a few days. We won't even talk about the dreaded dreadlock phase with Rohan, but it was Asmeret who made me feel like my hair was a crime; a strong yank was her way of humbling me.

Buzz. The abrupt sound snaps me out of my daydream. Dee-Dee seems nervous as she moves around my head. I figure it is because she has a lot on her mind and prays it doesn't mean that she somehow used the wrong clippers and cut me bald. After about ten minutes, all that heavy hair stops falling past the sides of my face. I can feel the slight breeze run over my scalp. While Dee-Dee stops to change the blades again, I drink some iced tea. Light wisps of hair fall around my face and neck for another ten minutes. I put my tea down and keep my mouth and eyes closed tight. When that part is over, Dee-Dee lowers the back of my head until my chin touches my collar bone, and turns my neck from side to side as she finishes me off with one of her famous linings. I can feel her warm breath on my head and ears. When she is done, she brushes me off and leads me to the sink to shampoo my head. For the first time my head is extra sensitive to the coolness and warmth of the faucet water. Dee-Dee's wash feels more like a massage than a shampoo. It feels good.

When she is done, she wraps my head with a soft towel, leads me by the hand to the mirror. She removes the towel from my head like a magician finishing a magic trick. "Wah-la."

I do a space shuttle countdown and open my eyes one at a time. I'm expressionless. I drop my shoulders and study every inch of my head. Dee-Dee leans back against the floral wallpaper awaiting my reaction. After a few moments of silence, I rub both my hands over my head and feel the soft bristles as they follow the backward direction of my hands only to spring back to forward attention. I turn around and look at Dee-Dee. "I love it."

She lets out a huge sigh of relief. "Good. I think it looks great and not just because I cut it." This time her smile is much more relaxed. "It compliments your face and eyes."

The nurse comes downstairs to tell Dee-Dee that she is leaving for the day and pauses when she sees me again. Dee-Dee isn't sure how much longer she'll be in New Jersey and she probably wouldn't make it to South Africa with me, but promises to send her cousin Vera instead. I'm going to miss my New York confidant, and secretly wish I can stay in New Jersey with her.

CHAPTER 22

Competition in the Motherland

I arrive in Johannesburg, South Africa the day before the show. The eighteen hour flight from New York to the world's largest inland city was tiring. I thought of nothing else but Erick Blak, South Africa, meeting my Ethiopian "cousin," Liya Kebede, and my new haircut, for the last two weeks. No one has seen the new me, except for Dee-Dee. I keep avoiding Laylah. I figure she can wait until the show like everyone else.

Johannesburg is spectacular. It is a cornucopia of black faces, diverse languages, wildlife, and vitality. I read some literature on the plane that said it was known as *E'goli*, a place of gold. The buzz in the modeling world is that Erick has outdone himself with what he has planned. I'm nervous and anxious. I arrive at the picturesque Gold Reef City Casino Hotel three hours before the show. Everyone who is anyone in the fashion world is expected to be in attendance. The entire hotel has been reserved just for this show. The entire stage is black and illuminated by black lights all along the sides. It even includes a wildlife safari scene complete with a waterfall. The word "BLAK" is projected in 3-D in silver letters on a black screen.

Many of the models are using Dee-Dee's staff for their makeup and hair needs. I wrap my head with a beautiful scarf my Aunt Fenayte gave me as a gift when I visited Brixton this summer. Vera meets me when I arrive. She is so excited for me, and can't wait to see my new look. I'm not quite ready for the unveiling.

Erick has chosen some bizarre designs for me. There are black leather ensembles, Queen Victorian-looking dresses, outfits made entirely out of blue jean material, wool shirts that pass for short dresses, and outlandish coats and sweaters in different shades of black and other drab colors. As I try on a few, some of the other Supermodels begin to arrive. I have shared the stage with Tyra before, and been in some of the same circles with Claudia and Naomi, but I am like a groupie waiting after the concert to get an autograph or just a glimpse of Liya.

All of a sudden, a loud voice shouts over a loud speaker. "Ladies, welcome to Johannesburg. I am Blak, Erick Blak, and in less than two hours each of you are about to make fashion history."

My heart races. Erick jumps off the chair he is standing on and marches straight over to me. He looks as if he has a secret to tell only me.

"Lime." He kisses my hand, looks at my head, and says, "I can't wait."

I smile, and then he is gone.

Vera comes over and starts to work on my makeup. As I close my eyes and raise my head so she could begin, I hear "Lime Prince?" I open them and there is my Ethiopian "cousin," standing in front of me. My heart races again.

"Hello, Liya." I say it more as a question than an actual greeting.

"So good to finally meet you," she responds as we embrace.

"Meet me? I've been dying to meet you."

"Well, Laylah has been telling me all about you and told me to make sure I introduce myself to you."

So maybe Laylah isn't so bad after all, I think.

"I know we won't have much time during the show, but afterward I would love for us to get together real soon."

"Absolutely. We have much to share." She hugs me again. "Have a great show."

"You, too." I'm ready now. I have met my motivation.

The show begins with a high energy performance by traditional Zulu dancers. The crowd goes wild. We watch on the television monitors in the back. My first scene is the leather scene. Erick wants us to wear wigs, multi-colored wigs. My wig is fuchsia. We strut in tight leather, knee high boots, colorful wigs, and suck on lollipops that match the color of our wigs. When I return from the stage, many of the models stare in my direction. Vera says the rumor is that I am bald. I decide to put an end to the rumors and to put a stop to all the wondering eyes in the room and remove the wig to reveal my new short mane. Vera grins in approval as Tyra walks up behind me and says close in my ear, "Hhhhhhot."

The last scene comes with wildlife. Only Erick would arrange for actual animals to walk down the runway with us in our safari type clothing. My companion is a playful, yet obedient monkey that I hold onto with a studded, black leather leash. I wear a hooded, dark green sporty outfit. The jacket is open to show my diamond studded sports bra, which lifts my small cleavage damn near up to my neck. As I walk, they bounce. The hood covers not only most of my face, but my entire head. Right before I do my turn back home, I grab the hood with my left hand and debut my head for the entire fashion world to see. As I blow a kiss into the crowd, I hear a thunderous applause and even a few whistles. It's invigorating. Liya follows me with a large white cockatoo perched on her shoulder. We wink at each other as we pass.

For the finale, we all take our final walk with "Blak shades" designed by Erick. They look like the mask Catwoman wears in the movie, except these are outlined with rhinestones. Erick is elated and kisses each of us on the cheek before taking his final bow. When he gets to me, he kisses me hard on both cheeks. I feel a bit uncomfortable and make a mental note to wipe my face backstage, but the show is a huge success and the fashion world knows it.

The after party is as extravagant as the show. Black balloons cover the floor and hired African dancers and drummers dance and play everywhere. The music blares and the food and drinks are flowing. The energy is as high as the music and the number of celebrities, models, and designers fill the room to capacity. As I look for Liya, I feel a hand rub the back of my head. It is none other than QT with Laylah. They are holding a bottle of champagne each, two glasses, and an extra glass for me.

"Ms. Thang, Ms. Thang." QT has had one too many.

Laylah follows, "I thought it was a good idea, but when you lifted that hood, it brought a tear to my eye. Did you hear me yelling your name?"

"Right in my ear." QT rolls his eyes at her.

"Lime, you did a monumental job, and I hope you're ready, because this…" she carelessly waves the champagne bottle around the room, "is only the beginning." She hands me a glass and pours some champagne in all our glasses while spilling the rest on the plush carpet. Laylah has had one too many as well. They lift their glasses in the air and gulp the champagne down with one swallow. We talk for a bit before others began to approach me. I have more offers to go on dates, appear in videos, movies, upcoming shows, you name it. I perfect my gracious smile and refer everyone to Laylah, who devours the attention.

As the party winds down, Erick tracks me down from across the room. He and an older, statuesque woman, who wears heels better than any of us models, stare at me and raise their champagne glasses in my direction. As he comes closer, the distinguished woman lowers her rectangular shaped glasses onto the bridge of her nose and studies me like a specimen under a microscope. Her glimmering gold Chanel dress, complemented by sparkling gold, drop earrings, shimmer in the room's light, and drape her body like royalty. Everything about her says wealth. Although she appears to be well into her seventies, her short bob styled jet black hair is immaculate; not a hair out of place and shows no sign of her true age.

Erick pulls me close to him and whispers his tobacco breath in my ear that he wants to introduce me to someone very important in the fashion industry.

"Lime Prince, I want you to meet the founder and CEO of Maier Modeling & Management, and a dear friend of mine, Ms. Sharon Maier."

I extend my hand to shake hers, but instead of accepting the offer, she switches her glass to the other hand, takes a slow sip, and repositions her glasses, without taking her eyes off me.

"Excellent show, as usual."

"Sharon has been to a few of your shows," Erick says like a doting parent.

"Oh really?"

Although I've been in the fashion business for just a little over a year, even I know that Maier Modeling & Management is top notch in the modeling world. It has not only launched the careers of hundreds of models, it also represents several actors. Maier makes Faces look amateur. The only thing I knew about Sharon Maier is that she's been married four times and is richer than all four combined. Her two daughters are her business partners and help to make Maier the empire it is today.

Erick keeps gushing over me while Sharon remains poised. "Yes, I would like to invite you to my annual Christmas bash at my villa on the French Rivera. Feel free to bring a friend."

Erick's ears perk up. It takes everything in me not to roll my eyes at him for even thinking we would go together.

"Thank you. I'd love to attend."

I pray I'll have someone special to take with me; if not, I know my dad will love it. Sharon smiles and whispers something in Erick's ear. Erick winks at me and excuses them both.

After no signs of Liya, I find QT again entertaining a small crowd while holding a martini glass in one hand and illustrating his point with the other. Everyone is very amused. When I walk up, he grabs me close and announces to the crowd "Make way for the 'baddest' bitch to ever walk in heels." He twirls me around to find a seat away from the crowd.

"Have you seen Liya?" I ask.

"No, not since the show. Why?"

"Well, we were supposed to meet here at the after party."

"Honey, she got a husband and a child probably waiting for her back at the hotel."

"Yeah, probably."

I try to hide my disappointment. Of course Liya had better things to do than to stay up all night drinking and grinning with a bunch of superficial strangers. For a moment, my mind pictures her back in her hotel room wrapped in her husband's arms while her darling baby clings to her chest. It is a picture I often try to paint for myself.

"So, I saw Erick panting all over you. Watch out, chile; he loves him some black women. The more exotic the better. You know he and Naomi dated for a few years, before his interest turned to Ms. Wek. He treated her so bad she refuses to even be in the same room with him. Since you are the new thirty-one flavors, I knew it was only a matter of time before he came sniffing. And what were you and Sharon Maier discussing?"

"You don't miss a thing do you? If you must know, she invited me to her Christmas bash."

"I bet she did." QT looks skeptical. "Sharon knows you're the hottest model on the runway right now, but she also knows you're with Laylah and let's just say the two of them are worse than stepchildren." I wasn't sure what QT meant and he could tell, so he leans closer "You got to watch your pretty ass in this business, Lime, or you'll get caught up in some silly fish fight. I'll bet my pinky ring that Sharon is going to try to convince you to sign with Maier and not Faces next year."

"Well, first, Erick is not nor will he ever be my type, plus he's eighteen years older than me, and as far as Maier Modeling is concerned, it's just a Christmas party, not a contract."

"Okay, Ms. Thang. You've been warned."

We share a few more laughs before I kiss him on the cheek and head back to the hotel. I kick off my shoes and plop down on the plush king sized bed. I'm not sleepy but I want to talk to someone familiar. It's six in the morning in Chicago and I figure AJ may have company. I wait another hour before calling my dad. He is happy for me, and knew I would do well. I tell him about the Christmas invitation to the French Rivera. I figure I will be dateless, so I invite him and Lona to attend. I figure one more guest isn't going to inconvenience Sharon. He tells me that he and Lona are coming to New York in November for his birthday. News of dad's visit in three months officially makes this trip the greatest trip ever. As the plane takes me back to the concrete jungle called New York the next day, I am thankful for the chance to have made my mark in my grandparent's homeland.

—ɯ—

By the first of November, the Tiffany ads are all over New York and every major city, and the magazine ads are featured in all the popular fashion magazines.

Laylah never brought up the Yanni incident again, and neither one of us heard from Yanni afterward. Maybe the slap slapped some sense into his arrogant head. I don't care. I have other things on my mind like preparing for dad and Lona's visit. They are arriving the following weekend, and in addition to meeting Lona for the first time, I haven't told dad about my new look. I have no idea how he is going to take it. He is very traditional when it comes to a woman's appearance and having a shaved head doesn't fit in his traditional view. I avoided telling him when the ads would debut.

When they arrive at my loft, I decide against the baseball cap or paper bag and just open the door, shaved head and all. While dad stands at the door with his eyes and mouth wide open, Lona breaks the ice right away with a pleasant, "Hi Lime, I'm Lona." We greet with a warm hug and I invite her inside.

"Apple." The way he calls me Apple this time lets me know he disapproves.

"Yes, dad, it's me. I didn't know how to tell you, so I didn't."

"So, why did you cut your hair?" You can hear the disappointment wrapped in his question.

"For a fashion show." I feel silly admitting that.

"Oh Apple. What next?"

"Nothing next. It will grow back. I'm still Apple." I smile and kiss him on the cheek.

"I think she looks very distinguished and sexy." Lona says. I like her already.

I arrange for a private birthday dinner for him. Since Lona is originally from New York, I invite a few of her family members to join us at Tavern on the Green on the Upper West Side. Dad is shocked and even makes a speech at the dinner about how much he appreciates everyone for coming and thanks me for organizing the dinner and for just being me, "the apple of his eye." At the conclusion of his speech, he asks me and Lona to come up to the head of the table and stand with him. Then he turns to Lona and kneels down on one knee, reaches into his pocket, and opens a silver box with a two karat white gold ring sparkling inside. He asks her to stay in his life forever. We both cover our mouths and scream. Lona shouts an emphatic "yes!" and plants a kiss on my dad so hard he stumbles backward into me.

I'm speechless, but so happy for them both. Lona is not only good for my dad, but good to him. I don't hesitate to give them my blessing. Afterwards, dad turns to me and asks if I'll be his "best man." At that moment, I think if he weren't my dad, I would kiss him harder than Lona.

I ask everyone to help me sing happy birthday to dad as he blows out the candles on his birthday cake. Once all the cake was served, I blindfold dad and escort him and the others out in front of the restaurant. I give the signal for my present to be brought in.

"Okay, dad, on the count of three, you can open your eyes."

As I count into his ear, I remove the blindfold. When he opens his eyes, he is standing in front of a Silver 2003 Jaguar with a huge red bow. He drops his hands onto his knees, shakes his head in disbelief, and hugs me tight.

"It's too much, Apple."

"Your love is too much."

CHAPTER 23

Confession is Good for the . . .

The end of the year comes too quick, and I am in Vegas for Thanksgiving attending a marketing campaign sponsored by Pepsi. Mr. Roberts did contact Laylah and between the two of them I became the Pepsi poster child complete with an upcoming commercial shoot. While trying my hand at a few slot machines, my phone beeps. The text message reads: *You are more beautiful than ever.* It is from another unrecognizable New York number. It's been months since I've received an anonymous call and now an anonymous text. It feels like Rohan. I think it is time to change this number. As I'm about to close my phone, another text comes through: *Nana died last nite, Dee.* I lay the phone against my heart.

According to Vera, Dee-Dee, Vera, Vera's father, and the nurse were all there when she died. For the past three days, her grandmother had refused to eat or take her insulin. Vera said she seemed ready to go. The funeral is scheduled for the following Friday. She always wanted to be buried in Cuba next to her son, Dee-Dee's father. After she died, Dee-Dee stayed in her grandmother's room all day, refusing to come out or let anyone in, so I didn't see her until the actual funeral.

At the funeral, Dee-Dee is quiet, yet strong, and gives a moving tribute, in English and Spanish, to the only mum she ever knew. Her grandmother died one day before her ninety-first birthday. I didn't hear from Dee-Dee for two weeks after the funeral. She spent time in Cuba for a week and then she stayed in Jersey to handle some of her grandmother's affairs.

—∞—

I was preparing for Sharon Maier's Christmas Bash in France. My dad and Lona are so excited about going that dad calls me every other day to confirm. I wish I could be as enthusiastic, but the death of Dee-Dee's grandmother just a month before, is still fresh in my mind. I think of Grandmother Genet more and more. I call her just to say hello. Then I call AJ to tell her about Dee-Dee's grandmother. She is finishing up her finals and plans to go to Tennessee for Christmas, but she and Jimmy plan to spend New Year's Eve together in Chicago.

We spend three days in France. The only thing that upstages Sharon's party is her home. It is almost a block long, three stories high, and nestled in the mountains. It sits right on the Rivera overlooking clear blue water. The view from every window in the house is majestic. She serves an international feast, complete with executive chefs. There is a variety of musicians, from an orchestra to a jazz ensemble. It is one of the most elaborate, yet elegant evenings I've ever experienced. Several models, agents, designers, celebrities, dignitaries, and even the President of France and his wife are here. Even Laylah makes an appearance, in light of what QT told me about Laylah and Sharon's ongoing rivalry. Not only is Laylah here, but she brought her husband and daughter. Knowing Laylah, her presence is more about appearances and business. I'm not sure what Laylah will think about me being here, but I notice the room is filled with other models who aren't with Maier either, so I just act calm.

"Lime?" Laylah looks startled.

"Happy holiday Laylah."

"Yes dear, happy holiday. I didn't know you knew Sharon."

"Well, I wouldn't say I know her, but she and Erick invited me after his show."

Laylah opens her eyes wide. "Oh…well, of course. Erick and Sharon are good friends."

After a few seconds of awkward silence, I decide to introduce my dad and Lona to Laylah. The tension is making everyone uncomfortable.

Sharon's daughters, Caryle and Candace, interrupt us and ask if we are enjoying ourselves. Laylah says "lovely," forces a smile and leaves. At the end of the evening, all the guests are given gifts of jewelry and assorted truffles. My dad keeps saying how he can't believe that a little pick-ninny, like him, from Jamaica is being treated like royalty. Lona also keeps thanking me throughout the night. I'm just glad that in a room full of strangers, for once, I have my family by my side.

When I arrive back in New York two days after Christmas, Dee-Dee's messages on my phone are marked "urgent." I call her right away. She doesn't want to talk about it over the phone, so she asks if she can come over. I wonder what's wrong now. When Dee-Dee arrives that afternoon, she is wearing makeup again, and gone are the sweat pants, sweaters, baseball caps, and gym shoes she wore while in Jersey. She is back in fashion mode. Although her physical appearance looks great, her countenance is serious.

We greet with a long hug and a warm smile. I take her hand and lead her to my couch in front of the fire where two cups of tea await us. I know something is up when Dee-Dee sits on the couch as if she is interviewing for a job instead of our usual yoga positions facing each other. After a few awkward moments of silence, Dee-Dee turns toward me. Her face shows the heaviness that is on her mind.

She bites her bottom lip, and takes her time before she speaks. "Lime, I need to share something with you." She takes in a deep breath of air and blows it out hard. "All year I've thought about how to approach you. I missed my opportunity when we sat on this very couch a few months ago talking about your frustrations with love, and when you came to Jersey for your haircut, but when Nana died, it taught me that ninety years is nothing in the whole scheme of life. I may not be fortunate enough to see ninety years, but I realize now that I must live life to the fullest and in truth."

I nod in agreement, but still have no idea where this conversation is going.

"I consider you a true friend, Lime, and I hope what I'm about to share with you will not change that."

She puts her tea down and I do the same.

"I can't imagine what you could share that would change our friendship, Dee."

She lets out another deep breath and peers into my eyes. "Lime, I'm a lesbian."

I close my eyes and jerk back as if to avoid some smoke, but what I'm really trying to do is to rewind what I just heard and replace the person who told me with someone else.

"Pardon me?"

"I'm gay, and I've known I was gay since college."

I look around the room to spot the hidden cameras. Dee-Dee waits for some reaction, but I can't muster one at that moment. So, I just look at her, clueless.

She bites her bottom lip again, and continues, "And here comes the hardest part. Knowing you and befriending you has been the best thing to happen to me in a long time; however, it has also been the most conflicting thing to happen to me in a long time." She hesitates for a moment and swallows hard. "I like you and somewhere in the course of our friendship, not intentionally, I've fallen in love with you."

I stand up, rubbing my hand over my head. "Dee, what are you saying? We're friends. I…I—"

"I know, and that's why I felt I could confide in you."

"Well, confiding is one thing, but telling me that you're in love with me is another." I stop pacing and sit back down, but this time on the arm of the couch. "This is just too much all at once. I mean, I just had no idea that you'd tell me something like this. No idea. Nor did I have any idea that you were gay."

"Really?" Dee-Dee asks as if she doesn't believe me.

"No. Why would I? You were seeing some guy, but you all broke up."

"It wasn't a guy."

Then I remember all the code language at Justin's when I told her about my childhood and my relationship with my mum, and I also remember the after party at my first runway show and how she and QT seemed to share some inside joke when QT found out we knew each other.

"Did you and QT plan this?"

"Plan what?"

"Remember at my first runway show and you and QT were making faces and laughing when he found out I knew you? Did you all set me up?"

"No, Lime. QT knows I'm gay and he assumed that something might be going on with us, but I swear I didn't start feeling this way about you until I got to know you. I was at that show to do my job, that's all."

Inside I know she's telling the truth, but I need something to make sense. We sit in complete silence for a while before I say, "Dee, I'm sorry, but what I want and need from you is friendship, nothing more."

Tears well up in her eyes, but I ignore them while I fight to hold back my own.

"Lime, I didn't mean to offend you."

"Look Dee, maybe it's best that we not work together." Now she looks angry. "I think you should go."

She takes her time getting up to leave. Right before she grabs the doorknob she stops and says with her back to me, "It's funny, because my friendship was never a problem for you, but I see that my sexuality is."

I don't respond. I just shut the door and put my head against it as my eyes begin to fill up. Dee is the one person who makes New York bearable. *Who will take Dee-Dee's place?*

All my engagements for the rest of the week are in New York and since there are only four more days until the New Year, I'm glad for time on the ground. New Year's Eve is another fashion show, but on a much smaller scale. I model for a private party for about 200 guests in upstate New York. They plan a gala event afterwards for the countdown, but I'm not in the mood, so after the show, I fake a migraine and head home. The headache isn't a complete lie. I feel tension every time I replay my conversation with Dee-Dee just four days ago.

I figure AJ is somewhere dancing the night away with Jimmy, and my dad and Lona are probably in the middle of a nice, romantic dinner, so I take a hot bath, turn on the telly, and nestle into my cozy bed, awaiting the countdown on Times Square. After a half hour, the telly is watching me sleep. I almost jump out of the bed when my phone rings. The caller ID reads "International."

"Hello," I whisper.

"Yes, I'm trying to reach Lime Prince."

"This is she. May I ask whose calling, please?"

"Lime?" The voice is distant and faint.

"Yes, this is Lime. Who is this?"

"This is your mum." My heart stops and I sit straight up in the bed.

"My mum? Asmeret Amde?"

"Yes. How are you?"

How am I? How I am supposed to answer that question when I haven't spoken to the person who asked the question in over ten years?

"I'm okay, I guess. How are you?" I ask mostly from lack of anything else to say.

"I've been better. Lime, Grandfather Dawit died yesterday evening."

I drop the phone. I can hear her calling my name. As my hands shake and my lips tremble, I manage to pick it back up.

"How did he die?"

"The cancer spread faster than they could remove the tumors. He died at home in his bed with Grandmother Genet."

I start crying. All I can see is him steadying himself on his walking stick to give me twenty pounds.

"When is the funeral?" I whimper.

"Next week in Brixton, but he will be buried back home in Ethiopia. Do you think you can attend?"

"I'll be there."

"Good. I'll tell everyone."

I'm not sure what else to say to her. Although she gave me life, the few years I spent with her were a living hell. Talking to her is like making small talk with a complete stranger. As I try to hang up, she begins talking again.

"Lime, I haven't had a peaceful night of sleep in years, because I was never the mum you deserved or needed. I put my desires before you, and I did things to you that God has never let me forget. I just want you to know before another day begins, that I am so very sorry for not being a good mum and I pray you can forgive me." Her voice is shaking. "I can't wait to—."

"I'll be at the funeral." I hang up.

My heart is beating out of my chest. Even though Asmeret wasn't screaming at me or taunting me, just the sound of her voice, twelve years later, still scares the bloody hell out of me. I go to the kitchen to fix some tea to try and calm my nerves, but I grow impatient with the boiling water. I need something now. I climb on the kitchen chair so I can reach the pack of Black & Mild I keep on top of the refrigerator. It has been almost two years since I've had a smoke. I remove the pot of water from the burner and light the clove until it sparks bright red. Three cloves later, I fall asleep.

The next day, the bright sun illuminates New Year snow, announcing the first day of 2003. I lie back down and put the covers over my head, wishing I could erase the entire week. A dear friend confesses her love for me. My grandfather is gone, and I hear Asmeret's voice for the first time in twelve years, asking for my forgiveness. They say confession is good for the soul, but I wonder whose soul.

CHAPTER 24

Too Late

AJ spent New Year's Eve alone. She and Jimmy got into a huge fight, so he drove back to D.C. that morning. When I asked her what the fight was about, she just kept saying "some dumb shit," and that she doesn't want to start the New Year off talking about it. She figured I was at some party, so she didn't bother calling after the fight. She brought in the New Year at watch service at her church. Since classes don't begin for another week, she is going to accompany me to Brixton for my grandfather's funeral. I relive the entire conversation with Asmeret and Dee-Dee to AJ on the flight.

—*—

The British press has gotten wind of my grandfather's funeral and my arrival in England. The paparazzi stalk my every move. For the first time, their cameras and questions irritate me. I just want to be with my family and say goodbye to my grandfather in peace. At the funeral, one photographer pushes his way through so hard that he shoves AJ in the back. It is almost the scene from *The Color Purple* all over again when that white man slapped Ms. Sophia after she refused to be a maid for his wife. I grab AJ and shove her inside before she crams that camera up his bum.

Despite the chaos outside, my family seems unaffected. I'm escorted to the front of the large, airy church on the same row as Grandmother Genet, Aunt Fenayte, Uncle Tesfai, Aunt Miriam, Uncle Hadgu, and Asmeret. The rest of my cousins are sitting on the row behind us. I want AJ to sit up front with me, but she insists on sitting a few rows back. The thought of seeing Asmeret again after all these years fills my stomach with monarch size butterflies.

I go down the row hugging and kissing everyone, and as fate would have it, Asmeret is the last person at the end of the row next to the space reserved for me. She is wearing a black Burberry Brit wool dress that conforms to her still muscular body. The dress has silk fur around the collar and sleeves. Her black leather Cesare Paciotti boots sport three inch heels, and she's wearing black shades. Her hair is pulled back into a smooth neat bun, but it appears shorter than I remembered, and has tiny strands of gray lying on top. She stands and removes the shades and we meet eye-to-eye for the first time since 1991. The slight dark circles under her eyes and the slight sag under her chin confirm her years of sleepless nights. She grabs my hand and pulls me down with her to take our seats. She holds my hand the entire funeral. As we stand at my grandfather's casket together, she whispers words in Amharic in his ear and plants a gentle kiss on his forehead. I wipe tears away and bid "good-bye" to my second father. As the condolences are read, I discover that Liya sent several large bouquets of Ethiopian roses, and Laylah also sent flowers.

We all gather at the café afterward, except for Grandmother Genet. She left for Ethiopia right after the funeral to prepare for the burial. Aunt Fenayte, Aunt Miriam, and Asmeret are also leaving for Ethiopia. I am unable to attend the burial because of contracted engagements with Pepsi. There are so many family and friends in the café that I'm sure we violate the fire code. AJ fits right in with the Amde family. As we talk, laugh, cry, eat, and share stories about Grandfather Dawit, tensions about seeing my mum are soon forgotten.

Asmeret remains to herself for most of the evening. You can tell she isn't comfortable around her sisters and relatives, because of the distance she put between them. Aunt Fenayte tells me that her relationship in Spain ended about a year ago, and that she isn't sure if she is going to stay in Spain or move back to England. She told Aunt Fenayte that if she did move back, she would live in London. While in Brixton, she stays with Grandmother Genet. Rumor has it that she is having some financial problems, because all the money she made running was spent traveling and taking care of her live in boyfriend in Spain. He stole a lot of her money and then left her when it ran out. She certainly didn't dress like she was broke. Aunt Fenayte had to take a call, so I was left in the corner by myself. Asmeret is sitting by the window with her arms crossed staring out onto the icy street. As I look at her, I replay all those times I too sat alone as a child waiting in this very café for her to come back to Brixton and spend time with me.

A friend of the family walks into the café and the brisk air from outside snaps me out of memory lane. I swallow my pride and walk over to her. I clear my throat to announce myself.

"Oh, hi, Lime. How are you?"

"I've been better. You don't seem okay."

She motions for me to sit down in the adjacent chair.

"Just thinking. I feel like the stranger here, and I know why. I was just thinking about all the time I spent away from my family, when they only wanted me near them." Her nervous laughter gives her permission to change the subject. "Well, anyway, tell me about you. I know you are a huge Supermodel in New York. I've seen your pictures in Spain. No one believed me when I—"

"Why didn't you like me? Why didn't you come see me when I moved back to the United States? All that time, you never came to see me. You never called. You never wrote. Nothing. You were in the 'ninety six Olympics in

Atlanta and you didn't even bother to call me. Why? What did I ever do to you?" My heart and the butterflies fill my throat.

She moves her chair closer to me, squeezes my hands, and looks me square in the eyes. "You didn't do anything, Lime. Nothing. Don't ever think that. I was a selfish, immature bitch who cared more about fame and fortune than what truly mattered in life; my only child and my family. I didn't realize that in 'ninety six."

I look away and meet AJ's eyes. She searches my face, and gives me the "you okay?" look. I nod. When Asmeret grabs my face with her hands and turns me back toward her, I jump. Her touches were always so painful, but this time her touch is surprisingly gentle.

"You are so lovely, and I missed out on all those lovely years, but I don't want to miss out on any more, if you'll give me another chance."

I snatch my head away and through tears, I ask her, "How do I do that? How do I get to know someone who never wanted to get to know me?"

Her almond shaped eyes are on the point of breaking. "You try."

I shake my head and bite my lip, fighting against the urge to break down in front of her and everyone in the cafe.

"Lime, I know I screwed up, but I've changed and I would love a second chance to prove it to you."

"I'm afraid it's too late, Asmeret."

I get up from the table and rejoin AJ leaving her sitting all alone in the corner staring at me as I walk away.

CHAPTER 25

Running

Laylah's call welcomes me back to New York. "*Coutuuure.*" She sings through the phone.

By now I know the game. "Couture?"

"Yes, dahling, in a couple of months, you will grace the front page of *Vogue* in a couture dress, and guess whose couture dress?"

"Whose?"

"None other than diva extraordinaire, Ms. Vera Wang." She lets out a squeal. "Lime, I told you in South Africa that this was only the beginning and I meant it. First Olympus, Dolce & Gabbana, Tiffany, Erick Blak, Pepsi, and now Coutuuuure. In sixteen years, I've only been wrong once, but with you I knew it the moment your photos crossed my desk."

I smile. The chance to model haute couture dresses means you are really high fashion. Those dresses cost as much as six figures.

"Wow, that's pretty exciting Laylah."

"Exciting? It's fantastic, stupendous, the rave. Shall I go on dahling?"

"No need. I get the point."

For the first time, Laylah and I share a laugh together, and after what I've just been through, I need one.

The shoot reunites me with the photographer Jung again. I wear a crimson, spaghetti strapped Wang couture gown with a choker made out of red roses as I lie on red satin sheets. I haven't spoken to Dee-Dee since she'd outed herself, so Vera does my makeup and hair. Either she doesn't know the truth about Dee-Dee or Dee-Dee didn't tell her about her secret crush on me; regardless, Vera gives no indication that she knows, and I never mention it.

It is already March and the arrival of spring is in the air. Asmeret keeps calling me, wanting to talk. I haven't spoken to her since the funeral. I ignore her calls and let them go into voice mail. I figure if it is an emergency she'd say so. Each time is about either about how good it is to see me, or details of the burial in Ethiopia, or how she understands I'm busy, but if she can just have a few minutes of my time. I debate on telling my dad about her calls. I convince myself that he is enjoying his newlywed life and doesn't want to be bothered with information about Asmeret, but I know he will tell me that I shouldn't avoid her.

For the next couple days, I think about her more than ever. At one point, she didn't call for over two weeks. *Maybe she has given up,* I thought. *Wasn't that what I wanted? For her to leave me alone? What can she say to me to erase years of total neglect and abuse? My life is fine without her, isn't it?* The questions roar in my head every day.

Early on a cool Thursday morning, my caller ID reads: The W Hotel from the 212 area code. I am more curious than I surprised, so I answer right away.

"Hello?"

"Lime, don't hang up. This is your mum again."

"Asmeret? What are you doing in New York?" I get up and sit on the edge of my bed.

"Hoping to see you. I know I am taking a chance coming out here without letting you know first, but I've been trying to reach you for weeks."

"So, you came all the way to New York just to see me?"

I try not to sound too skeptical, but I'm not sure if she is telling the truth.

"Yes Lime, I had to try. I'm staying at The W Hotel in Midtown until Sunday. After that, I'm heading back to London. I hope you can find the time to meet with me, if not, I won't bother you anymore." She sounds desperate.

I let out a long sigh. "I'll see, Asmeret. I'm very busy."

"I know."

I can't believe she flew all the way to New York to see me, and then tries to give me an ultimatum. Just so happens I have the next couple of days free, before more shoots and shows. I tell myself I'll sleep on it and make a decision in the morning. However, instead of sleeping, I toss and turn all night. At one point, I wake up in the middle of the night and fix a cup of herbal tea to drink with a smoke. I can't figure out if it is nerves or rage that is bothering me the most. I call AJ for advice.

"Lime?" What's wrong?"

Instead of sounding groggy at one thirty in the morning, she sounds as if she's been up for awhile.

"Hey. I thought you'd be asleep, but I'm glad you're not."

"No, I'm not." I can hear disappointment in her voice. "What's wrong?"

"Asmeret is here in New York. She came here to see me and to talk. She came without telling me and she's leaving Sunday, but she said if she doesn't get a chance to see me, she wouldn't bother me again. She's been calling me for weeks, but I just didn't have anything to say to her, so I guess she just decided to come out here, and take her chance, hoping we could talk."

I can't stop the speed of my words, but I know AJ understands.

"Did she say what she wanted to talk about?"

"No, but I figure it has something to do with making amends for being a shitty parent. I'm over that and I want her to be too—"

"Are you?"

"Am I what?"

"Are you truly over it like you say?"

"I haven't thought about her in years."

"But you *have* thought about her?"

"Some, but not enough to shake a stick at like your mum used to say."

"My point exactly, Lime. She is your mother and mine is gone. That doesn't mean you owe her anything, but you do owe yourself some peace of mind, and it's obvious by your early morning call to me that you don't have peace of mind when it comes to her. So, however you need to get it, whether it's meeting with her or not, that's what I think you should do."

Damn. AJ is right. I am silent for a few moments.

"Lime, you didn't hang up on me?" She starts laughing.

"No, I'm still here. I just want her to go away and leave me the bloody hell alone. She hasn't cared about me from day one and now she wants my forgiveness."

Instead of interrupting, AJ just lets me vent.

"Okay, I'll let you go to sleep and I'm going to try to do the same."

"You sure?"

"Yes, I'm sure."

"Okay, babe, I'm here if you need me."

"I know and I love you for that."

"Love you too."

I arrive at The W Hotel at nine o'clock the next morning. I lie in the bed until the sun tells me it is a decent hour to rise and start getting dressed. I put on a pair of jeans and a burnt orange V-neck, long sleeved fitted shirt, and a pair of soft mesh gym shoes. I wrap a matching scarf around my neck, throw on a denim jacket and hat and head out the door. I don't see a need to dress up in anything fancy today. I want to get to the hotel early before she starts her day. I decide to show up unannounced just as she has done by coming to New York. I don't want anything about my decision to meet with her to seem scripted.

As the hotel clerk rings her room, I fight every reason that whispers in my ear that it was a mistake to come and I can turn around and leave through those revolving doors just as I entered. After she doesn't answer right away, my feet turn toward the exit by themselves, and then I hear the clerk say, "Ms. Amde, someone is here to see you."

I tell him to tell her that I will wait for her in the lobby.

I find a secluded couch off to the side in the lobby, open up one of the magazines on the table and bury my face in it to distract any attention my way. Today, I don't want to be Lime Prince the Supermodel. Ten minutes later, I look up. There she is wearing a pair of tailored black pants, a white, long sleeved blouse with wide collars and sleeves, as she stands tall in a pair of black Christian Louboutin heels. Her pearl necklace matches her pearl earrings. She is carrying a black patent leather Salvatore Ferragamo hand held purse. Her hair is pinned up again in a small bun. Aunt Fenayte must have been wrong about her financial problems, because the W Hotel isn't cheap, and neither was that purse or her shoes. Her entire ensemble suggests she is headed for work in New York's business district. She stands in the center of the lobby searching for her mystery guest. I swallow hard to release the tightness in my throat, before I stand and call her name. Her face relaxes when she sees me and she begins a quick trot towards me.

She hugs me. "Thank you for coming." I nod and sit back down. "Do you want to go somewhere? Have you had breakfast?"

"No, I haven't."

"Then where would you like to go? My treat."

I have to chuckle to myself when she offers to pay. I guess it is a nice gesture, but it feels a bit over the top.

We decide to have breakfast at the hotel's restaurant. On the elevator ride up, we both keep our eyes straight ahead and let the elevator music do the talking. The hostess greets us as soon as we arrive. I ask to see the man-ager, hoping to get a private room or private section of the restaurant, if possible. When he recognizes me, he is more than happy to oblige. Asmeret keeps commenting on the decor of the restaurant and the hotel as we read the menu. After the waiter takes our order, she looks at me.

"When the hotel called my room this morning, I knew right away it was you. I was just getting out of the shower. I told myself that I would get up early every day and be ready just in case you decided to stop by or call."

She smiles and waits for me to respond. When I don't, she continues.

"Well, I know we spoke briefly at dad's funeral and something you asked me has been haunting me ever since. You asked me what you did to deserve the way I treated you, and you *did* do something."

When I fold my arms across my chest, she notices my posture and hur-ries to explain.

"You came into my life. I didn't know what to do, because running was all I knew how to do in life." She leans in closer to the table. "I ran not only for a living, but I ran from challenges, surprises, my mum and dad, Fenayte, Miriam, the café, Brixton, medical school, you and your dad. I ran and never looked back. When my maternal instincts made me think about you during those times I was away training or setting records, I ran even faster and further away. I kept telling myself you were in the hands of people who loved you more than I could, and better off without me, so I didn't bother calling you or seeing you. I was too ashamed. I know none of what I'm telling you is comforting or justifies my absence, but I thought it was worth flying to New York to tell you in person."

"A vegetable omelet for you and one for you too, ma'am. Enjoy."

The waiter has no idea what he just interrupted. We eat our omelets in silence, looking at everything except each other.

When we're done, I push my plate aside and bite my inside lip as I run my finger along the outside edge of my teacup. I wonder why she has suddenly grown a conscience. I wonder why we can't just have a normal mum-and-daughter breakfast without the drama. I wonder why I want to cry.

"Nothing you've said explains why you didn't like. Why you pulled my hair, pinched me, even spit in my face when I asked you to help me make dad a Father's Day card when I was five."

"I don't know what to say Lime, except that I was jealous of you and your love for your dad."

"And that justifies what you did."

I'm glad we are in a private room because I can't help but raise my voice.

"No. I'm just trying to be honest. I'm sorry for doing those horrible things to you."

She reaches for my hand and I snatch it away. She sits there not knowing what to do or say. When I don't look back at her, I can see her gathering her things out of my peripheral. Then she stands to leave.

"There you go running again." She slowly sits back down. "My life is so different now Asmeret and so much has happened to me without you, I just don't know where you fit. I think a part of me needed to meet with you more than I realized, and now that I have, I hope the restless nights can stop."

"Me too, Lime; me too. If you never want to see or talk to me again, I will respect that, but I couldn't let another day go by without telling you what has been weighing on my heart for years."

The truth is, I don't want her to disappear from my life again, but I'm not sure how we are supposed to stay connected and start over. So, instead of trying to come up with a plan of action for the rest of our lives, I decide to just let things happen as they should. I invite her to my loft the day before she leaves. She admires my photos and artwork. I see her looking at dad's wedding photo, but she never comments, although I can tell she wants to. She picks up the one photo I have of her and runs her finger along it before she puts it back down.

The one thing I always wanted to do was run with her. As a baby, dad said she often ran with me while I was strapped in a stroller, but we never ran together. I'm not even sure she knows about my love of running. As we sit on my couch, and stare at the telly, I mumble something about running. She looks puzzled, so I take another sip of tea and clear my throat.

"Do you still run?"

"Once in awhile, when I need to think."

I can't believe that we share the same reason for running.

"I ran cross-country in secondary school. Now I run when I need to think, too."

She looks pleased.

"Wow. Well, maybe one day we can run a race together." She chuckles as if she doesn't really believe it can happen.

"What about now?"

"Run now?"

"Yes. We can go for a quick run right now in Central Park. I have some running clothes and an extra pair of shoes, depending on your shoe size."

She's a bit hesitant, but I can tell she doesn't want to run the risk of disappointing me, so she agrees.

"Let's go."

Although Asmeret is turning forty-seven this year, she still has the physique of a stallion after all those years of running.

The run starts off easy. She seems to almost walk the first mile in an effort to stay the pace with me. I keep asking her if she wants to speed up, but she insists that the pace is fine, and she isn't as fast as she used to be. After mile three, I want to test her, so I pick up a little speed and with minimal effort she speeds up too. We keep up with each other as we turn corners and tackle small hills. She runs with the finesse of a gazelle. Instead of her feet pounding the pavement, they float to an almost inaudible, syncopated beat. Her thunderous thighs and long legs turn corners with master agility. Her breathing is effortless despite my occasional panting. I think running with me brings back memories of her glory days, and at one point she seems to forget I am beside her.

We run five miles before I initiate a turn that will send us back in the direction of my loft. At mile nine, I bump her on her arm and give her the signal to let the competition begin. She half smiles and gives me a look with her eyes that says "You're on."

I take a deep breath and kick my legs up in high gear. She does the same. Other runners and walkers can tell we are in a serious competition and dart out of our way. I visualize myself breaking that yellow ribbon to victory and make a move on her that leaves her wondering what happened. When I reach the starting point before her, I stretch out on the grass in desperate need of oxygen. She sits down beside me. Her breath is louder now, but she is still able to talk. After a few moments, she helps me up and puts her arm around my shoulder. "Great run."

Three days isn't long enough for two people who missed twelve years of each others' lives. On our last day together, we sit on my couch and talk about Grandfather Dawit and his cancer.

"Dad's mum died of cancer."

"I know."

Funny how I forget she was married to my dad. A wave of embarrassment flashes across my face.

"Well, I believe they are on the verge of eradicating cancer real soon."

I make an attempt to sound comforting while apologizing for telling her something she already knew. She nods her head in agreement and presses her lips together in an attempt to keep from crying. As her eyes began to water, she stands up and walks to the kitchen to pour a glass of water. I figure all the talk about cancer brought back memories of her dad.

"They found a lump in my breast two years ago while I was living in Barcelona." She says with her back to me. "The doctors were able to catch it in time, but I had to undergo chemotherapy." She turns to face me. That explains the shortness of her hair. "It was then that I began to realize what and who were truly important in my life." She smiles at me.

"Did you go back to Brixton?"

She laughs as if I am a child again who has said something that is incorrect.

"Mum and dad had enough to deal with at the time and since I was never there for any of them, I didn't expect them to be there for me."

"But they're your parents, and parents care about their children's well-being." In my mind, I want my words to sting. The look on her face confirms that they do.

"Yes and some daughter I turned out to be."

Her lips tremble. She places the glass on the counter and looks away. I feel sorry for her and for her loneliness. Before I can say anything, she seems to perk up.

"But the most important thing is that I'm fine now and I started eating better. I'm a vegetarian you know and after that run, my dear, I'm going to start back running more often. It got my adrenaline going."

"Asmeret, is there anything I can do?"

She cocks her head to the side, gazes into my eyes, and softly whispers, "Just stay in touch."

When she leaves, my home feels empty again.

CHAPTER 26

To Asia with Love

It is a month before my twenty-fifth birthday and I want to do something different. Last year, Dee-Dee surprised me with balloons at a photo shoot. I celebrated with a room full of strangers. AJ sent me a text a few weeks ago when she got accepted to a five week study program at Renmin People's University of Chinese School of Law in Beijing, China. It is China's premier law school. The program begins the first of June, so I decide to spend my birthday with my best and dearest friend in China.

This makes my third trip to Asia; however, it is my first trip to China. While AJ is in class, I walk around taking pictures and getting lost. We visited the Great Wall together. I even convinced AJ to run some of the stairs of the great edifice with me, but after ten minutes, she walked back down. We treated ourselves to $7.00 massages and took rides in rickshaws almost every day. The best part of being here is spending time with someone who wants nothing from me but my friendship.

After three days of being in China, curiosity gets the best of me. AJ hasn't mentioned Jimmy once. I find it odd, but I figure she doesn't want to seem rude and talk about him all the time while I am visiting. However, she just isn't her usual jovial self. When we do laugh and talk, it is just like old times, but I often find her staring off into space in the middle of our conversations or losing her train of thought whenever she sees a couple holding hands or kissing. I ask her about it at dinner.

"So, how are things with you and Jimmy? You haven't mentioned him at all. Matter of fact, I can't recall the *last time* you've mentioned him."

"Oh girl, I don't want to talk about that."

"Why not?"

"'Cause you're here and he's not, that's why."

"AJ, it's me. Something's going on. You don't go from fondling in the back of movie theaters to 'I don't want to talk about it,' for no reason. Talk to me."

She shakes her head back and forth and puts her hands over her face so I can't see her cry. The last time I can remember ever seeing AJ cry was at Ms. Henning's funeral. I know whatever it is, it's serious. She still doesn't say anything, so I start calling out some possible reasons.

"Did he cheat on you?" She shakes her head no. "Did he lie about something?" She shakes her head no, again. "Is he gay?" This time she closes her eyes and shakes her head no.

I am about to run out of possibilities, and that's when it comes to me, and I blurt it out before it is even a complete thought in my head, "AJ, did he hit you?"

Her tears begin to fall like raindrops. I can't believe it. The girl who came to my rescue in secondary school, and the woman who threatened to kick Rohan's, Waterfall's, and Yanni's bum if they even thought about bothering me again in New York. The woman, who took no shit from anyone, was admitting to me that some man put his hands on her *without* her permission.

It began in Cancun. He got a little physical with her during sex and when she complained about it, he called her a tease. On New Year's Eve, he pushed her up against a wall and grabbed her around her neck, because she didn't want to go to a party hosted by some of his fraternity brothers. They had planned a nice, quiet evening with dinner and board games, but at the last minute he wanted to go to the party. When she told him she didn't want to be around a bunch of "chauvinistic weed heads," he exploded, slammed her against the wall, and grabbed her by the throat. She was so shocked that she just sat on her kitchen floor where he'd left her, for an hour, before she decided to go to church.

"He's threatened me before."

"How? What did he say?"

"Something about if I ever cheated on him that he'd kill me. He always accuses me of flirting with other guys. He's just so jealous for no reason. I mean some guys at the law school flirt with me, but I've never cheated on Jimmy. He even gets pissed when I tell him I have to study. He says I'm too smart for my own good." She lets out a nervous laugh.

"Why didn't you tell me?"

She blows her nose hard. "So you could tell me what I already know… that Jimmy's ass is crazy and I need to get rid of him?"

"Exactly"

"Look, it wasn't always ideal, but when things were good he made me feel like a queen, but when things were bad, I just waited for them to get better." She starts crying again.

I just can't believe what I'm hearing. Even though marrying Rohan was the worst mistake of my life and I truly believed he cheated on me with Waterfall and probably others, he never raised his hand to me. I figured that AJ saw enough violence between her parents that it would deter her from anyone who was abusive, but I learn that evening that sometimes it is the very thing that attracts a person. I want to have that bastard arrested right now.

"I'm just glad you're here with me."

She tries to compose herself. AJ assures me that things are over with Jimmy and she told him so before he went back home to D.C. for the summer to intern with the Washington Redskins. I pray that it is over and that she will stay away from him for good. She doesn't want to talk about him anymore, so we spend my last four days enjoying each other and China as if no one else is in the world exist.

On the flight back to New York, an hour into the flight, the plane has to turn back around, because of smoke coming from one of the wings. Another plane has to be brought in, along with new pilots. As I sit in the terminal, watching the new pilots arrive, I notice how distinguished one of the pilots looks. He is tall and lean and his honey colored complexion shimmers in the Asian sun. He carries his hat under his left arm, and his clothing is crisp. His hair is short and soft like mine and cut low and neat. His very masculine face is smooth and angular, and as he shakes hands with the other pilots, I can't help but notice that his hands are large and well maintained. As he talks to the other pilots, his smile reveals porcelain like teeth that sparkle. The heat in Asia in June can't hold a candle to the heat I am feeling inside.

I didn't realize I was in a trance until the stewardess tells me it is time to board. I ask her about the new pilots and she asks me if I want to meet them before the flight.

I try not to act too excited, "Only if it's no trouble."

Both pilots stand as I approach the doorway. The other pilots are Asian. I don't pay attention to their names. Then the stewardess introduces us, "Pilot Peters, this is Ms. Lime Prince."

He turns around and faces me. "Very nice to meet you, Ms. Prince. I was hoping that I'd get a chance to meet you when I found out you were on the plane."

His voice is deep and silky. I can smell a hint of cologne. His eyes, like his skin, are also the color of honey. He looks so professional in his uniform. As I shake his hand, I take a quick peek at his left hand, and all fingers are bare. Either he is truly single or he is married and doesn't want anyone to know. I vow to find out.

"Nice to meet you, too, Mr. Peters."

"It's Nigel."

"Oh, okay, Nigel. Well, it's Lime."

We both smile as I linger by the door for a few moments longer until the other pilot says it is time to go. Nigel excuses himself and tells me to relax and enjoy the flight. My enjoyment began the moment I saw him.

Even though Nigel piques my interest, AJ is still heavy on my mind. As I sip my favorite tea, I think of her often and how scared she must have been when Jimmy was threatening her life and hurting her. I was ready to fight for her. I promise I will make more of an effort to talk to my friend more often and make sure Jimmy is leaving her the hell alone.

I am asleep when the plane lands in New York. It was such a smooth flight. Nigel and the other pilot are waiting at the doorway to say goodbye.

"Did you enjoy the flight?"

"Oh, I practically slept the entire time."

I have a car waiting for me and he asks if he can he walk me to my car. I'm glad, because I don't want my lame comment about sleeping on the flight to be our last words.

"Ginger peach."

"Pardon me?"

"I heard you requested ginger peach tea on the flight. It is my favorite flavor."

"How coincidental is that?"

As he opens the car door for me, he says with confidence, "I don't believe in coincidence."

He stands there as if he has more to say, so I roll down the window once inside. As he leans over to talk to me, I stare at his soft lips as if that is the only way to hear him.

"New York is home for me now and I would love to fly you again if the opportunity presents itself."

"Maybe." I try to sound flirtatious. "If you're serious about flying me again, I trust you'll make it happen."

"Well, is it possible to call you?"

I ask him for his cell phone number and put my number in. He changes my name in his phone to Ginger Peach, and promises that I will hear from him soon. As the car pulls off, I watch him walk away and the view is quite tempting.

CHAPTER 27

Pilot Peters

I don't hear from Nigel for a week. On the few occasions when I do give my phone number to guys, they are usually calling before I can walk away, but not Nigel. I try not to think about it, but the more I try not to the more I do. It is something about this man that makes me check my phone several times a day for any missed calls. Then one day on a break, in Los Angeles, at a group photo shoot for Jean-Paul Gaultier, to my pleasant surprise it is Nigel on the other end.

"Hello."

"Lime, is that you?"

I pretend like I don't recognize the voice. "Yes, it is. May I ask who's calling?"

"It's Nigel; Nigel Peters from your Beijing flight."

I am cheesing so hard I walk away from the other models and crew.

"Oh, hello, how are you?" I force myself to sound calm. "You sound so far away."

"That's because I'm in Japan, but I'm flying back to New York tomorrow." He pauses. "I have a couple of days off when I return and I was

wondering if I could prove to you that I am serious about flying you somewhere again?"

"I see. Hmm, I leave for Rio next week and I won't be back until Friday."

"Great, how about next Saturday?"

"I guess that can be arranged." Who am I kidding? It's official.

"Excellent. I'll call you when I'm on my way. See you soon."

He is so confident and smooth that I start the countdown to Saturday
as soon as I hang up the phone. Tiffany and Company wants me to do
another shoot in Rio De Janeiro, Brazil. Laylah assures me Tiffany is not
using Yanni to do the shoot. He's getting careless with his habit and showing up late and high to shoots.

When I return from Rio, I call AJ to check on her. It has been three
weeks since my visit to China. AJ is back in Chicago now, working as a law
clerk for a private legal practice.

"Hey." When AJ doesn't call me "babe," it usually means she has a lot
on her mind.

"Well hello. How are you?"

"Frustrated"

"Why?" I pray it's not Jimmy again.

"This one client just hung up on me when I asked him for some papers
he was supposed to fill out and get back to us before he goes to court
tomorrow."

"So why would he hang up on you?"

"Because I've been calling him all week and his ignorant ass said he
doesn't have time to go to the post office or take time from work to drop
them off to me."

"So what happens now?"

"The attorney could petition to be withdrawn from the case, but...
whatever, how are you doing?"

"Remember the pilot I met on the flight back from China?"

"Uh-huh."

"Looks like we are going out next Saturday." I beam into the phone.

"That's great babe. I want all the details."

"Will do." I change my tone from beaming to concern. "Have you heard from Jimmy?"

"He's been calling, but I don't answer and I delete all his emails and text messages. I'm through with him Lime."

I wonder what will happen when he comes back to school the following month.

—⁓—

Nigel has a driver pick me up Saturday morning in a luxury car. We drive to a landing area out in the middle of nowhere. Nigel tells me to dress casual. It is blazing hot in New York in August, so I wear a short blue jean skirt and a backless lavender top that ties behind my neck, and wide heeled sandals with denim straps. It is a welcome break from stilettos, long dresses, and outlandish outfits. The driver drives about a half a mile out onto the runway. Then he stops the car, gets out, and opens the door for me. He instructs me to put on my shades. Within minutes, the wind picks up and the sound of a chopper is deafening. I look up into the sky and a white helicopter is descending down in our direction. When it lands, the driver escorts me over to the helicopter and helps me in. Nigel lifts his shades onto his head and flashes those pearly whites at me. He holds out his hand to help me into the passenger seat. As we fly, he points out mountains, hills, and valleys, and then we begin our descent.

We land in Providence, Rhode Island where another luxury car is waiting for us. Nigel keeps looking at me and smiling. It is my first time seeing him in "civilian" clothes. He wears a pair of tan linen pants, a button down, tan, short sleeved shirt, a tan New York baseball cap rolled in and pulled down over his eyes, and a pair of brown leather, men's sandals. His feet are well groomed like his hands and face. He is also wearing the same cologne that he wore the day I met him on the plane, and as before, it isn't overpowering, but when he leaves a place, you know a man has been there.

He is tight lipped about where we are going, but he assures me I will enjoy it. The drive is pleasant. We listen to a soulful woman sing jazz, drank bottled water, and talk about my shoot in Brazil and his trip to Japan. The driver lets us out in front of a quaint little store on the harbor. The name above the store read: *Ti Time*. When we walk in, the aroma of tea fills every pore in your body. It is a tea lover's Mecca. There are barrels of tea all along the walls of the store and a buffet bar of teas in the middle. There are teas from as far as Russia and as close as Rhode Island. The owners also sell all kind of desserts to compliment your tea. There is indoor and outdoor seating in the back of the store. It is unbelievable.

An elderly Vietnamese woman greets Nigel when he enters. She and her husband own the little shop and when Nigel opens the door, they react as if he is their long lost son.

"Ni-jewel. Oh, so good to see you." They hug him several times and the husband keeps slapping him on the back and laughs. "And who is this boo-ti-ful lady?"

"Mr. & Mrs. Ti, this beautiful lady is Lime Prince."

They stretch out their arms for me to hug them just like they hugged Nigel. Mrs. Ti moves closer to my face as if to study me. At first I thought she recognized me, but instead she points towards my eyes.

"Your eyes color of special green tea. Come, let me show you."

She pours me a sample, and the special aroma and taste gave it a liquor-type quality. I thank her and give the rest to Nigel.

After we place our order for a "Tea Lover's Delight," which includes a sample of six small different kinds of teas and desserts, we sit outside and wait for them to bring our order to us. Nigel has been coming to this shop since he was a freshman at Brown. His college girlfriend introduced him to the place. He liked it so much that he used to come here three times a week to study and drink tea. He even volunteered to help out around the store from time to time. The Tis' don't have any children and many of the students at Brown became their "adopted" children.

Nigel shies away from talking about himself. He wants to know more about me; the things the world doesn't know.

"So tell me, what's your favorite meal, the last book you read, your favorite kind of music, and your favorite time of the year?"

I must admit his questions are unusual, but I tell him that those details are earned with time. I don't want to reveal everything about myself on the first date, because I am hoping for more. I do get an opportunity to pry into his background a little.

Nigel Thelonious Peters was born and raised in New Orleans, Louisiana. He is a southern Creole boy, true and true. He and his twin sister, Nia, were raised on the road with their jazz singing mum. That soulful voice we heard in the car was one of his mum's CDs. His dad died when he and his sister were seven. He had been a pilot in the Air Force and died in a rescue effort; Nigel's love of flying was inevitable. His mum was the lead vocalist in a jazz band from New Orleans called *Escapes*, in the '70s and '80s, and traveled all over the country performing. She took her children on the road with her as much as possible.

His sister, Nia, is married with two little girls, and runs a successful catering business back in New Orleans. Nigel was in the Air Force ROTC in college and an officer in the Air Force. He learned how to fly helicopters in the military, but today he is an international pilot; thirty, single, and as AJ says "delicious."

After the tea and light desserts, we walk along the harbor and have dinner at a wonderful restaurant overlooking the water. Nigel is attentive to every word that comes out of my mouth. He calls my accent melodious, and tells me my haircut compliments me well. Vera wasn't cutting it as close these days, so the wavy texture was coming back. What intrigues me the most is the fact that Nigel never mentions my life as a Supermodel.

He is well aware of whom I am and what I do for a living, but his interest is about me, not the person on the runway, on the cover of magazines, commercials, or billboards. He wants to know about Lime Prince. When the evening ends, we make our way back to the helicopter. Nigel decides to turn the tables on me again.

"So, you avoided talking about yourself all day."

"Avoided?"

"Yes, but that's okay. You will be the topic of conversation next time."

"Hmm. So when is next time?"

"After my next rotation this month." His confidence is sexy. "I fly four to five times a month for about four to five days at a time; the rest of the month is my time, which is when I'd like to see you again."

"Is there no one else who wants to see you on your days off?"

I try my best not to sound accusing.

When we arrive at the landing area, he hesitates before getting out of the car. Then he turns to me, leans forward, and says, "I don't play those games, but telling you and showing you are two different things, so I chose to show you. I'll see you, and *only* you, on my next couple of days off, if that's satisfactory to you, Ms. Prince?"

I smile and nod. He gets out of the car and opens the door for me, takes my hand, and escorts me into the helicopter. Something tells me that this is only the beginning of more pleasant experiences with Pilot Peters.

CHAPTER 28

Exes

I was so tired after my date with Nigel, I thought I heard a phone ringing in my sleep, but after three rings, I open my eyes and realize it's not a dream. The fluorescent numbers on the clock show 3:12 A.M. and I know that can only mean trouble is on the other end. It's dark, so I can't see the caller ID before I answer.

"Yes."

"Oh, my God . . . oh, my God, Lime." AJ's hysterical.

I jump up and turn on the light.

"What is it, AJ? What happened?"

My heart begins to beat out of my chest. All I can think about is our conversation in China about Jimmy.

"I'm going to kill somebody."

"What happened?" I yell.

"That fucker got his ex-girlfriend pregnant. She's been calling me all summer on his phone. I just got off the phone with her. I thought it was Jimmy calling all those times and I was going to cuss him out for calling me so much especially at two o'clock in the morning. Before I could say 'hello,' this woman starts going off. She wanted to know who I was and how did I know Jimmy. She said her name is Julia and she is his girlfriend and he just left her house, but he forgot his phone again. According to her, they've been dating since high school and they've been having sex all summer and now she's two months pregnant with his baby." AJ starts to cry. "I asked her why she was calling me. I told her I don't do drama, and I could care less what Jimmy does or who he does it with and I would appreciate if she'd stopped calling me before I call the police on her and Jimmy for harassment. That's when she got to cussing and threatening me to leave him alone or else—"

"Or else what?"

"I didn't even stay on the phone long enough to find out."

"So what did you do?"

"I called you."

"That wanker."

"Oh, my God, Lime. I don't need this. I'm through with Jimmy and I want him and his psychotic girlfriend to leave me the hell alone."

"And if they don't, you call the police like you said. Do you really think he is still in D.C., like she said, or is he back in Chicago?"

"I don't know. Classes don't begin for another month. I don't think he is."

"Well, listen, why don't you come here for a few days? You could travel with me or just stay here."

She thinks about it for a moment, before responding.

"No, I have to work and plus, I'm not afraid of them. I'm more pissed than anything. Although I ended things with Jimmy a part of me still loves him and I'm pissed about that. I'm pissed that some cracked out woman is calling me at fucking two in the morning with some nonsense. I'm a fucking law student who is about to graduate in less than a year and I don't need a case on my record for some bullshit."

"And you won't. Just try to be calm and remember if she calls again or if Jimmy starts calling, call the police. And I'm serious about you coming here."

"Yeah, I know."

"Try to get some sleep."

"Okay." She lets out a huge sigh.

"I love you."

"Me too."

After that call, I call AJ as often as I can. We make a point to touch base at least every other day. She did get a few more calls from Jimmy's phone, before she blocked the number. I still thought she should have called the police, but she didn't think it was necessary.

When classes began, she didn't hear from Jimmy and she didn't have any classes with him, so she didn't have to see him every day. The only time she has to see him now is twice a month at the Black Law Student Association meetings; AJ is the president this year and Jimmy is the treasurer. Since she blocked his number, he tries contacting her via email. She only responds if the messages involve BLSA business. She said he seems to be getting the hint; perhaps the emails will stop.

Even though AJ is dealing with her own issues, she still makes a point to ask me about Nigel from time to time. As promised, he spends his days off with me when I am in New York. I start to schedule my own off days these days and make sure they coincide with his days. It has been two months since our first introductions on the flight from China, and I'm liking him more and more with each passing day. In our short time together, we've flown to dinner in different states and he's taught me how to Rollerblade and play tennis. He even started running with me. He loves sports and although tennis and football are his favorites, he played both in high school and recreationally in college, he is enthusiastic about running.

Last year, I had a small, cameo role in a film, in which I played a sales representative at a makeup counter. I decide to invite him to attend the screening of the movie at Grauman's Chinese Theater in Hollywood with me. Although it's only been two months, I want him there with me. I decide to tell Laylah about my attendance at the premier, with Nigel, in advance before she reads about it in the tabloids the next day. She wants to know everything about Nigel, who he is, where he's from, and what he does for a living. I hadn't gotten this much interrogation from my dad when I married Rohan. I avoid her questions as best as I can and continue with my plans.

The day before we are set to leave for LA, I call Nigel to have a heart-to-heart talk with him about what to expect at the screening. I want him to be prepared for all the cameras, questions, and chaos.

"Hi."

"Hey, you." The sound of his voice makes me melt.

"You're not shy, are you?"

"No. Why?"

"Well, I know we don't talk much about my modeling career, but I just want you to know that overzealous photographers and nosy reporters are part of the package with me."

"Oooookay."

"I mean I don't want you to be intimidated by that."

"I'm not."

"Are you sure?"

"Yup."

"Because, I would understand if—"

"Lime, even though I don't talk about your Supermodel status, I'm well aware that you *are* a Supermodel, but that's not what I care about. I just want to be with you, whether that's at McDonalds or on the red carpet. If you're going to be there, that's where I want to be and no one else matters."

I want to jump through the phone and land in his arms. This man is too good to be true and it scares me a little. God knows I can't deal with another Rohan, Yanni, or even a Jimmy. I just take Grandmother Genet's advice about discernment and whisper a silent prayer that if Nigel is a wolf in sheep's clothing that I'll see the light before my heart is in too deep.

Nigel is the most handsome man at the screening. He wears a sharp, Calvin Klein navy blue, tailored suit with a crisp, beige shirt which he leaves open at the collar. He wears the jacket open as well, and a pair of brown, soft leather Paul Smith shoes. He accents my baby blue, ankle length skirt, white, fitted shirt, and high heeled blue stilettos. I feel so secure and special with him as he holds my hand and stands right next to me as the cameras flash. When they ask me his name, he looks at me as if to ask if it was okay if he introduces himself. I take a step back and let him. After the screening, we dance and mingle at the after party. Nigel is the perfect gentleman and all eyes are on us, and I can care less. It is the first time in my life a man, aside from my dad, is treating me like a queen and it doesn't hurt that the man is gorgeous.

When we return to New York, it is very late. I tell Nigel he doesn't have to drive back home if doesn't want to. This is the first time I've invited him to stay the evening. As attracted as I am to Nigel, I'm not ready to sleep with him yet. The truth is I'm afraid to. According to Rohan, I am terrible in bed, and since he was the only man I had ever had sex with, I didn't want to take the chance of disappointing Nigel in the same way. I just want him close to me for a little while longer. I want to fill the empty spaces in my home with more than just myself for once.

As I change into my silk pajama shorts and top, he takes off his shirt to reveal his lean, yet well cut frame. He keeps his suit pants on. We slide into bed together and I turn my back to him as I scoot closer. He wraps his arm around me as if to say "I got you forever." The warmth and scent of his body lull me into a deep sleep. It is my first deep sleep since arriving in New York.

CHAPTER 29

Won't Let Go

Thanksgiving is around the corner. Nigel is scheduled to fly to Africa, which means I'll be spending another holiday either by myself, working, or with my dad and Lona. AJ is unsure of her Thanksgiving plans. She just wants to chill by herself after all the drama with Jimmy, so I propose that she and I cook Thanksgiving dinner together at her place, just the two of us. Since I left Chicago, two years ago, I'd only been back twice and both times it was for very brief visits. Lona and dad are spending Thanksgiving with Lona's oldest son and his family in Ohio. Even though AJ and I only know how to cook the basics, we call her aunts back in Tennessee to guide us through.

When I arrive, AJ's face tells the story of her stress. Her eyes are dark, and she's lost some weight. Her hair isn't as stylish as I remember. You can tell her once a week visits to the hair salon have gone from weekly to monthly. As much as she tries to relax and enjoy Thanksgiving, her solemn spirit reveals the worries on her mind. However, we are excited to see each other and promise to focus only on enjoying our brief time together. As we peel sweet potatoes, wash greens, bake macaroni and cheese, roll dough for homemade rolls, season a turkey breast for AJ, and sip wine, we can't help but to reminisce about Ms. Henning's fish fry's and card parties.

—∿—

Friday nights, Maxine Henning could be found with a bottle of Corona in one hand, standing over a deep fryer of catfish as Johnny Taylor crooned how it is "cheaper to keep her "in the background. She was preparing for her Friday night bid whist parties with her co-workers from the post office. I would arrive just in time to help AJ set up the tables, vacuum, and clean the loo. Once everyone arrived with their pans of spaghetti, potato salad, and additional liquor, AJ and I were relegated to her room for the rest of the evening, only to emerge when it was time to eat or to pee. Within minutes, nicotine vapors mixed with fried grease and hot sauce filled every inch of the flat, and like clockwork Ms. Henning would yell at the top of her smoke filled lungs, "boston time, goddamnit." That meant at least three more hours of card slapping, high pitched laugher, and off key harmonizing with Johnny Taylor. Talking about Ms. Henning and cooking together helps us to find the humor in life and allow our spirits to laugh. We decide to play some Johnny Taylor in her honor.

Over dinner, AJ wants to hear more about Nigel. She says I have a glow about me. I tell her his whole life story as he has told it to me.

"So if he is the next best thing since ice cream, why doesn't he already have a woman?"

It wasn't that I didn't wonder that myself. I told her that he and his college girlfriend were both in AFROTC in college. They both went to the Air Force after college and at one point were engaged to be married; however, her father and only brother were killed in a tragic car accident, and she was transferred to another station closer to her family, and soon decided to call the engagement off. Nigel said she was never the same after the accident.

That was four years ago, and since then he's dated here and there, and even lived with a woman for a few months before they went their separate ways.

"Believe me I'm not in any rush to get my heart broken again."

"Look babe, not all men are like Rohan and Jimmy, and on the flip side, not all men are as special as your fine ass daddy, but when we meet the one truly for us, we'll know."

With that assurance, we grab hands, press our foreheads together, and smile.

I can only stay in Chicago for one more day. I have another photo shoot back in New York and some shows abroad. Since AJ has a one bedroom flat, we sleep in the same bed like we did as teenagers. We are both awakened when the phone rings at six in the morning. Without even looking at the caller ID, AJ grabs it, trying to keep it from waking me.

"Yeah?" She breathes into the phone. There is a pause. "Jimmy what part of 'don't call me' don't you understand?"

I sit up on my elbows. AJ motions for me to go into the other room and pick up the phone.

"I just want to apologize to you." His voice is softer now. "I'm sorry about everything. I've been trying to tell you that since classes began, but you won't even look at a brother, let alone respond to my emails."

"Because we don't have anything else to talk about, Jimmy. I don't like strange women calling me over dumb shit."

"I know, and I'm sorry about that. I don't know how she got your number—"

"From you."

"No, she didn't. I didn't tell her to call you."

"Whatever, Jimmy. You are about to be a father, so I wish you and Fatal Attraction the best."

He raises his voice. "I'm not about to be a father. That's not my baby, and I wish you would stop saying that. You're the only one I want to have my baby and no one else." AJ starts to laugh which makes Jimmy raise his voice even louder. "What the hell you laughing about? You know I love you."

AJ regains her composure. "Jimmy, stop calling me and enjoy your Thanksgiving with your new family." She hangs up the phone.

I come back in the room and sit on the edge of the bed. The phone rings again but she doesn't answer. AJ can't stop laughing about Jimmy and the phone call. She just keeps saying "Can you believe that nut?" You can tell she is tired of the whole situation and just wants to erase the day she ever met him, but she can't. As I listen to her rant about the whole "soap opera" affair, I have an uneasy feeling about Mr. Bryant and his state of mind. I can only hope that he gets the message this time.

—⁓—

When I get back to New York, work is waiting. Laylah calls, sounding upbeat. "Christmas show in Paris, dahling?"

"Excuse me?"

"Once again, Erick wants you for his special benefit Christmas show in Paris. Won't be able to join you, though, you know its Sharon's Christmas Bash and all, just business as usual." She sounds bored.

"Is the show the same day as Sharon's party?"

"No, it's two days before, but I have so much to do before the New Year, and I can't afford to be in Paris that long right now."

"Hmm, I did get an invitation this year, and since I will be there, I may stay a few extra days." For the first time since I'd met Laylah in June, 2001, she is speechless. Laylah knows that at the end of the year, my contract with Faces expires and I have the option not to renew with them, but I always do. Her silence tells me that this year, she is concerned.

"Well, dahling, I'm sure Sharon will be delighted." Now her sarcasm is showing.

My schedule is getting busier with the holidays and interferes with my time with Nigel, but he is very understanding. Once I find out his off days coincide with the show, I invite him to accompany me so we can attend Sharon's party on the Rivera together. I finally have that someone special to take.

Erick's show is as risqué as usual. It is a smaller production, though, with only seven models. The theme is Silver & Gold, and at one point in the show my face is painted with both colors. Although Erick's designs are controversial, they are always unique and garner a lot of press. The pace of the show is fast, and at one point I slip on the gold and silver glitter that covers the entire stage. A hush falls over the audience anticipating my fall, but I catch myself and make it look like it is part of the show. Everyone applauds my recovery.

I recognize some of Dee-Dee's staff at the show, but I don't see Dee-Dee. I have only seen her in passing since her confession, and I miss her. Nigel presents me with a bouquet of long stemmed yellow roses after the show. He arranged to have them there even before we arrived in Paris. As we laugh about how I almost kissed the pavement, Nigel turns his head to look behind me. I turn around and Dee-Dee is staring me in the face. I wasn't expecting to see her, but when I look at her and see her smile again, I am thankful for the reunion. We hug tight and I almost forget that Nigel is standing there before I introduce them. I tell Nigel she is a close friend, but we lost touch. Nigel can see that we want to talk in private, so he excuses himself to walk around. Dee-Dee is looking better than ever. Her hair, although still cut lower than mine, is no longer blond, but a complimentary shade of auburn. She is still a "fashion plate," and her makeup is as flawless as ever. She looks peaceful. I am so happy to see her.

"You look good, girl." I step back to take a look at her.

"No, Ms. Lime, all eyes were definitely on you tonight." She lets out a sigh. "It's so good to see you again."

"You, too, Dee-Dee." I pause to let the awkward silence pass. "Hey, about the way I reacted back then—"

"No need to explain. I'm past that, and I hope you are too, and from the looks of Nigel, I'd say you are more than 'past it.'" We both laugh.

We take a seat and I bring her up to date on my life. Dee-Dee said after our conversation she kind of went into seclusion. She only went to the office, worked a couple of shows and shoots, and stayed between Jersey and New York. She still has her grandmother's house in Jersey. It has become her getaway when work and life get to be too much. Her grandmother's cats now live with her and have become her babies, *and* she met someone. At first it is awkward to hear Dee-Dee describe a woman she met on a flight from Los Angeles, but she sounds so confident and excited that all I can do is listen and smile. I don't want to judge Dee-Dee or stir up the past, so I accept her for the friend she is to me and the one she will always be and keep listening.

CHAPTER 30

You, Me, & He

Sharon has outdone herself again. This year she hires performers from Cirque Du Soleil. These acrobatic wizards flip and twirl and contort all over her lawn. Everyone is amazed at the private show. Nigel is having a great time and everyone, even Sharon, makes him feel welcome. Laylah comes solo this time. Dee-Dee told me that Laylah's husband finally had had enough and filed for divorce. The thing about Laylah is that she doesn't let anything, not even the end of her twelve year marriage, interfere with what she does best; making money. She laughs and drinks all night long as if she hasn't a care in the world.

Whenever Sharon crosses my path throughout the night, I can feel Laylah's stares, but Sharon isn't stupid. She knows it was unethical to approach me about signing with Maier while I'm still with Faces, so she lets her lavish Christmas parties and subtle hints do the talking.

"Enjoying yourself, I hope?"

Her pleasant tone accompanies me as I stand on the terrace waiting for Nigel to come back from the loo. She is making her rounds to each guest.

"Absolutely. It's such a wonderful view from here."

She places her wine glass on the ledge, and inhales the view with me. "Yes, it's one of the main reasons I bought this house. I'm glad you could come again, Lime. You and your guests are always welcome." Right before she turns to go back into the party, she places her hand on my arm. "I'll be back in the States in a couple of days. If you need anything, Lime, don't hesitate to call me personally."

I nod and thank her. Just then Nigel returns with two glasses of Pinot Grigio and a smile that lights up the night sky, and erases Sharon's offer from my memory.

Nigel and I leave the party early to walk along the Eiffel Tower before it gets too late. We've both been to Paris before, but this is our first time together and we don't want to miss our share of the "City of Amore." The night air in Paris in December is brisk, so we bundle up with our coats and hats and walk arm in arm. We are so close that it reminds me of the couple I saw in the Chevy Impala on my drive to New York two years ago. We seem to meld together. As I nestle closer to Nigel, I begin to understand that woman's desire to be so close to her man. We talk about life and each other under the Eiffel Tower lights. It's been six months now since I stared out that airport window at Nigel; fate engineered our meeting.

Nigel keeps holding me close to him and places wet kisses on my forehead. I can tell he's been dying to say something the entire night.

"I feel so blessed to be with you right now at this moment, Lime. It's lonely out there, and the fact that you could have any man in the world and you allow me to be that man is unreal. I just hope we can continue to have more moments like this and you will allow me to be your man for a long time."

I want to interrupt him and tell him that I wrote the book on lonely and that I didn't want just "any" man. I want Nigel Thelonious Peters. Instead, I politely let him finish.

"Lime, I'm in love with you."

They are the words I have longed to hear. I bury myself deeper into his embrace and tell him that I love him too and I wish the night would never end.

Nigel only has one more day on the ground before he has to fly to back to Japan. He needs to rest, so we plan to see each other when he returns on December 30th. He insists that we will welcome 2004 in together, and I don't object. He already made our New Year Eve's plans. For the first time since Thanksgiving, I get to relax and do nothing until the New Year. I think about flying to Brixton to see my family. It has been months since I've heard from anyone there. Asmeret said Grandmother Genet planned to move back to Ethiopia to live in the New Year. She and her sisters made some changes to the café. They expanded the menu and added some entertainment on the weekends; everything from live music to spoken word. Addis Ababa Café was becoming the talk of Brixton and London. They were even talking about relocating to a bigger space in the New Year.

Since, Laylah had already promised me that 2004 was going to be bigger for me than 2003; I decide I really need to give my body and mind a rest. Actually, her exact words were "Two-thousand-four, dahling." Whenever she starts conversations with her "word games," I know she has something up her sleeve.

AJ and some of her law school girlfriends are taking a cruise to the Bahamas for New Year's Eve. I am glad to hear her excitement about getting away. It is what she needs and a great way to clear her mind for her last two quarters of law school. Jimmy did not call her again nor did his psychotic girlfriend, so she was able to take her finals in peace.

At the last minute, I decide to pack a small bag, rent a car, and drive up to upstate New York for two luxurious days of massages, manicures, pedicures, facials, and tranquility. For the first time in a long time, I don't think about shows, shoots, or interviews and that includes whether to re-sign with Faces or not. I know Maier is influential and means much more money and maybe even greater opportunities, but right now none of those things matter to me. I am in love. Truly in love for the first time in my life, and more money and greater opportunities can't compare.

When I return the morning of New Year's Eve, Nigel has already called. I call him as I drive back from the spa to my loft.

"Hello, you." His sweet voice fills my ear.

"Hello, honey," I say through my grin. "How was your flight?"

"Long, but safe. I would love to visit there with you one day. Hey, where are you? It sounds windy."

"I'm driving back from upstate New York. I treated myself to some pampering."

"Good for you. Are you all soft and glowing?"

"Just for you." I love flirting with him.

"Can't wait to see you tonight."

"Me, neither. What time should I expect you?"

"Well, I thought I would pick you up at seven. Is that okay?"

"Perfect. Oh, what should I wear?"

"Whatever you want, because you look good in everything." Now I am glowing.

We hang up and I press on the gas. I have to get home and get ready for my date with Pilot Peters.

Nigel arrives at 7:00 P.M. on the nose, looking and smelling good enough to eat. He is wearing black jeans, a sexy cashmere black turtleneck, black cowboy boots, and a soft leather black jacket. I can tell he just cut his hair, because it is neater and has that afro sheen smell they spray at the barbershop. He plants a series of warm kisses all over my face, and tells me that he misses me every day, in between each one.

I am overdressed in my black evening gown and stilettos. Nigel thinks I look wonderful and what I'm wearing is fine, but I work in this attire all during the week and I welcome any opportunity to dress more casual. I change into a sexy black pants suit to match my man. The jacket drops low enough to see the curvature of my breasts. I change my jewelry to a silver choker with one of those colorful diamonds hanging on the end, compliments of Tiffany. After I brush my hair back with my hands, retouch my makeup, reapply some more lipstick, and grab my handbag, I head back downstairs where my prince waits. He stands and shakes his head in amazement.

I love how Nigel always thinks ahead and how he listens to my likes and dislikes and my wishes and does his level best to surprise me by making each one come true for me, but I still want to know where we were going. All he will say is "You will see when we get there."

We pull up to one of my favorite restaurants in New York, the Spice Market in West Village. This restaurant is "the" spot for celebrity events and shows. The food is great and I am starving. The valet takes the car and Nigel takes my hand. I always feel comfortable at the Spice Market, because most New Yorkers who come here are almost immune to celebrity presence; however, there are always those who didn't get the memo. To avoid any interruptions, Nigel arranges for us to have a private room. Janet Jackson and Jermaine Dupri are in the next room. We giggle and talk as usual as we eat from each other's plates and feed each other like teenagers on a date.

"Lime, I've been thinking and I want you to meet my mom and sister and the rest of my family in New Orleans. I've told them all about you and I feel like the time is right."

I too have told AJ and my dad about Nigel, but he hasn't met them either. The last man my dad met returned me back to him like pants that were too tight. I love Nigel, but I am still cautious. I mean what if in a few months he gets tired of me, or like these other guys who are all into me in the beginning and then one day I never hear from them again. I ask myself, *what would be the point of meeting his family then?*

"That's a big step, Nigel."

"I know and flying over continents gave me a lot of time to think about it, but I can't explain it Lime. It just feels right and I want them to get to know you." He can feel my resistance. "Are you having doubts about us?"

"Noooo, I...I...just want to be sure. What if you introduce me to your family now and then you change your mind about me, about us?"

"I don't think that's going to happen."

"But it could and then—"

"Sounds like you are the one having doubts." He sits back in his seat, and I can see the fear in his eyes.

I scoot closer. "I'm not. I just want you to be sure, that's all."

I kiss him on the lips and promise him the first opportunity I can get away; we will go to New Orleans.

We finish dinner and dessert around eight forty five. He wants to make sure we leave in time so we don't miss the rest of our evening. I'm anxious and persuade him to at least give me a hint.

"A friend of mine from high school plays in a jazz band and they are performing tonight at a club in Brooklyn. They are scheduled to go on at nine thirty."

I know Nigel is a jazz lover, because of his mum. He and his sister's middle names are in honor of some great jazz legends, Thelonious Monk and Nina Simone. What he said next sent an electric shock through me.

"The name of the band is Red Velvet. My boy Pepper is the percussionist, but I heard the trumpet player is out of this world." I look at him as if he's a ghost.

I excuse myself to the ladies' room as soon as we arrive. I burst through the door and rush into the first stall ready to throw up everything I'd eaten right onto the floor. I can't believe that I am about to be reunited with Rohan and Pepper again. The last time that happened was one of the worst nights of my life. Almost three years in New York, and never have our paths crossed. God really has an odd sense of humor. I had no idea Pepper was from New Orleans. I thought he was from New York and moved to Chicago where he and Rohan met. I'm having trouble breathing and feel a bit light headed. I sit on the toilet with my head buried between my legs. I suck in all the air I can to fill my lungs, before blowing it out slowly.

I have to find out if Nigel told Pepper about me and how I can change our plans. I decide to fake an upset stomach. I will blame it on the food and ask if we can just go back to his place. Nigel is waiting for me outside holding our coats.

"You okay, baby?"

He looks so concerned and sweet. I can't lie to him. He is so anxious to get going, because he doesn't want to miss the opening selection.

What are the chances that Nigel would know Pepper? At the restaurant he said he and Stephon Pepper had met in high school. The joke became Peters and Peppers as in "Peter Piper picked a pack of peppers . . ." They were in the band together. Nigel played the saxophone and Pepper the drums, and soon they became good friends. Nigel said Pepper was the best high school percussionist in the state of Louisiana. After college, Pepper went to DePaul on a music scholarship. His father's job relocated them to Chicago after Pepper's graduation, but Pepper quit college and decided to start his own jazz band and that is when he and Rohan met. They reconnected when Pepper moved to New York six years ago. I asked him if Pepper knew he was bringing me tonight and he said "no." He planned to introduce us tonight.

It isn't enough to just see Rohan again. I'm being forced to see two reminders of my ugly past. Rohan, I can explain. Nigel knows I'm divorced and that my marriage was less than ideal, but I have no idea how I will explain Rohan *and* Pepper, especially if they both decide to relive the past tonight for some reason. I need to talk to AJ. She will know what to do, but she is on a cruise ship in the middle of the Atlantic Ocean. She's trying to escape all the craziness with Jimmy and here I am ready to reintroduce her to more, but I need to call. I excuse myself to the loo again right before the band begins. Nigel furrows his brow. I blame it on all the tea and wine at the restaurant. I slip into a stall and speed dial AJ's number. As the phone rings for what seems like eternity, I pray she answers.

"Hey, babe." It sounds like AJ is at a party.

"AJ, I'm in trouble."

"Hold on, I can barely hear you. I'm about to enter a limbo contest." It gets quiet for a few seconds, and then she comes back on the phone. "Okay, I can hear you now. I almost didn't hear this phone ring. I was in line and about to take it down low." She cackles.

"AJ, you are not going to believe this. Nigel *and* Pepper are friends and I'm at a club in Brooklyn to see Rohan and Pepper's band perform in five minutes."

"Did you just say you are somewhere with Rohan and Pepper?"

"Not *with* them, I'm at a club with Nigel to see *them* perform. Pepper is a close friend of his."

"Where are you?"

"I'm in a stall in the loo. AJ, what the bloody hell do I do? What do I do? Nigel wants to introduce me to Pepper after the show. If those bastards decide to get cute and Nigel finds out about what happened that night, he will end things between us for sure."

I put my hand over my mouth to stop a panic attack from coming on.

"No, he won't, because he won't find out. You go in there and enjoy the show and after it's over—" Her phone breaks up.

I forget I'm in a public place and start yelling into the phone. "AJ, I can't hear you. You're breaking up . . . AJ!"

"Babe . . . can you hear me? . . . Li—?"

The phone goes dead. I redial her number, but it keeps going into her voice mail. *Shit.* I've been in here for awhile, and I know Nigel is getting anxious about seeing the show. I do my best to straighten my face before leaving the loo.

This time he looks a bit upset. "Lime, are you okay?"

I might as well get it over with and confess. Just as I open my mouth to tell him the truth, the club goes dark and the crowd goes wild. When the crowd settles down, the spotlight illuminates the mic on the stage, and all you can see is a gold trumpet surrounded by long fingers. It looks as if the trumpet and fingers are suspended in midair. A few seconds later, an upbeat, jazzy, a cappella melody flows from the trumpet and penetrates our ears. The other instruments join in one at a time, until the entire stage is lit and the ensemble is alive.

I haven't laid eyes on Rohan in four years. His locs are well past his shoulders now, and pulled back into a long ponytail. He is much more muscular than I remember. His army green cargo pants, black T-shirt with Miles Davis face on the front, and black combat boots, give him a kind of prominence that I had never seen before. He plays with his eyes closed and sweat dripping from every pore on his body. He always put his heart and soul into his music and tonight is no different.

Pepper looks the same, except he is sporting a bald head now. The one nice feature about Pepper is his lips. He has LL Cool J lips and licks them several times as he beats the bloody hell out those drums. He also plays the bongos at different points in the show, and makes those drums breathe. Although I'm still nervous throughout the entire show, I must admit they put on one hell of a performance.

Nigel is on fire. He rocks and taps his fingers with the same fervor in which Rohan plays. I try to be calm, and enjoy the evening, for him. The band plays the countdown to the New Year, and at midnight confetti falls from the ceiling and Nigel leans over the table and kisses me hard.

After their last number, Nigel is excited to meet Rohan and introduce me to Pepper. I try to tell him before we go backstage that I know them both, but he is so engrossed in finding out how to get backstage, that doesn't hear a word I say. The security is tight, but Pepper left Nigel's name, "with guest" on the VIP list. We walk down a long corridor. There are people everywhere, and Nigel is navigating the crowd while holding my hand. I do my best to keep up with him and while preparing myself for the worst.

Pepper is smoking a cigarette and talking close in some white woman's ear in the hall with his back to us. Nigel sneaks up behind him and puts his head in a choke hold. "Peter Piper Punk."

Pepper turns around and slaps Nigel's hand so hard the smack echoes in the hall for a few moments. When they hug, Pepper freezes.

"Well, shit, Lime Prince?"

"You too know each other?" Nigel asks.

"Hell yeah. Lime and I go way back. How are you?" He gives me a bear hug.

"I'm fine, Pepper. How are you?" I refuse to put my arms around him. I keep my eyes on Nigel the whole time.

"Real good . . . real good." He turns to Nigel. "So how long you two been dating?"

"Six months," Nigel and I say in unison.

Nigel looks at me and kisses my hand. I force a smile.

"So how do you two know each other?" Nigel asks us both.

Before I can answer, Pepper bites his bottom lip and squints his eyes in my direction, "Through a mutual friend, when I lived in Chicago, and today she is a Supermodel and still fine as ever. Nigel, you got gold, man."

Just then Rohan walks out into the hall calling Pepper's name. We all turn around. Rohan stops in his tracks when he sees me. Pepper introduces Nigel to Rohan, and as they exchange "dap." Rohan stares at me in disbelief.

I turn to Nigel. "Nigel, Rohan is my ex-husband."

"What? *This* is your ex-husband?" He rubs his hand across his chin a couple of times. "You know Pepper *and* the trumpet player? What's really going on?" he asks all of us.

Rohan interjects, "Mi nah see Lime in, mek me tink, four year ah so, but me nah worry."

"And plus, I had no idea we were coming to see them tonight, remember?" I plead to Nigel to understand.

Nigel inhales and let out a long sigh. "Wow."

Just then, Pepper pulls him aside into a room and leaves Rohan and me in the hall alone.

"Kiss me neck baack, Lime. Me nevah know I would come cross you but for a million year."

"That makes two of us." My tone is dry.

"Yuh hair look real nice. Me caan help but to see you all bout New Yahk, pon de tee vee, all kind ah street postah, but me tink dat yuh waan see me."

"You figured right."

All I could think about was this very day January 1, 2000 when Rohan gave me back to my dad and left for New York never to be heard from again, until now.

"Me deserve dat. Look Lime, yuh no believe dis but me saari—"

"Rohan don't. Your 'sorries' are the furthest thing from my mind right now. I didn't come here for an apology from you. I came to enjoy the evening with my man."

He looks over his shoulder at the room Nigel and Pepper entered. "Now, tell me, you and yuh *mon* enjoy de show?"

I can't believe he has the nerve to be sarcastic.

"Yes, you all put on a good performance, but then again your music has always been your only true love." Now it is my turn to be sarcastic.

"Ah why yuh haf fe be suh rude?" Me say me saari."

"And I said I'm not interested in your sorries. You and I are history, so it really doesn't matter to me anymore."

Nigel and Pepper come out of the room laughing and holding on to each other. I feel my stomach churn again. Nigel slaps hands with Rohan again and tells him he made love to that trumpet tonight. Pepper grabs my hand and tells me it is good to see me again and that no one on earth has eyes as gorgeous as mine. I can't wait to wash my hand as soon as I get a chance. Rohan doesn't touch me. Instead he just says good-bye as if he has lost his best friend. Nigel helps me with my coat, and hugs Pepper and tells him that he will talk to him soon.

We left Rohan and Pepper in the hall watching us hold hands and walking away. I can feel the heat on my back from their stares. My phone rings and the call read "urgent." I stop to answer it, but can't get good reception in the hollow hallways.

"Hello . . . hello . . . can you hear me?"

I motion to Nigel that I can't hear and start walking farther back down the hall to see if the reception is any better. Nigel mouths that he will go get the car.

"Hello."

"Lime . . . it's me . . . you okay?"

"AJ? The reception is awful. I can barely hear you."

"I asked are you okay?" AJ shouts.

"Yes, Nigel and I are leaving now."

"Did you see Rohan and Pepper?"

"Yes, but let me call you later, okay?"

I wait a few seconds, but I never hear AJ's response. "AJ?" I close my phone and start heading back to the exit door. I realize that I walked back down the hall to almost the same spot that Rohan, Pepper, Nigel, and I had been standing minutes ago. I shudder at the thought of seeing them again, drop my phone in my purse, and stop at the water fountain behind me for a quick sip. The entire reunion with Rohan and Pepper leaves my mouth dry.

"See, I told you, man. I told you one day she'd do something to try and embarrass you." I almost choke.

It's Pepper. He is yelling at someone as they walk up the hall in my direction. I slip behind the wall next to the water fountain.

"She brought that nigga here to get back at you. I mean Nigel is cool and all but this is about paper and Lime got plenty of it. I say it's time to send her a little reminder from her past."

I peek from behind the wall, careful to not be seen. Pepper is holding a cigarette between two fingers while pointing them in Rohan's chest as if he is scolding him. Rohan looks as if he wants to say something, but instead he just nods in agreement. They turn down another hallway before passing me. *What the bloody hell did Pepper mean about sending me a little reminder from my past?* I start breathing so hard I'm afraid someone will hear me. When I can't hear Pepper's voice anymore, I take off down the hall. This night is turning into the night from hell. Nigel is waiting and I just want to get home and far away from this place. After all these years, Pepper and Rohan are still up to no good.

Nigel is sitting in the car with his head leaned back against the head rest, listening to his jazz CDs. My frantic entrance into the passenger seat startles him. I do my best to regain my composure, but Nigel can tell something isn't right. This time instead of asking me if I am okay, he doesn't say a word to me. I just want to run, open up the car door and run as far away from this night as possible. With each silent moment, I die inside.

Just when I decide to break the silence, Nigel speaks. "Lime, now I know why you were so nervous tonight. You knew this was your ex-husband's band, but you didn't know how to tell me, because you didn't want to ruin the evening for me, but I remembered that you told me once that the marriage was a nightmare for you. If I had known, I would have never taken you to see him play. Sweetheart, you have to communicate with me better. I don't ever want to put you in an awkward situation, ever."

I put my hand on top of his hand and squeeze it tight. Then I lean my head back against the seat thanking God for small favors. This New Year's morning, I don't just want Nigel to lie next to me when we get back to my place. This time, I want to express all the love I'm feeling for this man at this very moment, and just forget everything and everyone else. I'm ready to make love for the first time with Nigel Peters.

CHAPTER 31

Small Packages

I open my eyes at ten o'clock the next morning. Sunlight beams through my bay window straight into my face. I roll over. Nigel sleeps on his stomach with his face buried in a pillow. My satin sheets cover only some of his bum, but his muscular, honey dipped legs and calves glow in the sun's rays. I want to get my camera and freeze this moment in time, but I don't want to take the chance of disturbing his sleep and this perfect view. Instead, I just prop my head on my left hand and stare at him from the top of his soft head to the bottom of his long feet. I grab the sheets and pull them close to my nose and inhale the sweet smell of cologne, sweat, and love making. What I experienced with Nigel was like eating cotton candy after the newest and wildest ride at the amusement park, and at the height of the ride, I touched heaven.

I can feel my phone vibrating in my purse at the foot of my bed. I slip out of the covers, grab an oversized T-shirt, and take the phone into the living room. Before I can say hello, Laylah announces the New Year.

"Happy New Year, dahling."

"Happy New Year to you, too, Laylah."

"What did I tell you about two-thousand-four?" She doesn't give me a chance to answer before she continues. "I told you it was going to be bigger than two-thousand-three, right? Well, I'm no shorter than my word. Lime Prince, you are the new face of Clinique Cosmetics."

"What?"

"Yes, dahling, you and Clinique are about to take this world by storm."

"Laylah, my goodness, how did you arrange that? That is incredible. Thank you so much."

"I've been working on this deal for the past six months. Clinique, and I agree, thinks *you* are fabulous. So, meet me in my office first thing Monday morning at nine for a conference call with Clinique executives. I would suggest you start familiarizing yourself with their products and tell Ms. Divine to start stocking her supply with Clinique."

I hang up the phone and pause for a moment. Life is good, despite an almost disastrous night. I can't wait to share its goodness with Nigel.

Nigel and I decide to spend the entire day inside. We play card games, watch movies, order in, and seal the evening with another round of wonderful love making. Since he needs to prepare for some flights, and I need to start my homework on Clinique, we end our slumber party that evening.

After a weekend of relaxing, I arrive at Laylah's office bright and early. She meets me at the door so we can celebrate at the Fashion Café. Laylah insists that we have champagne although it is nine in the morning. She explains everything about Clinique, the numerous magazine shoots, commercials, etc. The contract is for two years and I will be joining the ranks of my fellow Supermodels like Liya, Tyra, Carolyn, and several others as a cosmetic spokesperson. Laylah brings the contract, and takes a huge gulp of champagne before she announces that it is a multi-million-dollar deal. Every time she says "multi-million," her pupils seem to transform into dollar signs. I can't believe it. As I listen to her, I keep thinking about my journey to this point. Everything is happening so fast, and although the road to get here wasn't easy, AJ is right, "I have already made it."

When we arrive back at Faces, Elmira tells me that a package has arrived for me while we were out and it is marked urgent. It is a mustard colored padded envelope about the size of a book. I figure it is some fan mail or promotional materials. The protocol is to hold onto my mail at Faces and sort through it unless it looks important. Even though there is no return address and it is sealed several times with clear tape, I guess that makes it important. I start to open it when Laylah calls me into her office for the conference call. I stuff it into my purse to open when I get home.

Although February is the month of *amour*, I will be spending Valentine's Day working for the Spring Olympus Fashion Week in New York. Nigel is flying overseas again, but he promises his first day off is our time together. This time I am taking him to Aspen for a romantic weekend of skiing and fireplaces. I decide to call AJ on Valentine's Day and give her my love. It is her first Valentine's Day without Jimmy, and I want to see what she is doing, and if she is okay.

"Hey, babe. Hold on for a sec."

I hear her tell someone "thank you," and that she will call them later. "Okay, I'm back. What you doing calling me on Valentine's Day? Where is Pilot Peters?"

"Flying." I don't want to think that she is talking to Jimmy, so I try to ask her about the person she is addressing without accusing her of anything. "So, who was that?"

"Oh, that was another law student named Scott. We have a class together this quarter and we study together from time to time, and since neither of us has anyone special in our lives right now we grabbed a bite at this new Cajun restaurant in Hyde Park. He was just dropping me off."

"Is he someone of interest?"

"Oh, no, girl. He's just cool as hell and he makes me laugh. I'm through with men right now. I'm only focused on graduating and passing that bar, plus Scott is about three-hundred-plus pounds and that is way too much meat for mama." We both crack up.

"Well, I wanted to tell you—"

"Damn, I need to go back out to my car to get something."

I start talking about Clinique, when AJ cuts me off.

"Hold up! Is that . . . what the fu—?"

"What's going on, AJ?"

"Girl, I think I just saw Jimmy sitting on his motorcycle across the street."

"What?! Are you sure?"

"I think so. Yeah, that was him. He pulled off when I looked at him."

"Oh my goodness, AJ. What the bloody hell was he doing?"

"I don't know. He doesn't live over here. I got to get my keys from that fool."

"He still has keys to your flat? Why didn't you get those from him months ago, like when he tried to strangle you?"

I know I sound reprimanding, but I don't care. Jimmy is on some stalker shit.

"I've been meaning to but I don't talk to him anymore. He's in my Evidence class this quarter with me and Scott and I don't even look in his direction, but don't worry, I will."

"AJ, make sure you do, but in the meantime get your locks changed. I can call my dad and have him come over there and do it."

"Okay. All right, babe, CSI comes on in five minutes."

"Okay, don't forget, AJ."

"I won't. I promise."

When she mentions Jimmy's name, Clinique just didn't seem relevant anymore. *What was he doing outside her flat just sitting on his motorcycle? Did he follow her and Scott to dinner and then back home?* I call dad and tell him the entire situation. I give him AJ's cell number and ask him to give her a call tomorrow to schedule a time to change her locks. AJ is being too casual about the whole situation. My bad feeling about Jimmy began in China last summer and his stunt tonight just confirms what I was feeling.

When Nigel returns, I tell him all about it on our trip to Aspen.

"Jimmy Bryant…Jimmy Bryant. Ooooh yeah, I remember him now. He was a Defensive End with the Bears. Pretty good too until he got cut. Never knew why they cut him 'cause he had an impressive record."

"AJ said it had something to do with a back injury."

"Hmm, I don't know, but AJ should be more cautious and if she sees him again she should definitely call the police."

Nigel and I have a ball on the slopes of Aspen. I am a novice skier, but Nigel skied from time to time in college with friends. He whisks down those slopes like a pro, and looks extra debonair in his black ski goggles and outfit. I'm regulated to the bunny slopes the entire time. I fall so many times, I bruise my bum. Back at our private lodge, we spend time in the hot tub and drink wine by the fireplace. It is so cozy. Later, as I lay on Nigel's lap, I tell him that I can get away for a couple days before my obligations with Clinique begin next month and would love to go to New Orleans to visit his family. He is elated and starts making plans right then.

—⚬—

A few weeks after we returned to New York, I decide to start packing a couple days before our trip to New Orleans. I am nervous about meeting Nigel's family and figure if I start early I won't forget anything. As I go through my purses deciding which ones to take, the package I received from Elmira falls out. I'd forgotten all about it with Fashion Week, Jimmy's nonsense, and Aspen. I find a pair of scissors in my kitchen drawer and cut it open. A small note falls out. In oversized handwriting, it reads, *HOW SOON WE FORGET* followed by a telephone number. I reach back into the package and pull out a blank DVD. *What in the world is this?* I say out loud. I pop it into the player and stand back so I can view it better, and as soon as it begins, I drop to my knees onto the hardwood floor. Heat sweeps through me in waves as I watch.

There I am, sitting on Rohan's and my bed in my nighties with Waterfall beside me staring at each other. She is dressed in a red lace bra and matching panties. She grabs the side of my face and starts kissing me. Although my eyes are wide open, Waterfall looks as if she is enjoying every minute of it. Then two male bodies enter the picture, first Pepper then Rohan. They are wearing their underwear and begin massaging our shoulders before they start climbing all over us. The pain in my chest is unbearable. I fast forward and Waterfall is engaging in sex with Pepper and Rohan and I'm rubbing on her while Rohan is touching me. I bang the player off and cover my mouth to stop my insides from escaping. Too late the force of it releases itself all over my coffee table and floor. I'm sweating more than usual and having trouble swallowing.

Those wankers must have used a tripod to set up a video camera in the closest that night unbeknownst to me and now they are trying to blackmail me with them. *Wait…a video.* Oh my God, I'm watching the video that Waterfall agreed to make for Rohan and Pepper. They lied about paying her and that is why she was harassing me, but I had no idea *this* was the video. Shit. It has been three years and no word from Waterfall. I figured by now she had resolved things with Rohan and Pepper and that is why she stopped contacting me. I can hear Pepper's loud voice, at the club, telling Rohan that it is time to send me a reminder from my past. All three of them are trying to blackmail me.

I can't go to the police with this video, because it will only be a matter of time before the press gets word and all that I have been blessed to achieve will be destroyed in less time than it took to bring the Twin Towers down. There is no way I can call my dad. AJ is going through so much these days that I feel selfish calling her yet again to solve one more problem of mine. I won't dare confide in Nigel, for this is the one part of my past that I hope he will never have to know. For a split second, I think about calling Asmeret, but despite our recent efforts, we still aren't close. Only I, Rohan, Pepper, Waterfall, and AJ know the truth about the video. So, I call the number on the note. I figure if I can just talk to Rohan maybe . . . just maybe we can handle this like adults. My fingers are trembling so much that I have to redial the number twice. The all too familiar butterflies warn me that if Rohan was a mature adult, he would have never sent me the video in the first place. The phone echoes with each ring. After three rings, a male voice answers. I can hear traffic in the background.

"We were waiting on your call," Pepper said on cue.

"Pepper?" I yell. "Where is Rohan?"

"He's not here at the moment. You can talk to me."

"Pepper, what in the bloody hell is going on, sending me this video? Are you, Rohan, and Waterfall trying to blackmail me or something?"

"If that is what you want to call it, Ms. Supermodel. Sometimes we all need to be reminded of our past."

"Damnit, Pepper, videotaping me without my permission is illegal, and plus you know I left before the night was through."

"Do you think the media will give a damn if we got your permission or not or the fact that you and some stripper are exchanging saliva and having sex with each other and two men?"

I bang my fist on the island in my kitchen again.

"I didn't have sex with a stripper or two men and you know that, Pepper."

"Look, you obviously want to deal or you wouldn't have called, so let's deal."

"Deal? Who do you think I am, Pepper? I'm not that naïve, timid girl Rohan coerced into marrying or into being a part of sick fantasy that night. Something tells me that you are more to blame for this than Rohan. I want to talk to him."

"Like I said, you can talk to me. If you want all of this to disappear, then let's deal, if not, we go to the press. It's up to you, sweetheart. You have two days to call us back with your answer."

He hangs up the phone before I could say another word.

Nigel and I are leaving for New Orleans in two days. *How am I supposed to figure this out by then? What possible reason can I give Nigel for canceling a trip he's been planning for weeks?* I'm too angry to cry. I need solutions. I call AJ. She is the only one I can trust right now and I need her comfort, and her legal advice.

As her phone rings, lightening flashes across the evening sky, followed by clashing thunder. When thunderstorms scared most children, I always slept right through. Grandmother Genet would come into my room to check on me, only to find me cuddling my teddy bear sound asleep. The smell and sound of rain sedates me; however, tonight it only reminds me how complicated my life has just become in a matter of minutes. For the first time, AJ's voice mail message thanking whomever for calling and to have a blessed day or evening annoys me.

"AJ . . . AJ . . . please call me as soon as you get this message. Pepper, Rohan, and Waterfall are trying to blackmail me. Please call me tonight."

My phone beeps as I end my message, and I hope it's AJ calling me back, but the caller ID displays Nigel's number. I let it go into voice mail.

Thirty minutes later and still no word from AJ. I am still in my kitchen listening to the hail like sound of rain hitting my windows. I am sure the streets of New York are full of dirty puddles by now. I turn off all the lights and sit in total darkness, listening to "God's tears," as Grandmother Genet called them. After a few more minutes, I can't help but join Him. The more I replay my conversation with Pepper, the more the silent tears fall. I run my finger down the center of my head just as my phone rings. When I see AJ's face, I answer on the first ring.

"Lime, I'm sorry I didn't call you back right away. I was in a BLSA meeting. It just ended and I ran into our office and listened to your voice message. What do you mean they're trying to blackmail you? With what?"

I tell her about the package Elmira gave me. I tell her Pepper and Rohan videotaped that night without my permission.

"The video came with a note that said 'how soon we forget' and there was a phone number. I'm afraid to call the police, because I know the press will find out and since you are the only other person who knows what really happened, I had to call you. I know you're dealing with a lot right now, AJ, but I didn't know what else to do." I sniff and wipe a tear away.

"I don't care what I'm going through or you're going through, you can always call me. Damn, Lime, leave it to Rohan and Pepper to pull a bitch ass move like this. Did the note say what they wanted?"

"No. So I called the number and Pepper answered."

"And what did he say?"

"Something about they were waiting on my call and I needed to be reminded of my past, like I heard him say that night in the hallway at that club, and the fact that I called must mean I want to strike a deal."

"A deal?"

"Right. I told him I wasn't interested in any deal and I wanted to speak with Rohan. I truly believe this is more Pepper's doing than Rohan's. Rohan is too much of a follower to do something like this, which is how I was put in that situation in the first place. Pepper gave me two days to make a decision about making a deal, so I called you."

She lets out a sigh. "Well, the only thing you can do legally is file a police report for extortion; otherwise unless the video has been doctored in any way, truth is an absolute defense. In other words, babe, unless you can get the original copy from them without stabbing them both in their jugulars with an ice pick and turning it to make sure they die for certain, that's about all you can do."

I know AJ is kidding, but for the first time in my life I want someone dead. AJ calls my name.

"Yeah, I'm still here. Just thinking." I am silent for a moment more. "I'm going to talk to Rohan alone. I think I can reach him."

"Really?"

"You didn't see that look on his face when he saw me that night at the club and how he looked when Nigel and I walked away. It was as if for the first time in his selfish life he realized that he had made a mistake for treating me like he did when we were married."

"Hmm. Well, I wasn't there and Rohan has never been high on my list, but if you feel you can reason with him, although most animals lack that skill, then go for it. Just be careful, Lime."

"I will. Hey, before I go. Was Jimmy at the meeting tonight?"

"No, I didn't tell you. He sent an email to the executive committee last week, resigning as treasurer. He gave some weak excuse about taking on more than he could handle this quarter. I didn't even respond. So aside from our Evidence class twice a week, I don't have to see him at all."

"Good. Well, goodnight, babe."

"Goodnight."

Instead of calling Nigel back, I open up my laptop and send Rohan an immediate email. I pray he hasn't changed his email address since we were married. In the subject I put NEED TO TALK in all caps. I ask if he and I can meet somewhere in private tomorrow to talk; if so, to email me back right away. Before I hit "send" I wonder if I should say more, but Rohan knows why I want to meet and if he gets the message, I think he'll agree to it. I close my laptop and lay on my couch listening to the rain subside until I fall asleep.

CHAPTER 32

Trumpet is My Life

Another restless night. I wake up at three in the morning and check my email. Rohan hasn't responded. Since the message hasn't bounced back to me, means it made it to that address. Now the question is does he still check it? Somehow, I go back to sleep only to wake up two hours later. Still no response. I'm losing faith and options. I mill around the loft in slow motion, wondering what to do next. I sit back on my couch and flip through the channels as if on automatic. After an hour of cheesy infomercials, I can't take it anymore and I check again. Only new junk mail. *Ugh.* I tap my fingers on my forehead as I await an answer.

Maybe I can contact Waterfall. She knows what really happened that night. She knows I didn't want to go through with that night and when she began calling me about the money she was promised, at first we seemed to connect. She was pleasant and well spoken. She even shared with me that she was a single parent of a young son with Down Syndrome and his medical expenses were more than her stripper salary. I guess I felt sorry for her. I wasn't sure what she could do or what I would say, but I had to try. I have no idea about the longevity of a stripper's career, but I do a search for the Back Room in Harvey, Illinois. Just as it comes up on the screen, a pop-up box appears on the lower right hand corner of my computer screen telling me I have just received a message from "Trumpetismylife." I can't stop shaking. Rohan agrees to a meeting at three at Cuny Brooklyn College in the Music Building. I start getting dressed even though our meeting is hours away.

I find the place with no problem. The building is quiet, with only a handful of students in various rooms practicing their respective instruments. The rooms are all soundproof so you have to rely on the view of the students through the small window on the door to tell that they are practicing. Rohan's email instructs me to go to the last room on the left. It is the only room without a window on the front, but it has a sign on the door that says Occupied or Vacant. The sign read "vacant" so I let myself in. There is a large piano that takes up most of the space, two windows, and large mirrors full of smudges. There is a seat at the piano and a bench along the opposite wall. The dingy white tile is covered with black streaks from student's shoes. The air in the room is stale, so I crack open a window to circulate some fresh air from last night's rain. The clock on the wall reads 3:02 P.M. I had hoped that Rohan would be here, already waiting.

I try to sit still and await his arrival, but with each passing minute, I have to move around. At 3:08 P.M., I begin to think the worst. *What if Rohan set me up? What if he told Pepper about our meeting and they planned to meet me and do God only knows what?* I tell myself that I will leave at 3:10 P.M. and not a second later. *Why did I ever think I could trust Rohan in the first place?*

3:10 P.M., I turn around to reach for the door handle and it opens before I can touch it. It is Rohan and he is alone with only his trumpet case strapped around his chest. His abrupt stop puts us almost nose to nose. I step back and let him in.

"I didn't think you were coming."

"Well, me de ya."

He sets the case down on the piano and takes a seat on the bench. He avoids eye contact with me, so I sit down beside him and cut to the chase.

"Rohan, why are you doing this?"

Instead of answering me, he puts his elbows on his knees, cups his hands, and gazes down at the floor.

"Rohan, you and I both know what really happened that night. I told you I couldn't go through with it and left. I stayed at Kevin's flat that night. You know that. So, why are you, Pepper, and Waterfall trying to blackmail me? I've never done anything to you except tried to be a good wife, but you treated me like you hated me. I tried to do everything I could to please you, but nothing was good enough and then you gave me back to my dad like I was a pair of britches that didn't fit. I never bothered you again after that or asked you for one thing. Now, I've been able to do something with my life and you all want to try to take that away from me. Why? If its money you need, is blackmailing me really going to help? I saw the way you looked at me at the club after your show. You seemed sincere about seeking my forgiveness, which is why I wanted to talk to *you*." I grab his face in my hands and look into his eyes. "I don't know what hold Pepper has on you, but if you ever loved me, you won't do this."

He looks away and licks his lips. We can hear an occasional door opening and closing down the hall.

"Me nah av de fus one."

"Can you get it?"

"Me nah know."

I rub my forehead and blow hard out of my nose.

"Look, I have to go out of town tomorrow. Do you really think Pepper will go to the press?"

"Pepper waan pay."

For what? I wonder. *What did Pepper ever do to deserve to get paid?*

"What do you want, Rohan?"

He takes his time to answer before he mumbles, "Fe play mi music til heaven hear me."

I understand what he means. I ask Rohan to stall Pepper until I get back. I need more time for truth and past love to prevail.

CHAPTER 33

Flick of a Flame

I need to call Nigel before he starts to worry. I'm afraid if I hear his sweet voice that I'll break down and cry, so I send him a text message: *Hey luv, some things came up, xcited bout tmrw."* I go straight home and finish packing with thoughts of Rohan and Pepper heavy on my mind.

—m—

Naw'lins, Bourbon Street, French Quarter, gumbo, jazz, and above ground coffins. Nigel was so eager to get there that he stayed up all night packing and talking to his family about our arrival. He seems so relaxed in his southern home. In fact, everyone in New Orleans seems relaxed, without a care in the world. I'm a city girl to my core having lived in Chicago, Brixton, and now New York, but here my soul seems to rest. His mum and sister live in a peaceful community in New Orleans East. Everyone is waiting for us at his sister's house.

We rent a car, because Nigel wants to show me all of New Orleans. When we pull up at his sister's home, his mum is the first person to come out to meet us. She is a short, petite woman, with dark chocolate skin, and a short afro. She calls to the family that we are here and about fifteen more people pour out of the house to greet us and help us with our bags. The mixture of half-white, Creole looking people, Nigel's father's family, and dark chocolate, Nigel's mum's family, harmonize like keys on a piano.

Everyone plants tight hugs and kind kisses on us. Nigel's nieces run up to him as soon as he walks through the door, screaming, "Uncle Nigel!" as they wrap their little arms around his legs. As he holds them both in his lap, I'm glad I brought my camera. I take picture after picture of this gentle giant play and laugh with his nieces, Carrie and Anayah. As my camera clicks, I think about the type of father Nigel will be. My dad showed me that nothing is more important to a man than his family, and I will settle for nothing less in my future husband. Carrie and Anayah are the most darling Creole girls I have ever seen, with their long, sandy brown hair, and peanut butter colored skin. Nigel introduces us and in a polite southern drawl they recite their names one by one and call me, "Ma'am."

Nigel's sister is still in the kitchen preparing food. I can't wait to meet the woman I have heard so much about. Her husband, Andrew, calls her name and tells her to take a break and come out and greet us. Her catering business, Nigel's Catering & Event Planning named in honor of their late father, is known all over New Orleans. A few minutes later, a stunning female version of Nigel walks out of the kitchen's French doors, wearing a red apron that reads, "Cooking is an Art." Nia is tall and lean like Nigel, with light brown eyes and deep dimples. She looks more like a model to me than I do. Nigel stands to hug her, and after they hug she gives him a fake punch to his stomach. Nigel doubles over and fakes a groan. When he stands, he lands a fake karate chop to her neck. She jumps on his back and they fall on the couch with the girls jumping on top of them. Nigel's mum shakes her head.

"They've been doing that since they were kids."

I admire their closeness.

"Now, where is the most desirable woman in the world and what are you doing with this guy?"

Her deep, soft, southern drawl and her warm hug are sincere. She asks me if she can have my eyes when I'm done with them. Her humor is natural and reminds me of AJ. I feel comfortable and welcome.

As we wait for dinner to be served, I think about the video, and my conversations with Rohan and Pepper. Every time I think about the video in the hands of the press, I shift in my seat. However, the constant attention from Nigel's family breaks my thoughts. His uncles, aunts and cousins, gather around me grinning from ear to ear.

"You all act like you've never seen anyone from Chicago before." Nia winks at me.

I laugh, because I know they are just trying to be polite, although to them I'm a celebrity.

Andrew taps a silver triangle, announcing that dinner is served. Nigel grabs my hand and his nieces grab my other hand and lead me to a huge back yard under a silver tent. Inside is exquisite. The two tables, one for the adults and one for the kids, are draped with burgundy chiffon with big ribbons, bows, and freshly cut flowers in pretty vases everywhere. The centerpieces and place settings make you think you are at a wedding reception. The scene is magical to me, but I seem to be the only one mesmerized by it. According to Nigel, Nia does this type of decorating each time the family gets together. Nia's business partner, Keenan, is in the tent helping to put the final preparations on the food and the decorations. Keenan grew up with Nia and Nigel and he is like part of the family. Nigel told me that Keenan was always more interested in playing double-dutch and imitating female singers with Nia and her girlfriends than playing football and riding bikes with him and the other boys in the neighborhood. According to Nigel, Keenan loved the "softer things in life."

Keenan handles the party/event planning and decorating side of the business, while Nia concentrates on the cooking, catering, and anything else. You wouldn't suspect Keenan was gay based on his appearance. Aside from the two, small, gold hoop earrings in each ear, and well manicured hands, he looks just like another professional, handsome man in loose fitting blue jeans, polo shirt, and gym shoes. However, when he opens his mouth to greet us, the lisp mixed with the southern drawl gives him away. Nigel gives him dap and Keenan returns it with masculine confidence. Then he turns to me, puts one hand over his mouth and the other over his heart, shakes his head before saying, "The diva of all divas is standing in front me. Now I can die."

Nia walks past him, and hits him upside his head. "Calm down RuPaul, and let's eat."

When everyone is seated, Nigel's mum stands to bless the food. She asks that everyone hold hands. Before she prays, she hums a soothing version of "Amazing Grace," which everyone continues to hum while she prays. I recognize the song from Ms. Henning's funeral.

"Dear Heavenly Father, what a privilege it is for our family to be together again. We thank you for that. We also thank you for new friends like Lime. Now Lord, we give thanks for this meal and for the hands that prepared it. And we pray for those who have not. In Jesus name let us all say together…Amen."

After the chorus of "amen's," Nigel squeezes my hand in agreement and everyone makes a mad dash to the buffet. As Nigel scoots my chair back for me, my phone rings. It scares me. My gut tells me it is Laylah in hysterics about the video or Pepper threatening me again, because it is day two of his ultimatum. I reach down in my purse to grab it and notice my dad's face with Marley. I breathe a huge sigh of relief and ask dad to hold on while I walked out of the tent to talk to him.

"Hey dad, what's up?"

"Lime." He is breathing fast and when he calls me Lime I know it's serious. "You need to come to Chicago right now. There's been an accident."

"What accident? What's wrong? Are you okay?

"Not me, AJ. Lona just called me from the hospital. She overhead some nurses talking about a young woman from Northwestern Law School being brought in who was in really bad shape. Lona remembered AJ attends Northwestern Law School, and thought she would check just to see who it was, and that's when she found out it was AJ. She was taken to the Burn Unit."

I scream "Nooooooo!" out loud and grab my head. Nigel and Nia run outside toward me followed by the rest of the family.

"Baby, what's wrong?"

Nigel tries to put his arms around me. I back away. I need to listen.

"I think it was that boyfriend of hers, Jimmy. I tried to call her a couple times after you told me about her locks needing to be changed. I kept getting her voice mail. I had planned to call her again today, since today is my off day. Can you come to Chicago today?"

"I'm on my way now. I'll call from the airport when I know my flight and arrival time." My voice and hands are shaking.

"Okay. I'll pick you up. I love you, Apple."

I hang up before I tell him, "I love you more."

I pace back and forth and grab my heart. I didn't want to waste any more time. Everyone is silent.

Nigel approaches me again. "Lime, what's the matter?"

"AJ. She's in the hospital. Jimmy hurt her. I've got to go to Chicago now." My voice cracks.

"Okay, I'll go with you."

"No, you stay here with your family. I can go alone. Can you take me to the airport now?"

"Of course."

Nigel tells his family there is an emergency and he will be right back. After all the sad good-byes, everyone waves to me as I get into the car. I don't have the energy to wave back.

Nigel doesn't ask any questions in the car. He just holds my hand and drives as fast as he can without getting a ticket. For the second time in my life, I'm comatose. My eyes cloud with tears as I replay my dad's words: *She was taken to the burn unit. I think it was Jimmy.* My head makes a litany out of it: *Jimmy, Jimmy, Jimmy, Burn Unit, Burn Unit, Burn Unit. What did he do? Where were they? Was she all alone?* When Nigel pulls up to the airport, he helps me with my bags. I turn to him, but no words come out. He kisses me on my lips.

"Please call me when you get there. I love you."

I just nod and turn to leave. I file his words in my heart for later, because right now my mind is empty.

Dad is at O'Hare waiting for me as promised. As we drive to the hospital, he fills me in on what he knows. AJ suffered burns on the left side of her body. It appears she was set on fire. The police discovered an empty can of gasoline in a dumpster about a mile away. Her neighbor in the flat next to her heard her screaming and called the police, and they rushed her to Northwestern Hospital downtown.

Everything is like a dream from the time my dad called me to the moment I enter AJ's hospital room. I do a light sprint down the hall toward AJ's room once the elevator doors open on the eighth floor. Two police officers are outside of her room talking to Ms. Gordon, AJ's next door neighbor. Ms. Gordon is an elderly white woman who lives alone, and wears her glasses around her neck on a rusty chain with floral house-coats. AJ always complains about how nosy Ms. Gordon is and how she sometimes keeps her door cracked just to hear and see what was going on. AJ always threatened to go get the mail butt naked one day to really give her something to see. Times like these everyone needs a Ms. Gordon.

I have to pass the police in order to enter AJ's room. The police officers put their pencils and notepads down and smile at me. They recognize me right away and seem more interested in me than getting pertinent information from Ms. Gordon.

"Hello, Ms. Prince," they both say in chorus like school boys asking a girl to the dance.

"Hello, officers. AJ, I mean Angela, is like a sister to me. Can you tell me anything about what happened and if you've caught the bastard who did this?"

The officer with the broad shoulders and thick neck answers before his partner has a chance to open his mouth.

"Well, no one has been apprehended yet. We're still waiting to speak with Ms. Henning, but Ms. Gordon has been a very helpful witness."

I smile at Ms. Gordon. I can't understand why Jimmy hasn't been arrested.

"His name is Jimmy Bryant. *He* did this."

The volume of my voice make people look in our direction.

The silent partner speaks while trying to calm me down. "Again, we need to speak to Ms. Henning, but I assure you that we are doing everything to find the person responsible."

I can't figure out why the bloody hell they keep calling him "the person" when I just told them his name? I let out a loud sigh of frustration and rub my finger down the center of my head. The police are being tight lipped and I am getting anxious to see AJ, so I excuse myself. Before, I enter AJ's room; I ask Ms. Gordon if she can wait until I come back out. Ms. Gordon knows AJ and I are friends because AJ introduced us last year when I spent Thanksgiving at her place. I'm hoping I can get more information from her than the police.

I stayed in AJ's room all night. The nurses were kind enough to bring me a cot and a blanket. The high pitched ring of my phone wakes me out of my sleep early the next morning. I flip it open, after the first ring without looking at the number as not to disturb AJ.

"This is Lime." I cup my hand over my mouth.

"Times up."

I sit up. "What?...Who is—

"You know who the fuck this is. Times up."

"Look Pepper, I—"

A nurse pushing a squeaking cart with what looks like a first aid kit enters the room right, so I slam the phone shut and put it on vibrate. She needs to change AJ's dressing. I take a deep breath to calm myself down, and move into the corner to watch the procedure. I keep trying to figure out how this happened to AJ? She's protected me since secondary school and where was I when she needed protecting? Instead of being here, I was off in my fantasy land fattening the pockets of bloody designers who can care less about life outside of the runway, my life. If I never see another couture dress, stilettos, or Fashion Week, it will be too soon. I swear this is it. I'm sick of it all. Chicago is my home; not New York, and AJ, and my dad are my family not those fake Botox model bitches. We won't even discuss Laylah, because if it doesn't make money, Laylah doesn't have the time or the interest.

The nurse turns around and tosses her gloves into the bin. Before leaving the room, she flashes a gentle smile in my direction to assure me that she's healing. I put my phone on vibrate before walking back over to AJ's bed. The twitches and uncomfortable grimaces remain, but her breathing is more relaxed. I thought I saw AJ open her eyes and smile at me, or maybe I just want her to. After a closer look, the smile is nothing more than a tightening of her lips followed by a brief gaze at the ceiling. I hover over her for a few moments more, hoping the next time she opens her eyes, she will know that I'm here. After a few minutes, I concede defeat. She's resting, and I need a smoke.

I'm sure by now some unscrupulous reporter is getting off on which headline to print: "Supermodel, Lime Prince, has two days to live" or "Supermodel attempts to take own life after recent scandal." *To bloody hell with 'em.* I throw on my hooded sweat shirt, sun glasses; grab my phone, and smokes. My phone begins vibrating as soon as I step outside. I had two missed calls and three text messages already. *Damn that Pepper.* I breathe a quick sigh of relief when I see both missed calls are from my sweetheart, Nigel. I left New Orleans in such a panic after my dad called about AJ that I forgot to let Nigel know that I had made it to Chicago safely.

The texts are one stupid threat after another: *This is not a game…Pay up or else…My patience is running thin…K bitch, u made your choice.* I want to run upstairs and grab AJ so we can drive to New York and kick Pepper's ass together, but the reality is I can't grab AJ and kicking Pepper's ass won't make him and his blackmailing threats go away. I light a Black and Mild and let the sweet flavor fill my fears. AJ needs me now and no matter how much I need her protection, I have to be strong for her.

As I stand off in my corner, away from the "No smoking within fifteen feet of the building" sign and the other smokers who are gathering, I keep thinking someone has to know what happened. *Shit, I forgot about Ms. Gordon.* I asked her to wait for me while I was in AJ's room. When I get back to the nurse's station, they said Ms. Gordon left a number for me to call her. I call her right away.

"Hello, Ms. Gordon. This is Lime. A.J…, I mean Angela's friend. I'm sorry I missed you yesterday. I fell asleep in the room with Angela."

"That's okay, dear. I had to get home to let my dog out and feed my fish. That poor girl. How is she doing?"

"I really don't know at this point. The nurses are with her now. Ms. Gordon, can you tell me what happened?"

"Well, it was late, and I couldn't sleep for some reason. Lady, that's my French poodle, kept running to the door barking and growling. I knew something had to be wrong, because it woke her up out of her sleep. I decided to just crack my door to take a peek, through the chain, to see if something was going on in the hallway. All I could see was a black man pacing back in forth in front of Angela's door with something in his hand. I'm not one to pry so I just watched him for a few moments, and then closed my door again."

"Did you recognize him?"

"It was so dark, dear, but I thought it must have been the young man she was dating from the law school coming by to see her. He has come late before. Lady and I went back to bed, but I still couldn't sleep and that's when I heard that poor girl scream. I tell you I'll never forget that scream as long as I live. I jumped out of bed and ran over there. Some of the other neighbors came outside as well. I ran back in to call the police. Her door was open and some of the neighbors went in to help her. I could hear them yelling, 'She's on fire! She's on fire!'"

I lower my head and shut my eyes tight and try to catch my breath.

"Thank you, Ms. Gordon. Thank you for helping her."

"I said a prayer to St. Michael for her recovery, dear."

I need some more air. I do a brisk walk back outside to my secluded spot and reach into my pocket for another smoke, but I can't find one. I know I didn't smoke a whole pack. I do a frantic search of my clothes as the tears roll down my face. "She's on fire…she's on fire" is all I hear. I don't want to break down outside of the hospital in case someone passes by and starts asking questions, and I don't want to cry in AJ's room. God, how I wish Nigel was here. *Nigel.* I do a hard wipe of both of my eyes, and dial his number. He answers on the first ring. He's watching a basketball game with his brother-in-law. I tell him what I know and he tells me that he and Andrew remember the real reason Jimmy Bryant was cut from the Bears.

"He assaulted his girlfriend, and a Chicago Bears cheerleader had also accused him of attempted rape, but that charge was dropped."

"So he lied when he told AJ that he was cut from the Bears for a back injury."

"I didn't think that sounded right when you told me."

"I had my suspicions about him early on."

"How is she doing?"

"It's hard to tell. She's been asleep since I've been here and I haven't talked to her doctor yet."

"How are you holding up?"

"Barely."

"I wanted to be there with you."

"I know. I just don't know how long I will be in Chicago, and I know you have some upcoming flights. I'm sorry for ruining your family dinner. I know you wanted this to be a special trip."

"You didn't ruin anything. Everyone was quiet for awhile until I told them it wasn't a funeral and everything would be okay. That's when mom sang a song to lighten the mood and we were eating and laughing again as usual. I hope *we* can come back one day soon."

Before I hang up, I say, "Nigel, I heard what you said when you took me to the airport, and I love you too."

Talking to Nigel seems to give me strength, so I check my voice message and it is dad checking on me and letting me know he will pick me up whenever I'm ready. Someone walks past me and flicks a cigarette butt toward my feet. I step on the butt and think how one flick of a flame changed the entire life of someone I truly love.

CHAPTER 34

Who's Going to Want Me Now?

I stay another night in AJ's hospital room. AJ is in and out of consciousness all night, but stable. Lona wakes me the next day when she comes to work. She works in the Geriatric Ward on the third floor of the hospital. It is eight o'clock, and she wants to know if I need anything or want to get something to eat. I don't want to miss when AJ opens her eyes, but Lona assures me we will be right back. We eat in the nurse's private lounge and it's a good thing we do, because word spreads quick that I'm in the hospital and the stares and whispers increase by the minute.

I tell Lona what the nurses tell me about AJ's condition, but I ask her to explain everything to me.

"So, how long are you planning on staying?" Lona asks.

"I don't know. I'm still supposed to be in New Orleans with Nigel and I have some promotional shoots in New York and Paris for Clinique at the end of the month."

I don't feel like eating. I push my yogurt away. "Two…three weeks maybe."

"Well, if you want to go back to the house this evening. My shift ends at five."

I'm not sure of anything. I just want to take AJ back to New York with me and keep her safe forever, but right now, she needs to heal under the doctor's supervision. I thank Lona for breakfast and tell her I will let her know.

AJ's doctor and nurse are in the room with her when I return. I panic, but the nurses give me the "she's okay" look. I nod and step back out of the room until they were done. I think about AJ's family in Tennessee. I call Ms. Gordon again to see if she can go into AJ's flat and find her phone for me, but she tells me the police have put yellow tape all over AJ's door and no one can enter. Something about it being a crime scene. *Police.* James Armstrong pops into my head. For whatever reason, I kept his card buried in my wallet. I'm not sure what he can do, but he is a cop; a state trooper and maybe he can help. His cell phone number is written on the back. When he doesn't answer, I leave a message for him to call me right away and that is an emergency.

When the doctor and nurse come out I stop them in the hall. Dr. Gupta looks like he just graduated from medical school. His messy hair and hairless face makes him look like an older teenager.

"Hello doctor. I'm AJ's best friend. How is she was doing?"

"She has second degree burns, which means the epidermis tissue or outer layer was burned. We were able to do auto grafting. We took some skin from her buttocks and applied it to her arm, thigh, and leg. She seems to be a fighter. Because second degree burns are more superficial than third degree, that penetrates deeper into the skin, it looks like her recovery time will be about six to eight weeks. We will want to keep her in the hospital for a little while longer to watch the grafting, and then she can recover at home with outpatient follow up."

"Is she awake? Can I see her?"

"Yes, but be sure to let her rest when she wants."

Just as I was about to open the door, one of the officers from before shows up, but this time he is accompanied by a female officer. They ask Dr.

Gupta if they can talk with AJ for a few minutes. I want to go in with them, but I figure the sooner AJ can answer their questions, the sooner Jimmy will be behind bars. We all step aside to let them enter.

Five minutes turns into ten, and then fifteen before the officers emerge. Their faces are stoic. I stand to go in after them and they both hold the door for me. I wonder what they are thinking, but more importantly, what did AJ tell them.

I take a deep breath before facing AJ. Her head is turned away from me, and she seems to be staring out the window. She doesn't turn her head or even flinch when I enter. I walk around to face her and that is when she bursts into tears. I try as hard as I can to hold back my tears, but I always feel what AJ feels.

AJ speaks first.

"Why are *you* crying?" Her voice is low and breathy.

"I don't know."

"Some sight, huh?"

"Yeah, that hospital gown is dreadful."

I smile, but AJ isn't in the mood for our usual antics. She cries harder. I pull up a chair and gently rub her head.

"Can you believe this shit? Why didn't I change my locks like you told me? What was so important that I couldn't take time to return your dad's phone calls?"

"Sshh. It's okay. I know you just talked to the police, but they won't tell me anything. What happened, babe?"

She licks her tears away and clears her throat. "I was at a bid whist party at Scott's house with some other law students. I had one too many, so Scott drove me home. It was about one in the morning, I think and I was a bit tipsy, so Scott made sure I made it in my apartment okay. All I remember was taking off some of my clothes and then going to sleep. The next thing I remember I was on fire, and then I woke up here." She pauses to take a deep breath. "Jimmy must have followed me again. Scott told me to lock the door after he left, but I was so out of it." More tears fall onto her gown. She looks so helpless. "Half of my body is burned to a crisp. Why did this happen? What is going to happen to me? Who's going to want me now?"

She rattles off question after question, pleading for an answer that makes sense. My heart breaks in two with each question. AJ cries like a baby and all I can do is hold the hand that isn't burned and continue to stroke her head until she drifts back off to sleep. About an hour later, my cell phone starts vibrating in my bag. I slip out of the bed and tiptoe into the loo. This time before answering, I look at the caller ID.

"Hello?" I whisper.

"Hello, Lime. This is James. I'm returning your call."

"Oh, hi, James." I forgot that I called him. "Thank you so much for calling me back."

"You said it was an emergency. Are you okay?"

"I'm okay, but AJ isn't."

"Who?"

"Angela Henning from Hurston high school."

"What's wrong?"

I explain the entire situation. I tell him Jimmy is still on the run. I give him a description and tell him that he is from D.C. When I tell him Jimmy played for the Chicago Bears, he knows who I am talking about right away. He says he has police friends in Chicago. He does his best to calm me down and explains that if AJ knows her assailant, it will be easy for the police to figure out what happened and to capture him. The fact that Jimmy is a former professional football player who was once in the public eye means he won't get very far after the Chicago police notify the local media, airports, other police departments, and enter him in the National Crime Information Center.

We continue to talk for awhile and even reminisce about AJ in secondary school. The more we talk the more I wish James had not been such an asshole back then. Before we hang up, he promises he will call back if he hears anything and to check on AJ.

As I stand outside the loo door, watching AJ as she sleeps, I feel the urge to take pictures. I slip my camera out of my bag. I'm not sure why, but I feel a need to photograph her. I need to capture this moment. I change the lens and begin the photo shoot. I walk around her ever so careful not to wake her, zooming in and out, taking one picture after another. There is a soft knock at the door and a man and two women enter as I take my last shot. They jump when they see me. I'm not sure if AJ told them that she and I were best friends or not, but at first they look as if they have the wrong room.

"Oh, we're sorry. They said she was alone." The man speaks for everyone.

"Hi. I'm Lime. Angela's best friend."

"Hi. I'm Scott."

"I'm Janine."

"And I'm Dianna."

"We are classmates with Angela." Scott speaks again.

Scott is a portly man with a round, smooth baby face, complimented by a thin, evenly cut mustache and goatee. I'm pretty sure AJ doesn't want anyone to see her like this, but I let them in, because I know she and Scott have become close, but I tell them just for a few minutes. I go outside to find Lona, but I stop at the nurse's station first. They are all engrossed in charts and answering patient calls, so I just stand and wait. One nurse turns around and ends her call right away when she sees me standing there.

"Hi, can I help you, Ms. Prince?"

"Yes, if Angela asks for me, can you tell her that I went home for a few minutes and I'll be back later?"

By now all the nurses are staring in my direction. I can tell they all want to say something to me, but they don't know how. I decide to break the ice.

"I truly want to thank each of you for taking such good care of Angela. It really means a lot to me."

After that they begin to open up and one by one they ask me for my autograph and if they can take some pictures with me. I am more than happy to oblige and even take a few pictures of them with my camera.

Lona drops me off at my dad's studio and goes home to prepare dinner for us. Dad is still there, helping a few customers. After I kiss him on the cheek, I head straight for the dark room. As I bathe the film, the black and white images of AJ's body began to emerge. You can see the intricacies of burned skin, but the image that burns in my mind is how peaceful AJ looks as she sleeps. Gone are the grimaces from when I first arrived. Her soul seems to accept its new temple. I wanted to find a way to capture that peacefulness, because in the end that is what matters the most.

My dad waits until he can enter the room. He watches me as I lay the pictures on the drying cabinet. His demeanor changes as he folds his arms across his chest and studies each one. After he's done looking, he holds me in his arms and kisses the top of my head as I bury my face deep into his chest and weep.

CHAPTER 35

Waiting Game

When AJ is released from the hospital, she no longer has a flat to go home to, so she moves in with dad and Lona. There is plenty of room in their three bedroom house, and since Lona is a nurse, she can take care of AJ's medical needs. I decide to stay for two more weeks before heading back to New York. It's like our slumber parties in secondary school all over again, except AJ isn't as talkative and comedic as before. AJ seems to be suffering from slight depression. She sobs and sleeps a lot during the day. She refuses all company and even phone calls, and demands that all mirrors be taken out of her room. We do our best to accommodate her wishes. Lona says some depression is normal, but she will watch her to make sure it doesn't get any worse. AJ is set to graduate from law school in three months; I'm not sure if she is thinking about that at all.

James calls me back to check on AJ. I tell him that Jimmy hasn't been captured yet, but the police issued a warrant for his arrest for heinous battery. I've heard about rewards for criminals so I ask James about it.

"James, can I offer some sort of incentive for Jimmy's arrest?"

"By incentive, do you mean money?"

"Well, yes. I've heard about people offering rewards in criminal cases before, so I was just wondering if I could do that as well."

"You certainly can offer a reward for information leading to the arrest and conviction of the person responsible. However, that's done with the press and not necessarily the police. I'm sure once the press realizes its Lime Prince the Supermodel offering the reward they'll be more than eager to publicize it."

"I'm certainly not looking for any press for myself. Can I remain anonymous?"

I'm sure if my name is advertised with the money it will take the focus off Jimmy's arrest.

"Sure. Talk to the police there so they can explain how to post the reward with the press."

"Thanks again, James. I know you are very busy."

"I'm never too busy for the girl, I mean, woman I've had a crush on from the day you walked into Biology class."

I take a deep breath and exhale because I'm not sure how to respond, so I just thank him again.

The next day I call the Chicago Police Department about the reward and they direct me to the *Chicago Sun-Times* and *Tribune*. Since my dad used to do freelance photography work for the *Sun-Times*, I ask him to go with me. Although they are eager to slap my picture and story on the front page, I tell them I want to remain anonymous and offer the reward under the guise of AJ's family. I offer $100,000 to anyone whose leads led to Jimmy's arrest and conviction like James said. I just need to do something.

The day I leave for New York, AJ doesn't say more than two words to me. I talk to her as I pack.

"I'll be back in a couple of weeks. Do you want to come to New York and stay with me for awhile?"

AJ just rocks in the oversized rocking chair without making a sound or even looking in my direction. Her burns are still raw and tender and glisten from the salve that Lona has to apply three times a day. I walk over to her and put my hands on the arms of the chair to stop it from rocking. AJ turns her head to the other side and stares at the wall. I put my fingers under her chin and turn her face toward me.

She gazes into my eyes as if she is seeing me for the very first time.

"You really do have beautiful eyes."

Her comment blows me away. It is the first time in the history of our friendship that she's ever complimented me like that. Our physical appearances mean nothing to us. We love each other from the inside out. I kiss her on the forehead.

"I'll call you when I get to New York."

Nigel had just gotten back from South America the day before I arrive. He is at my place that evening. I'm drained from the last few weeks and just want to hear about his life. He fills me in on the rest of his stay in New Orleans, his flights, and how much he's missed me. Its eight o'clock, and I have to be at my photo shoot at ten the next morning and I truly need some rest. I fall asleep on Nigel's lap as he talks and rubs my head.

I'm not sure how Clinique will react to my hair these days. It hasn't been cut in weeks and has grown out a lot. I called Dee-Dee early in the morning and ask if she can meet me at the studio before the shoot. She already has a commitment, but sends Vera. Dee-Dee is known for her trims, cuts, and linings, but she has taught Vera well, because Clinique likes it. I found out later that the Clinique executives had been hoping that I'd grow my hair back soon anyway. My hair is such an insignificant issue in my world these days, and I can really careless what anybody thinks about it.

The shoot is long, but successful. Somehow, I manage to fake a smile for hours. I call home to check on AJ during a break.

Dad answers the phone. "Hi Apple."

"Hi dad. How are you?"

"Oh, I'm okay. Lona's working late, so I'm heating up some left overs."

"Dad, how is AJ doing?"

"She pretty much stays in the room. We bring her food, but she doesn't really eat. She won't let me enter so I have to leave it outside the door." AJ is becoming a prisoner in her own little cell. "But her aunts called yesterday and they are coming up for the weekend to see her, so that should help."

I wonder if AJ plans to go to Tennessee for awhile.

I finally decide to tell Laylah what happened before she hears about it in a tabloid or is asked about it in public. I tell her my sister was a victim of a violent crime. Instead of sympathizing with me, Laylah reminds me that I am an only child. I swear as soon as someone invents a phone that allows you to reach through and choke the bloody hell out of the person on the other end, I will not only buy every phone; I will also buy the damn patent. Until that day, I tell Laylah that for what it is worth; AJ is and always will be my sister, regardless of our parentage. She doesn't press the issue further.

In all the tragedy with AJ, I forget about my own dilemma. I check my email when I get off the phone with Laylah to see if Rohan has written, but he hasn't. Maybe he was able to change Pepper's mind, and convince him to destroy the original video. Deep down, I don't think that it's over, for good. I walk over to the drawer where I've hidden the video, break it into little pieces and then flush it down the toilet. All I can do is wait, because it is out of my hands now.

CHAPTER 36

Outsiders

April 1, 2004, they catch Jimmy. CPD officials and James call me within an hour of each other to deliver the satisfying news. According to James, after Jimmy set AJ on fire, he drove his car all the way to D.C. He'd been planning on repeating the same crime; this time the victim was his baby's mum, Julia, and their two-month-old daughter. When he arrived at her house, he broke into a window of the garden level flat. Julia woke up and pleaded with Jimmy not to hurt her or their daughter as he doused the room, the bed, and the bassinette with the baby still in it, with gasoline. Mrs. Parker, Julia's mom was visiting from out of town, and was sleeping in the next room. When she heard her daughter screaming, she sneaked into the kitchen and grabbed a butcher knife, and punctured Jimmy in his right shoulder blade so deep that the tip of the knife came out the other end. Mrs. Parker grabbed the baby, and she and Julia sprinted out of the flat in nothing but their nightgowns, screaming for help.

Somehow Jimmy got the strength to make it out of the flat and into his car. He hid at the home of one of the Washington Wizard players whom he befriended when he interned with them two summers ago. The player was out of town and had no idea that Jimmy was there, but figured Jimmy remembered how to get into the place, because they would go there with some other players to play poker and watch the games. Jimmy knew he didn't lock the back door, because the place was so secluded.

The lieutenant from CPD told me that it was Julia who'd made the late night call to the D.C. police. Although Jimmy threatened to end her life, her child's life, and almost ended AJ's life, she was still reluctant to tell the police everything. Jimmy had some sick hold on her, and she didn't want the cure. Then after a couple of days, she called the police back in the middle of the night in a frantic state and confessed all she knew and they should check the Wizard's player's home. Julia had a restraining order against Jimmy, because of his violent threats against her when she was six months pregnant. I hoped she'd put the reward money to good use for herself and her baby; a baby girl who would now grow up without a dad.

I call AJ to give her the good news. I wish I could be there with her to share in her elation and relief. Lona tells me AJ doesn't sleep well. She turns the telly on and off several times during the night, and sometimes cries out loud. I hope news of Jimmy's capture will put her mind and spirit at ease.

"AJ, they caught Jimmy! They caught him. He went to D.C. to do the same thing to Julia and her baby and Julia's mum stabbed him in his shoulder, but he got away and hid in a home in the woods, but Julia turned him in and he's going to prison for the rest of his miserable life."

I exhale. AJ is silent.

I yell into the phone. "AJ, did you hear me? They caught Jimmy. You don't have to worry anymore. He'll never come near you again."

Again, she is silent. I can't understand why she isn't responding, no emotion, no sarcastic comment, no profanity, nothing. I try again this time much calmer.

"AJ, why won't you talk to me?"

"What difference does it make? The damage has already been done. I'll never be the same, Lime, don't you understand?"

I don't. I thought catching Jimmy would somehow erase all her fears and pain. I thought it was the news that AJ needed so she could smile, laugh, just be AJ again. I thought the answer to all of AJ's problems lay in Jimmy being punished. I guess I thought wrong.

—◊◊—

Clinique makes me earn my pay for the next few weeks. It is one photo shoot, commercial, or appearance after another. I have no time for myself, let alone AJ or Nigel. I do my best to stay in touch with them both as much as I can. Lona and AJ's aunts convince AJ to get some counseling, but after two sessions she stops going. Dad tells me she is finishing her studies, but within the confines of their home. Her professors allow her to miss classes with no penalty. Scott drops off notes and reading assignments for her, but they only communicate via text messages. AJ isn't comfortable going out in public and the few times she does, she covers herself from head to toe. It is early May and although Chicago is not known for the warmest temperatures in May, AJ wears turtlenecks, neck scarves, long sleeved shirts, pants, and even boots. It's obvious that she is hiding something. I too start text messaging AJ only to receive short, formal, empty replies. *No. Yes. Maybe. Good-bye.* She is building a wall around her and not even I am allowed to enter.

On a rare evening when Nigel and I are in New York together, we decide to spend a quiet evening at his place watching one of my favorite movies, *Love and Basketball,* in bed. I just love how true love prevails for Monica and Quincy in the end. Lying under Nigel and inhaling his scent while listening to the rhythmic beat of his heart always calms my spirit and massages my heart. Being in his presence centers me. My phone rings and I jump, because I thought I put it on vibrate. Even though it has been months since I've heard from Pepper or Rohan, I never know when they will surface again. It's a Chicago number, so I answer it.

"Hello, Lime? It's Scott. Angela's friend." He sounds anxious.

"Hi, Scott, what's going on?" Scott has never called me before.

"Sorry to bother you, but I'm real worried about Angela."

"Worried? Did something happen?"

"Whenever we text, she sounds more and more depressed. It's not enough that she doesn't plan to attend the graduation, but her comments—" He pauses. "Well, honestly, they sound suicidal."

"Suicidal? What do you mean?" I stand up, which makes Nigel jump up.

"Well, lately she keeps saying things like, 'What's the point of a law degree if you never plan to use it,' and 'Life is fucked up,' and 'If she wasn't here, who would know?' She won an award from the law school last year for Student Leader of the Year for all the work she's done with BLSA. They also gave her a fourteen karat gold watch. She keeps talking about giving it to me, along with some other things that she has in storage, and she is always comparing herself to you."

"To me, how?"

"Just the other day she said the world doesn't care about how many degrees you acquire. She said it's about being beautiful like Lime and look at her. She also said she's a creature compared to you. She mentions you at least twice a day."

No matter how I try, I can't swallow the lump that is now logged in my throat. I can't believe what I'm hearing. I don't recognize this AJ that Scott is describing. Suicide and comparisons to me aren't part of AJ's vocabulary. My head is hot as the blood rushes to my face. I start to feel dizzy and sit back down on the bed. Nigel stares at me, wondering what is going on. I tell Scott I can be there over the weekend. I thank him for calling me and being such a caring friend. When I hang up with Scott, I press the speed dial for dad and Lona. Dad answers. I recount everything Scott told me and he promises to call Lona at work, the doctors, and counselors, and to keep an even closer watch on AJ. I tell him I'm coming to Chicago in two days.

As if Nigel had held his breath for as long as he could, he blurts out "Lime, what is going on with AJ?"

"That was Scott. Something about AJ being suicidal."

"Yes, I heard you say that."

"AJ is giving things away, could care less about graduating, saying things like if she wasn't here, and now she's starting to compare herself to me." I start pacing and talking fast.

"Did she *say* she was going to kill herself?" Nigel's question is calm and rationale.

"No," I snap. "But this is not AJ." I sniff so hard it dries any tears that want to form. "This is that fucking Jimmy's—"

Nigel's eyes grow large. It is the first time he has heard me swear and the first time he witnesses my rage. Although Nigel is an arm's length away from me, I direct my anger toward the sky.

"Fuck him for putting his hands on her. Fuck him for lying to her, following her, burning her!" And then I remember AJ's dad. "Fuck Mr. Henning for beating Mrs. Henning. Fuck…fuck…fuck!"

I plop down on my recliner and put my face in my hands. I can feel the warmth of Nigel's body as he places his arms around me. I'm out of rage. When I look up, Nigel is still holding on tight. This time I direct my comments to him.

"AJ is the sister I never had. Her mum was the mum I never had and as long as we have been friends she has never been envious of how I look, never. Now whenever she dares to look in the mirror she hates what she sees. She is comparing herself to me; to me, Nigel."

"Baby, she's been to hell and back. Give her time. She'll come around."

Nigel sounds so confident, but my confidence is quickly waning.

—⁓—

When I arrive at dad and Lona's house, I ask them if they can give AJ and me some privacy. They decide to go see a movie. I can tell they are eager to have some alone time. I asked them not to tell AJ I was coming. As I climb the stairs to my old room, I think about what to say to her, so I say a silent prayer for wisdom with each step. I listen by the door before I enter, but all I hear are muffled sounds of AJ's favorite CD, R. Kelly's *Chocolate Factory*. I take a deep breath and open the door instead of knocking.

AJ is lying on her back. It is hard to tell if she is sleeping or just gazing up at the ceiling. An enormous book is opened by her side. The room is black except for a night light casting a dim glow from the corner of the room. She didn't hear me come in, so I tiptoe over to the stereo and turn the volume down. That's when she sits up. I flick on the light switch. AJ begins straightening her clothes and hair as if I'm an intruder who has caught her naked. I stand by the door watching her every move.

"Lime, what are doing here?"

"I came to see you." I fold my arms across my chest.

"You should have told me you were coming."

She fusses with her clothes to make herself presentable while turning away from me. I just look at her.

"AJ, what are you doing?"

"Nothing, I was reading this damn encyclopedia they call a law book and must have fallen asleep. Finals are on Monday."

I didn't give a damn about finals or how she looks. I want to know what AJ is doing with her life. I walk over to the bed and kneel down in front of her. She avoids direct eye contact with me and tries to hide her face and neck with her hands. I can't take it anymore. I grab her hands.

"Listen to me. I'm not going to pretend that I understand what you're going through, nor am I going to feed you some crap about how things are going to get better. I'm just going to agree with you that what happened to you was fucked up, and that you have a right to hurt, grieve, complain, and even ask why, but what you don't have a right to do, Angela Juanita Henning, is to give up on life. Your life was *not* taken on that night and no matter how dismal it looks to you now, it's not yours for the taking."

Tears form in her eyes, but I can't stop.

"If you give up, I give up. If you stop trying, I stop trying. If you stop breathing, I stop breathing. This body you have is just a shell that houses something so majestic and beautiful. Why can't you see that? You have something that I wish I had."

She looks at me as if I am speaking another language.

"But Lime, you are gorgeous. You are the most attractive and gorgeous woman in the world and the whole world knows it. What good does it do to have it going on in the inside if all everyone sees is the outside? Look at me, I've never been and I never will be as gorgeous as you. I can't even look at myself in the mirror anymore. I have no peace with myself. I know you don't understand, but I don't want to live like this."

Her tears are uncontrollable, and she cries from the pit of her belly. I plead with her.

"AJ, don't look at me like the world sees me. They don't know me, and they don't know you. You and Ms. Henning gave me a confidence that my looks can never afford. My own mum didn't even want me, and a man married me for my looks, not for me. I'm an object to this world; a figment of society's imagination about what they consider beautiful for all women, but my peace comes from witnessing and experiencing how you and your mum loved life and loved yourselves, and loved me. You two gave me purpose."

She averts her eyes again, so I reposition myself so she has to see me.

"Don't give up on yourself. Fight those voices that want to take you out. Fight, AJ! Fight!"

I put my arms around her so tight, I think I'm going to break her, but she holds on and we both cry until daybreak.

Before I leave, I convince AJ to go back to counseling. The counselor tells AJ that a loss of self-worth after a tragedy like hers is expected, but now that she has committed to the first step of getting help, true recovery can begin.

CHAPTER 37

Flip the Script

AJ's graduation is in two weeks. We all encourage her to attend. She is in the top ten percent of her graduating class and the dean of the law school called her to make sure she attends, and asked if she would say a few words at the commencement. Dad said she has started coming out of the room more and more to eat dinner with dad and Lona and even allowed Scott to come by the house from time to time. Nigel and I both are able to attend the graduation together. It is the first time the two most important people in my life, my dad and AJ, will meet the man who is becoming the third most important person in my life. My dad and Nigel hit it off well. Dad is fascinated with flying and asks Nigel a million questions every opportunity he gets, even during the ceremony. Lona and I have to shush them both like misbehaving school children. By the end of the day, dad and Nigel are laughing and talking like old buddies.

I treat AJ to an entire day at Channings and Red 7, a luxurious spa and salon in downtown Chicago for the graduation. She sparkles. The cap and gown cover up most of AJ's body. Although she is feeling a lot better about herself, you can still tell by the way she moves and fidgets with herself and her clothes that it is still a day-to-day struggle.

After the dean makes a few remarks about the future of the class of 2004, he gives AJ a warm introduction.

"As dean of this fine law school, I spend the majority of my time traveling, speaking, planning, strategizing, problem solving, and in meeting after meeting, but the meeting I'll never forget is the one I had three years ago with Angela Henning. She made an appointment with me the first week of classes. She just wanted to introduce herself to me, and I could tell from her firm handshake and her unflinching eye contact that she was a mover and shaker and introducing herself to me was more for my benefit than hers. Today, she is still a mover and a shaker, but also a survivor who despite it all, graduates today in the top ten percent of this year's class. I asked Angela to enlighten us for a few moments about true courage and perseverance . . . traits that define an outstanding attorney."

When AJ takes the stand, an eerie hush falls over the crowd. You can hear a pin drop in the large stadium. Even babies stop fussing. AJ hesitates as she organizes her notes, but when she lifts her head to look at the sea of anticipating faces, she decides to speak from the heart.

"What Dean Edmond failed to tell everyone is that he had just gotten back from a conference in Ghana the day before our meeting, and literally dozed off twice in the ten minutes we met."

And with that ice breaker, the crowd exhales and explodes in laughter. Dean Edmond laughs so hard he turns red. AJ chuckles to herself for a brief moment, and then as if struck with a new idea, she tightens her mouth and studies the crowd before she speaks again. Her words trickle into the mic like water dripping from a faucet.

"Here's what I know. Life can flip the script on you sometimes. Things happen without your permission and leave you wondering why. I was eight when the Greyhound bus brought my mother and me to Chicago from Memphis, Tennessee. We left because life in Memphis flipped the script on us. When she died, leaving me with no other family here, life flipped the script on me again, and when my body was set on fire, the script was flipped yet again."

She blows out hard through her nostrils and lowers her head. Just when everyone thinks she can't continue, she raises her head high and begins again as if just awaken from a bad dream.

"But, and I thank God for 'buts,' you can start again."

Her words are full of faith and hope. She educates us on persistence and determination, humble beginnings, hard work and as she makes eye contact with me, the importance of true friendship. But before she is through, she takes us back to that hellish night when Jimmy's actions changed her perspective on life forever.

"After that night, I wasn't sure if life was worth living or if the last three years of law school were worth this moment, but as I stand here, a little country girl from Tennessee, I realize that my life is by design and all that is required of me is to live it."

When she is done, there isn't a dry eye in the stadium. The ovation is tremendous, and I know my friend is on her way.

CHAPTER 38

Internet Therapy

AJ, Scott, and some other law students start studying for the Illinois Bar Exam right after graduation. AJ moves out of dad and Lona's house and finds a two bedroom condo in Hyde Park on Chicago's south side. She didn't want anything from the old flat, aside from a few personal items, because of the memories of times with Jimmy and "that" night.

Life seems to be better for everyone this summer. I even start running again. Between traveling and AJ, I just didn't have the energy or the time. I decide to take a long morning run with Ms. India Arie serenading in my ears the importance of slowing down. It is a mild New York summer day and New Yorkers are out taking advantage of it. When I return, the concierge, Corey, hands me a package. It is another gold envelope the same size as the one Pepper and Rohan sent me four months ago. I hold my breath.

"How was your run, Ms. Prince?"

"It was great, Corey, thank you."

It has been three months since I've heard hide or hair from Pepper or Rohan. After the incident with AJ, I didn't get an email from Rohan so I left it alone, now this.

The package is addressed to me with no return address on it; however, the handwriting looks familiar. I flip it over and breathe an immediate sigh of relief. It's stamped Apple of My Eye Studio; it is from my dad. I rip it open and find a note inside.

"AJ left this in a drawer in your old room. It's addressed to you. Love you, Dad."

It looks like a diary. It is all black with red stucco lettering on the front that says *Thoughts*. I grab some bottled water from the fridge, and start reading the first entry, and that's when my knees buckle.

Dearest Lime:

Remember how we used to write notes to each other during study hall in high school? They were always filled with stupid jokes, silly crushes (most of them were about how many boys had crushes on you), and what college we were going to attend. It all seems so superficial and meaningless now in the whole scheme of life. As I sit in your old room, day after day, staring out the window at the cars passing by, I am too ashamed to be among the living. I sit here surrounded by your presence. I can feel your beauty and spirit in this room and it suffocates me, because I can never be beautiful again. Jimmy took that from me. So, I sit here writing you another meaningless note, because inside this room and inside myself, I am not living. I am dead like my charred skin. I am dead, Lime, but I want you to have this journal. I began writing in it last year when Jimmy first hit me and today is my last and final entry. I will be okay. Just know that I am with you always.
Love Eternally,
AJ

I search for the date. April 30, 2004 was the day Scott called me. I sit in the middle of my floor for two straight hours reading every word.

August 24, 2003
Its 2:00 in the morning and I'm here, in Cancun on vacation, on the fucking bathroom floor. I just don't understand him. He says he loves me, but tonight,

he just took it too far. I used to love sex with Jimmy. We used to kiss for what seemed like hours and even have foreplay. Now he just wants to mount me like some damn horse and he's starting to ask me to do things that I'm not comfortable doing. He asked me about anal sex again tonight and I'm like what part of "not in this lifetime" don't you understand? He keeps calling me a tease and a baby and telling me to stop being so damned scared, but he didn't stop there. He put his hands around my throat when we were having sex tonight, and kept tightening them each time I told him I couldn't breathe. He acted like he didn't hear me and didn't let go until I almost blacked out. I had to literally beat that motherfucker off of me. It was the look in his eyes, like he was possessed or something. I don't know, but I think Jimmy tried to kill me. I can't wait to go back home tomorrow. I need to get away from him for awhile.

AJ

AJ chronicled everything from sex with Jimmy, the numerous verbal and physical fights, to waking up in the hospital after she was burned. One day, Jimmy even stole her car keys from her because she was late coming over to his house. She had to take the bus for two days, because she was too embarrassed to tell anyone. All her emotions mixed with detailed description are right here in black and white. Toward the end, every entry comments on beauty.

May 1, 2004

I just saw Halle Berry advertising makeup on television. Shit, if Halle Berry can't keep a man and she's drop dead gorgeous, I can forget it. Who am I kidding? I can't even stand to look at myself in the mirror. At least I'm not throwing up anymore, but I still can't look. Everyone is prettier than me. I look like a damn beast. No one cares if you are a good person anymore. All they see is how you look on the outside. I can't watch television, read a magazine, or even sit in this house without being reminded of how ugly I am. Lona is attractive and

Lime is, well . . . Lime is stunning. Even ugly men can get dates, but life for a hideous woman is hell . . . PURE HELLLLLLLLLLLLL!!!!!!!!!!!!!!!!
AJ

It is one gloomy entry after another. She lists every person who she and society considers beautiful, and I'm number one on the list written in great big red letters with several exclamation marks. She points out our physical features like she is taking inventory. The list is full of Supermodels, actresses, singers, dancers, college classmates, and even some girls in secondary school. What we all have in common is that we have, according to AJ, "bodies to die for" and "stop traffic" faces. While reading it, I find myself underlining and making notes off to the side like university. Like AJ, I'm consumed with it. I know she is in a different mental place these days, but after reading her journal, I call just to make sure.

"Hey you." She seems to sing her greeting after picking up on the first ring.

"Hey," I say as if just remembering why I called. "What are you doing?"

I can hear pots and plates banging in the background.

"Girl, taking a much needed study break. I haven't eaten all day. Scott, Janine, Dianna and I are meeting again at the law school in about an hour."

"Oh, okay."

"Why, what's up?"

"Nothing, just checking on you." I try hard to sound unconcerned.

"Right. You sure?"

"I just want to make sure you are okay."

"I'm doing what I need to do to keep my sanity, babe, and believe me, studying for this Bar is doing it, but if you're worried that I'm going to have some sort of relapse, it will have to wait until after the Bar."

I can feel her smile through the phone. Her humor is coming back. I don't mention about her journal. I'm sure she has forgotten about it, but I can't.

The next day, I call Nigel to tell him about the journal. When I call he is eating dinner with some other pilots in Amsterdam, but he can hear the concern in my voice and agrees to step away to talk to me for a few minutes.

"Is something wrong?"

I hesitate because I realize that although my man is halfway around the world, instead of calling him to tell him how much I miss him or just want to hear his voice, I'm ready to burn a hole in his ear about AJ again.

"Well, how are you?"

"Missing you."

Now I really feel bad.

"I miss you, too, sweetie." I get to the point. "Dad sent me this package today, from AJ. She left her journal in my old drawer addressed to me. She wrote me a suicide note, Nigel. I just can't believe she contemplated killing herself over an illusion of what is beautiful and what is not. I stayed up half the night reading it over and over again, and what bothered me the most was her obsession with beauty."

"Hmm, but she seemed so happy at the graduation."

"I know and I started to think that was a façade, so I called her after I read the journal. She really does sound focused. I think studying for this Bar is giving her new purpose now."

"Did you talk about the journal?"

"No, I didn't mention it. I just wanted to check to make sure she was okay."

"Well, then, look at her journal as a way of healing."

My slow response lets him know that I'm confused.

"When my dad died, my mom bought Nia and me journals so we could write our feelings down about his death. She never read them, because she said they were our feelings and therefore they were private, but they needed to be expressed. I wrote for a little while and it did help, but Nia still writes in one today. They say writing is cathartic."

He sounds so knowledgeable.

"I never thought about it that way."

"Oh yeah, millions of people are journaling online now. It's called blogging."

Nigel explains that blogs are like personal diaries for anyone to read. We talk for a few minutes more about blogging, before he remembers that his food is getting cold and the other pilots are probably starting to wonder about him.

"Thank you, sweetie, for just listening to me all the way in Amsterdam."

"Anytime. Now, let me finish this food. The Red Light District is calling my name."

"What?!" I yell.

"I'm just kidding, baby."

"I love you, Nigel." And I mean it.

"I love you, too."

It's not that I'm computer illiterate. I do own a laptop, but only use it to check or send emails, and to check or to make additions or deletions to my modeling schedule. I just don't have the time to spend on the internet. At one point, Laylah created a fan website for me and insisted that I respond to some of the emails from fans. At first, it was fun. I was getting emails from all around the world about everything from advice about breaking into the modeling industry to marriage proposals, but as my schedule increased, I couldn't keep up and Laylah assigned someone at Faces to filter the messages for me and often sent canned responses, along with a photo.

This notion of journaling and writing with others as a form of therapy intrigues me. Since I can remember, running has been my therapy, but it doesn't allow for much communication. I talk to AJ, Nigel, and my dad when I need a shoulder to cry on or just a listening ear, but what I feel inside with regards to AJ and her inner turmoil, and to some degree my own, talking to them right now seems self-defeating. I need objectivity; a way to understand my friend's obsession with physical beauty. I want us to get back to accepting each other as we are. I decide to do some research on blogs.

—∽—

Tuesday is another commercial shoot for Clinique. As Dee-Dee shapes my sides, tapers the back of my head and spikes the top of my hair, I keep thinking about AJ's journal. All that time I was traveling, posing in front of camera after camera, meeting and drinking with celebrities, walking down runways, and making more money than I can spend in this lifetime or the next, AJ was experiencing a reality that my fantasy life can't begin to comprehend. I've spent so much time away from my dad and AJ that I feel guilt settle in my bones. Then when Yanni, Rohan, Pepper, and Waterfall tried to destroy me, AJ was the first person I ran to. I sit in the chair, emotionless, as Dee-Dee works her magic.

"A portabella mushroom for your thoughts?" Dee-Dee smiles as she reminds me of our times together.

"Oh . . . nothing."

It has been a long time since Dee-Dee and I have had a heart-to-heart. She knows about AJ's assault and about the encounters with Yanni, but I didn't dare tell her about the video and how my ex-husband, his low life friend, and a stripper are trying to blackmail me. Although I still consider Dee-Dee a friend, she has been replaced with Nigel.

"Do you ever get tired of this life?"

"What life? Fashion?"

"Yeah."

"No, I love what I do. I mean it gets hectic, but that's with anything, I guess."

"Right."

She stops painting my face and looks at me with a puzzled look.

"You thinking about quitting?"

"No, I'm not saying that. It's just that this year has put some things in perspective for me. Things that matter more, you know?"

Dee-Dee nods, and for a moment I think she is going to cry. I can tell she is thinking about her grandmother.

After AJ's accident, modeling is kind of losing its zest. It's something about AJ's words that night in my old bedroom when she and I confronted her demons that stay in my head: *What good does it do to have it going on in the inside if all everyone sees is the outside?* Every time I look in the mirror now, her words look back at me. I need to understand them, but when Dee-Dee is done, I put on the selected outfit, and my "fashion game face." For the next few days, my personal issues will have to wait.

CHAPTER 39

Unpretty

I call AJ the day before she takes the Bar exam. She sounds calm and reflective when she answers the phone.

"Hey, babe."

"Hey, how you feeling?"

"Hmm, just ready for it to be over, I guess."

"What are you doing now?"

"Nothing. Just thinking."

For the first time in a long time, I hear sadness in her voice as R. Kelly's *Chocolate Factory* CD hums in the background.

"A million dollars for your thoughts."

I laugh, but the way I've been feeling these days, I would gladly hand her a million dollars in cash, if I it could erase this whole year and allow us to start over.

She chuckles. "I was just thinking about my mama and how if she was here how proud she would be and how instead of Jimmy going to prison, he would be dead already."

"Amen to that." We share a quick laugh, before AJ's laughter turns serious.

"I don't know, Lime. I don't get it. What was the point of it all? What's the point of the Bar?"

"The point is that this is your preparation for your greater good. You got criminals like Jimmy to prosecute. You are going to help to make this world better for the next woman."

"So, I had to get burned to a crisp to help make this world a better place?"

She's not feeling my answer, so I take a deep breath.

"I'm not saying that, I'm just saying we need you."

After a long pause, she replies, "Riiight."

"You're not thinking about *not* taking the exam tomorrow?"

"Oh, hell no. I'm going to make it do what it do, but I just want you to know as my best friend, if someone had told me years ago that my life would have turned out this way, I would hit them in the head with two cast iron skillets instead of one like my mama did to my daddy the night we left Memphis.

AJ has come a long way, but I can tell the affects of the burns have left scars on the inside as well as the outside. When I hang up with her, I plug in my laptop and let the keyboard be the catalyst to my blogging journey. I search for sites that deal with domestic violence.

July 23, 2004

Three months ago, my best friend in life wrote me a suicide note after a horrible assault which disfigured the left side of her body. She didn't think that life was worth living and for months she isolated herself from the world. Not only is she full of life, but she is full of beauty. In her suicide note she said that she can never be beautiful again, because "he" took that away from her. It angers and saddens me that he put his hands on her without her permission and scarred her for life. It angers and saddens me that her laughter has been replaced with melancholy. It angers and saddens me that now she compares her physical appearance to every other woman society labels "The Most Beautiful Women in the

World." Now whenever she allows herself to look into a mirror, she sees herself through the eyes of others. She even compares herself to me. True, we are physical opposites, but kindred spirits, and all my life, I wished I had just an ounce of the self-esteem that she used to possess. I wished I loved my thighs, my breasts, my bum, my lips, my hair a fraction of the way she loved herself. I had to learn the hard way, through her attack, that I am more than what society sees on the outside. Aren't we more than the shell in which our souls are housed? I need to understand her obsession with beauty, but the problem is I wasn't the one who was attacked, nor have I ever been attacked. I wasn't the one who was left for dead and have to face daily reminders of that heinous night. I am not the one that society now looks at with pity. How do I understand? What is my role? Who gave birth to this fascination with beauty? Does it matter? Why doesn't she still see what I see whenever I look at her, whenever I am in her presence, whenever I hear her voice? Why? Because all I see is beautiful.

I sit back in my chair, exhausted. My emotions pour on the screen with a fury that takes my breath away. I reread it several times before creating my profile. I ponder over a name for awhile. I want a name that reflects the purpose of my blog. I prop my elbows on my coffee table and run my index finger down the center of my head as I stare out of my window. "Unpretty," whispers in my ear. I remember it was the title of a song in the 90s, and the title says it all. AJ feels unpretty. I create an email address just for Unpretty and await insight from others.

The next day, I can't believe I have 15 comments between the hour after I wrote my entry and now. Women are responding from all over the globe. It's amazing. The first post is from a woman from England who was the victim of her ex-husband's drunken rages.

Dear Unpretty-
Five years ago, I had to undergo Ocular Prosthesis (a glass eye) after my ex-husband punched me so hard in my right eye that he split my eyeball in three

different places. The doctors couldn't save it. I was a cheerleader all my life and even a NBA cheerleader in the United States for two years, which is where I met my husband. Everyone used to describe me as a "looker," but after what he did to me, now all I get are confused stares. It's very difficult to feel good about yourself after an attack like that, despite what others who care about you may say. After five years, I'm still resentful, and at times, very self-conscious.
Nora, UK

The ones that follow are even more heart wrenching.

You're lucky that your friend only got as far as writing you a suicide note, because I attempted it. The only thing that saved my life was the door to the garage where I locked myself inside my car with the motor running wasn't completely shut and a neighbor saw the exhaust coming from underneath. I was sexually molested by my favorite uncle from the age of four to eight. During my first year in college, I was raped by three fraternity pigs as part of their initiation, and the final straw for me was being shot in the face by my daughter's father, because he suspected me of cheating on him with his cousin. Half of my jaw is missing because of his jealousy and need to control. My own daughter was afraid to look at me at times, so I decided to spare everyone anymore of the freak show and sent my daughter off to school, called in sick to work, and prepared to awake on the other side. That was eight years ago, and today after more surgeries than I can count, I'm not as gruesome as before. With the support of my church and my family, I found myself again. They say beauty is in the eye of the beholder, but the beholder is never the one with the "Cain-like" mark. If we lived in Utopia, I still don't think, even there, women would be valued. It is our appearance that defines us. Just ask someone to describe any woman and the first thing out of their mouth is how she looks. So, Unpretty, welcome to our world… the Unpretties!
Sandra, California

Unpretty-
I wear two huge keloid scars on my face after I was robbed at an ATM last
year. A teenage thug cut me in my face twice with a box cutter over $20. You
don't know the pain unless you've been there. It's not fair, but women are judged
on their looks. Every day, we are faced with images of beauty and sexiness and
none of those images show who we are on the inside. My keloid scars cost me
$20, but no money can erase that night or the scars I wear on the outside and
on the inside.
Valerie, Mississippi

My cell phone rings. It's Nigel. I know he's getting back into town
today, but I can't stop reading their comments. I let it go into voice mail
and promise myself to call him back as soon as I'm done. I put the phone
on vibrate, stretch out on my couch, and place my laptop on my lap. I
don't want to miss reading one word.

It's one painful story after another. Women, bonded by their abuse,
are recounting their own vicious attacks with vivid details and doing their
best to help me understand what AJ is going through. I want to respond to
them all, but what can I say? I feel like I'm the student and they are teach-
ing me about a world in which I know nothing about.

I write almost every day for weeks. I stop attending the shows' after
parties. Instead, I rush back to my hotel room for more conversation with
my new global girlfriends. After three weeks, I have quite a following and
the number of posts to my blog is increasing every day. After two months,
Unpretty is getting posts left and right. Women are allowing themselves to
share their innermost feelings about themselves before the attack and after
and about their attackers. The majority of them have been abused by men
they knew and it isn't only physical abuse. They are educating me about
an area I never considered: mental and sexual abuse. Regardless, the issue
that confronts them all is their feelings of self-worth and beauty. The comments are candid and the details of physical scars are often too horrific to

read, but for the first time since AJ's torture, I am beginning to understand the women behind the scars. One post in particular strikes a personal cord with me.

Unpretty:
I'm the invisible woman, because my scars are invisible. I married my high school sweetheart right after college. We were so in love, so I thought. In high school, he was a bit of a loner, but he was sweet to me. I was considered one of the popular girls…president of the student council, captain of the volleyball team, chair of the prom committee, you name it, and I did it. I remember in high school how he would get upset when I had meetings or just hung out with my friends. He just seemed to want me all to himself. Once we decided to get married, I thought he would come out of his shell a bit more, but instead he became more possessive of me and my time. He began yelling at me about everything from working late to talking on the phone. Soon the yelling turned into insults about how I dressed, cooked, drove…it didn't matter. He always had something negative to say. Then one day, he did the unthinkable. I was throwing a birthday party for my sister. He didn't want to attend. I had a few glasses of wine. When I arrived home, he was waiting up for me and accused me of being drunk and called my entire family a bunch of alcoholics. I ignored him and just walked away. He followed me, grabbed the back of my head, and forced me to have sex with him while he yelled derogatory names at me and slapped and punched me. When he was done, he told me that it was my duty to have sex with him whenever and however he wanted it. So you see my scars are invisible to outsiders, but larger than life to me. I was raped numerous times by my husband for years. Sexual abuse is often not even in the same category as physical abuse, but the scars are just as real.
Signed,
Invisible

I put my hand over my mouth and think about all those times Rohan climbed on top of me when I often told him no or that I wasn't in the mood.

He would just ignore me. My mind flashes back to that night he brought Pepper and Waterfall to our home for a planned sexual orgy against my will. He degraded me so in front of them that I unwillingly agreed thinking that maybe…just maybe when it was over he would love me more. When he saw how upset I was, he tried to sweet talk me and handed me a clove cigar, because he said it would relax me. After a few puffs, I felt light-headed, dizzy, and almost drunk. He insisted that I smoke another. I was an emotional mess during those two years with Rohan and after reading some of these comments; I think I too was a victim of sexual abuse.

CHAPTER 40

True Identity

"It's a wrap." AJ is ecstatic.

She calls me early on an October morning with the good news. It's the afternoon in London.

"You passed?!" I scream into the phone.

"Oh, Lime. We did it!"

"You and Scott?"

"Yes, but I'm talking about us. If it weren't for you and your encouragement, I wouldn't be holding this bottle of Chardonnay at nine in the morning." She lets out a hearty laugh.

Her enthusiasm is infectious. I'm so happy for her and so glad she didn't give up. I have yet to tell AJ about my blog, and I'm not sure why since she is the reason I started blogging in the first place. I don't want to ruin her moment and remind her of that experience any more than she reminds herself.

—·—

My time in London is short, but Asmeret and I meet for dinner. It has been over a year since her visit to New York. We talked on the phone from time to time and even sent a few emails. She looks the same as when she came to New York, and seems somewhat at peace now that she's settled back in Brixton. Grandmother Genet moved back to Ethiopia and Asmeret has the house all to herself. The café is doing better than ever. They moved it to a larger space, hired more staff, and welcomed some of London's finest musicians, spoken word artists, and writers. London's own, a musical spoken word female group called Floetry, is performing at the café tomorrow night.

"So tell me. What's going on with you these days?"

She does her best to sound sincere.

"Oh, God. Where do I begin?" I wipe the corners of my mouth with my napkin. "My best friend and closest thing to a sister—"

"AJ?"

She cuts me off. I can't believe she remembered. Maybe she is being sincere. I try to let my guard down some.

"Yes, AJ. Well, she was burned by a crazy, jealous boyfriend earlier this year."

Her eyes buck. "What do you mean, burned?"

"He broke into her flat and poured gasoline all over her and lit a match." She's speechless. "Yes, it was devastating, but today after months of turmoil, she is so much better and even passed the Illinois Bar today."

I decide to skip a lot of the details. It is just too painful to recount again.

"I am so sorry to hear that. I can't imagine. She's lucky to have a friend . . . I mean, sister like you." Her smile is gentle as if she understands the importance of family now.

"Sometimes, I feel like the lucky one." I look away.

A tall gentleman about Nigel's height and build walks past our table, leading a young woman by the hand. They're being escorted to their table by the hostess. Just then, I remember Nigel. I tell her how we met and how great he is. She can't wait to meet Nigel and says he sounds a lot like my dad. I promise to bring Nigel to Brixton next time I visit. As the evening ends, the awkward silence that lingers between she and I each time we meet is back. As I sip my tea and she plays with her crème brulee, I think about my blog. I haven't written anything in days.

She finally puts her spoon down, and looks up at me, pressing her lips together.

"The cancer is back." Her eyes are doleful.

I put my tea down and blink my eyes as if bringing her words into focus.

"When did that happen?"

"I found out this summer. It has spread to my other breast, and I may have to start chemo treatments again, but they are watching me closely."

"Does Aunt Miriam and Aunt Fenayte know? Does Grandmother Genet know?"

"Miriam and Fenayte went to the hospital with me and heard the diagnosis themselves. Mum doesn't need this news in her life right now."

She pushes the dessert away from her. I don't know what to do or what to say. Yes, she is my mum, but our relationship feels more like distant friends. I put my hand on top of her hand and she puts her other hand on top of mine.

"Is there anything I can do?"

"Pray"

When I arrive back in New York, I do what I do best whenever I need to think, I run. When I return almost an hour later, I call Nigel and leave him a voice message on his cell phone that I'm back and how much I miss him. This time instead of flying, he is attending his ten year college reunion at Brown. The timing of it conflicted with my trip to London, so he went alone. I'm not sure who to tell about the news of Asmeret's cancer. AJ is celebrating her Bar results with friends and whereas dad would be sympathetic, I just don't want to bother him and Lona with unpleasant news. So, I plug in my laptop ready to share the news with my global friends.

Before I can gather my thoughts, I notice that something new is happening on my blog. Women are posting pictures of themselves; pictures of their scars. What I see frightens and disturbs me at the same time. There are pictures of missing fingers and hands, now stubby mounds of black and white flesh. Faces with sideway smiles, bruised eyes, gashes in cheeks, and permanent cuts across foreheads and lips. The more I stroll the more revealing the pictures are. A few women show their bare shoulders, chest, stomachs, and even bums. Discolored bodies with a scary mixture of black, blue, and green bruises and raised keloid scars from stab wounds almost an arm's length long cover their private parts.

And then there are the burns. Melded flesh after melded flesh replace smooth, soft skin. One woman is covered with small, circular red marks on her entire back. According to her, her stepfather used her back for an ashtray for years. There are images of burns that make AJ's burns look like child's play. Every posting is a result of undeserved and unwelcome attacks. I feel hurt and confused at the same time. Something needs to be done to stop this senseless violence against women and to give them hope that there are people in the world who care about more than their physical appearance.

The next thing I read is from a former model from New York who posted a picture of her scars from a brutal rape. The rapist used a piece of broken glass to pry her legs open and cut one inch deep slits all over her inner and outer thighs. Under her pictures she writes:

The son of a bitch who did this to me stalked me for months. I was just breaking into the modeling profession and my career looked promising. Now my modeling career is just a pipe dream. I don't wear swimsuits or shorts anymore. Although my face is still intact and not a day goes by when people don't ask me if I am a model, my decision to quit has really opened my eyes to how superficial

the modeling world really is. These models today are just pretty faces with waif-
like bodies. The idea of posing seductively again to sell a product for a man's
enjoyment disgusts me. Supermodels like Naomi, Tyra, and now Lime, are just
illusions of beauty for women, especially black women.
Donna, New York

Her words aren't bitter, just honest and full of emotion. Many of the
women on the site who identify themselves as black engage in a heated discussion about beauty for the black woman, and even discuss me, and other
black Supermodels, in detail. The comments range from my ethnicity; they
question if I'm black or not, to men's fascination with me. I close my laptop
and wonder if they would even be having this discussion if they had never
been attacked. How did they feel about themselves before the attacks and
if somewhere in their subconscious they blame my looks and status in life
on their scars? I wonder if AJ felt the same.

I'm so conflicted by the discussions that I don't write anything for a
week. Nigel and I decide to take some time and get away together for the
Thanksgiving holiday. It's been months since we've spent any significant
time together, and I'm missing his touch. We decide to go back to Paris,
the first place we ever traveled together. This time we opt for a cozy cottage
in Paris' countryside forty miles outside of Paris. Nigel and I need some
quiet time, surrounded by God's green earth and tranquility. We talk into
the wee hours of the night about everything from where we see ourselves
in the next five years to the war in Iraq. Nigel is so verse on almost any
topic and his opinions are sensible and interesting. As much I try to avoid
talking about my blog, I just can't. I can tell Nigel is a bit tired of hearing
about it, because every time I call him these days it is the first thing out of
my mouth, but I need his sensible opinion now.

On our last night in Paris, we lay in the jacuzzi tub submerged in
bubbles and scented oils. As my back presses against his tight chest, he
squeezes his thighs around me.

"Asmeret's cancer is back."

Nigel hugs me tighter. "How is she doing?"

"She's going to start chemo again."

"How do you feel about it?"

"I don't know, Nigel. It just didn't hit me as hard as when I found out Grandfather Dawit had cancer."

Nigel knows that Asmeret and I have an estranged relationship; therefore, I don't feel the need to justify my feelings further. I close my eyes for a moment and listen to the subtle movement of the warm, bubbly bath water.

"Nigel?" I ask with my eyes closed. "Is a woman's beauty the most important thing to a man?"

I can feel he is contemplating his answer before he responds by the way his breathing slows down in his chest.

"We are visual creatures, Lime, and only a few men can really look past a woman's physical appearance and see something genuine."

"So, if I didn't look like I look, would you have been attracted to me?"

I open my eyes in anticipation of his answer.

"I know I would have been attracted to your personality and spirit . . . yes, but if you want me to be honest, it was your physical beauty first."

"AJ's mum always told us that one day the world is going to stop taking good looks for currency and then what will we do? I'm starting to see what she means." Our silence seems to make the bath water cooler. "If it had been me who'd suffered second-degree burns, would you still want me?"

Nigel turns the side of my face toward him and whispers, "I hope so or I would have missed out on someone wonderful."

I turn to face him and kiss him long and hard on his soft lips; however, I still haven't gotten an answer to my true problem for the past few days. Do I reveal my identity to the women on my blog? I take a deep breath and begin to tell Nigel about the pictures and the ongoing conversations that the women are having about me and issues of beauty. I feel like an eavesdropper and an outsider on my own blog. I want to ease their concerns and misconceptions, but I also want to help them feel better about themselves. I just don't know how.

"Then you owe it to them to tell them who you are. It may not turn out as bad as you think it will."

He begins to massage my neck and shoulders.

I thank him for being so patient with my new hobby and promise to relax for the rest of the night and just enjoy each other.

CHAPTER 41

Bright Idea

On the long flight back to New York from Paris, I'm wide awake thinking. All I can think about is my life and how Laylah would have never called me, three years ago, to come to New York, because of my IQ or even my personality. My looks have afforded me some opportunities that others only wish they could have. It's a shame all the struggles women go through in the name of someone's definition of what is beautiful. I want to dispel the myth and to somehow show the world that the true measure of a woman is on the inside.

As Nigel sleeps with his head on my shoulder, I stare at an aerial view of his body; his well-defined chest, rounded shoulders, muscular arms, firm yet gentle hands, and lean legs. Everything but his face is in my direct view, and I realize what keeps me attracted and satisfied month after month to this man, is just Nigel, not his physical appearance. I reposition Nigel's head in the other direction, careful not to wake him, and locate my laptop in the overhead compartment. My typing races to keep up with my thoughts.

December 1, 2004

I took a bit of a hiatus. I needed to gather my thoughts and process all of the conversations that my blog started four months ago. What began as a way for me to understand my best friend after a life changing attack has developed into a female community bonded by our need to give voice to our personal tragedies. Yes, I am including myself in this community, because although my tragedy was not a physical one, I have shared in each of your tragedies for the past four months. Our collective voices let the world know that real, tangible women with careers, ambitions, families, etc., exist and that we are more than the physical scars that the world sees. We are irreplaceable beings that the world needs to recognize, see, and respect. Your words and your pictures speak truth; an internet reality show, and for some of you your truth is somehow tied to the unrealistic world of Hollywood, celebrities, and Supermodels. Please don't make the same mistake that society does when they look at each of you and judge us for the same reasons that you are unfairly judged. Many of your comments suggest that you have forgotten what it feels like to be judged. I logged onto my blog this evening for the sole purpose to reveal my identity and to let you know that I think I have found a way to bring positive attention to each of you in light of your attacks. Each of you has helped my understanding of violence against women and what is truly beautiful for women in your own unique way, and for that I am grateful. I want to show the world who we are as women. I want to photograph each of you in a way that shows your unique beauty. Allow me to create a new face for women forever changed by violence.

Bonded,

Lime Prince, New York

As I post my comment, butterflies dance in my stomach, like no one is watching. They keep telling me that revealing my identity is a mistake, and try to convince me that the women will feel betrayed, used, and suspicious. *What was I thinking?* I rarely have anytime to call my best friend or spend time with Nigel, let alone agree to photograph hundreds of women, but I want to do this. I need to do this. Back in New York, I call dad right away.

"Hi, dad."

"Hey, Apple. How are you?"

"Busy . . . always busy. How are you?"

"Well, you know it's Christmas season so everyone and their mother want pictures, but I'm managing."

Dad knows I started blogging, but he has no idea what I'm planning.

"Dad, I want to talk to you about something?"

"Sure, what's up?"

"Remember the blog I started months ago and how I was learning more and more about violence against women?"

"I think I recall something about that. Why?"

"Well, it's taken on a life of its own. Women are sharing their innermost feelings about their attacks and now they are posting pictures of themselves on my blog."

"What kind of pictures?" He sounds puzzled.

"Pictures of their scars, kind of like how I took pictures of AJ's burns when she was in the hospital. Dad, these women are hurting because they feel as if society doesn't care about the well-being of women, period. I know this is going to sound crazy, but I want to try and make society care. For the first time since becoming a model, I want to do something with my fame and fortune that doesn't involve selling a product or making others rich."

"So what do you want to do?"

"I want to photograph these women in a way that brings some positive attention to their attacks, but also shows how beautiful all women are who are victims of violence."

"Okay?" I can tell he still doesn't understand.

"Dad, I need your help. You are the best photographer I know—"

"You want me to photograph them?"

"I want *us* to photograph them together."

"Apple, you know I want to help, but I'm swamped right now. Can't you get some of those New York photographers to do it? I mean their equipment and studios are much more high tech than mine."

"If it's not about fashion and making millions of dollars, they aren't interested, plus they wouldn't understand why I want to do this, and they wouldn't care. I don't want these women to be exploited and used for some media frenzy. I want something positive to come out of this. I can't explain it fully, I just know I want to do it and I want to do it with you."

He lets out a heavy sigh into the phone and asks when and how many women need to be photographed, but I don't know. I haven't thought that far ahead. I just need to know that I can count on him.

CHAPTER 42

News Travels Fast

Within days, Unpretty is on fire. There are more posts than I can read and news of my blog is starting to reach the media's ears. Editorials are being written about it and radio stations are dedicating entire shows to it. One editorial reads "Supermodel Lime Prince Has a New Job."

AJ calls me one afternoon after hearing about it on the radio in her car. "Hey, babe."

I was on my way to Faces to meet with Laylah.

"Uh, Lime, today on V103, Ramonski Love and Joe Soto were discussing some internet blog that you created. Something called Unpretty. They are asking people to call in to give their opinions on beauty for women. What's that all about?"

I try to explain the best I can.

"I've been writing on this blog I created about four months ago. I needed to understand what you were going through after the attack. I began to question what you thought about me after reading the letter you wrote me."

"What letter?"

"The one in your diary. You left it in my room when you were staying with dad and Lona."

AJ is silent.

"Oh my God, I forgot all about that. Lime, I wrote that at a low point in my life. All those comparisons to you came from that place. Babe, if I ain't killed myself by now, I don't when I would have time. I hope you understand that."

"What I understand AJ is that what happened to you happens to women all across the globe every day. It even happened to me while I was married to Rohan. Through this blog, I realized that he sexually, mentally, and emotionally abused me and although no one can see the scars on the outside, I live with them every day. The women on my blog feel worthless and undesirable, and some of them compare themselves to women like me. Unpretty was my way of understanding what you, and they, are going through and now I want to help."

"Help how?"

"I'm going to try to show the world their true beauty and what it means for all women."

"Hmm, that's an ambitions task. How are you going to do that?"

"I don't have it all worked out now, but I will."

"Well, you know I support you, babe. Just don't let me turn on the radio and hear folks talking about you and I don't know what's going on. That makes mama nervous."

We share a much needed laugh. I finish explaining the blog to her and describe the women and their various stories.

"I want to photograph these women in a way that helps to bring positive attention instead of negative attention to their attacks, and I would love for you to be a part of it."

"Sure. What do you need?"

"I want to photograph you, too."

"Oh, hell no—"

"AJ, you don't even know how I'm going to photograph everyone."

"With a camera, and again, hell to the no."

"Why not?"

"I'm not about to pose this half-baked body in front of a camera for no one, not even you, babe."

Good thing I didn't tell her about the pictures I'd taken of her when she was in the hospital.

"I promise you it will be very tasteful."

"Good. I'm sure *the women* you photograph will appreciate that."

"Did I mention that my dad is helping me take some of the pictures? My *fine ass* daddy."

"You want me to pose in front of your *fine ass* daddy? Lime, please."

"Can you just think about it, please? Your experience inspired me to do this, so without you it would be incomplete."

She huffs before saying, "Good-bye, babe."

When I arrive at Faces, Elmira says Laylah wants to see me right away. Before I go into her office, I notice that an enormous life like photograph of me from my first Couture shoot on the cover of *Vogue* is hanging big as day in the front hallway. It is right next to Liya Kebede's photo. Although I know Laylah is very impatient, I take a moment to look at it and smile to myself about how far I have come. Elmira smiles with me. Laylah is on the phone in a loud discussion in what sounds like Japanese. I open the door and her eyes flare when she sees me. I sit down, oblivious to her reaction. After five minutes, she finishes her conversation, takes off her headset, and begins massaging her temples.

"Foreign models are the worst." Then she addresses me with her eyes closed. "Lime, I've been getting one phone call after another all week from newspapers, magazines, television, and radio stations across the country for an interview with you. Something about a blog called Unpretty. What is this about you being involved with some crusade for women, and now you are anti the modeling world?"

She massages her temples again, opens her eyes, and looks at me square in the eyes.

"Only half of that is true."

"Okay dahling, no games, which half is true?"

She sits back in her leather chair and folds her arms across her chest.

"Yes, I have been writing on a blog, and the blog is called Unpretty, and women who are victims of heinous, violent crimes, like my sister, have been blogging with me. No one is anti anything. Don't believe everything you hear, Laylah."

I copy her, sit back in my chair, and fold my arms across my chest.

"What I hear is my phone ringing and when I don't know what the hell they are talking about it vexes me."

I can tell that she is uneasy with the attention, because it isn't fashion related. I share as much information about the blog as I feel Laylah needs to know. I'm not ready to reveal my plan to photograph the women until my dad and I and the women work out the logistics. Laylah's biggest concern when it comes to me is Clinique, couture, and multi-million dollar contracts; anything that makes her money from my looks.

"I assure you that my blogging won't, and hasn't interfered with my modeling career. It's what I do in my personal time, but as usual, even that isn't off limits to the press."

"Well, let's just see that this blogging doesn't get out of control. I will do my best to handle the press." She seems to relax for a minute and eases back into her high backed leather chair. "Did you notice anything in the hallway?" We both grin. "I had it installed two weeks ago and wanted to surprise you. It is rather striking, don't you think?"

After a few moments of reliving the couture photo shoot, Laylah informs me that she and her daughter are leaving for Iran next week until the New Year.

"No Sharon soiree for me this year."

She fans her left hand in the air minus her three-carat diamond wedding ring. I can tell she is fishing to see if I'm going to attend or not. I didn't hear from Sharon much after the last Christmas party. Everyone keeps telling me that signing with Maier will take my career to new heights like movies, and possibly my own television show, but that's just not what I want. I forgot about a meeting with her once, and when I tried to reschedule, I never heard from her again. Another model warned me that Sharon doesn't like to be snubbed. I haven't received a personal invitation this year like before, and don't expect to. Sharon's party is the furthest thing from my mind right now unbeknownst to Laylah.

"Yeah, I think I'm just going to head home for the holiday as well."

My plans seem to satisfy Laylah. I have a major photo shoot of my own to plan.

CHAPTER 43

A Little Help from my Friends

SPECIAL PHOTO SHOOT

It's time to show the world our true beauty. I'm organizing a special photo shoot in Chicago for you, my internet sisters. You show bravery through your stories and pictures, and you've helped me to understand violence against women. Now I want to do something for you. Let me use my lens to bring your stories to life, in hopes that senseless attacks on women will stop.

The next day, women respond from all over. Many are thrilled by the idea that I, a Supermodel, care so much or that I am willing to help. Others seem more interested in just meeting me and coming to Chicago. I spend the rest of that month corresponding with the women who are not only humbled by the opportunity, but also willing to help out anyway they can. After AJ advises me on all the legal issues, and even helps me to draft a written agreement, dad and I discuss scheduling.

2005 seems to come overnight. Laylah is back and as usual my schedule is booked. I have no idea how I will keep up with the demands of modeling and organize the photo shoot, especially with Fashion Week coming up next month. I need more help than what my dad and I can do. AJ has accepted a position as a prosecutor, which means she has no time to breathe. Nigel seems to have one flight after another and Lona is working a lot of late shifts in the New Year. The only other person who I know in Chicago and can trust is Kevin. It has been some time since we last spoke, but I decide to take a chance and give him a call from my hotel in Milan.

"Kevin."

He answers the phone as if telling someone his name for the first time. The noise in the background makes it difficult to hear him.

"Hello is this Kevin Hawley?"

"Yes, it is. Is this who I think it is? Quiet everyone, I can't hear. Is this Lime Prince?"

"Yes, how did you know it was me?"

"Are you kidding me? I know that accent anywhere. Where are you? You sound so far away."

"I'm in Milan—"

"And you thought about me?"

"Matter of fact, I did. How are you? I hope I'm not interrupting."

"Oh, not at all. I'm at work, well, kind of."

"Isn't it like seven or eight at night there? Why are you working so late at the office?"

"I guess you didn't get the memo. I quit Boyd & Woods at the beginning of last year. They passed me over again for a senior accounting position, plus they were just a little too free with the F word."

"The F word? Fuck?"

"No, faggot. You know how chauvinistic and homophobic those guys were; at least they pretended to be. The jury is still out on half of them. So, I started a consulting business and now I've combined my two loves, accounting and theater. I do accounting work for small theater companies in Chicago and all over the Midwest, and I've even started doing some acting again. Just small roles, but I love it. Right now, they're rehearsing for a ten thirty show. But never mind that, what are you up to? I see your Clinique commercials all the time and I tell everyone that we used to work together, and how you sent me tickets to New Zealand last year."

"I see. I got your letter that you had a fantastic time."

"I had an orgasmic time and that had nothing to do with the guy I went with." He laughs.

"Well, I'm still modeling, but I'm also working on another project, which is why I called you."

I begin at the beginning with AJ's attack, how I began blogging, the women on the blog, and the photo shoot.

"Kevin, I need some help. I need someone who is organized and business minded to help me coordinate this effort, someone who is in Chicago. Someone I can trust; someone like you."

"What do you need me to do?"

He says as if he is ready to start right now. We spend the next thirty minutes talking about how he can help. Before the conversation is over, Kevin maps out the entire shoot from start to finish.

Fashion Week in New York is another huge success. Once again, I share the runway with Liya. Like everyone else, Liya has heard about all the controversy surrounding my blog. This time we are able to connect after the show. Liya pulls me away from a dull conversation between Laylah and a buyer for Barneys.

"You looked like you were having fun." Liya's sarcasm is a welcome relief. We find two seats at the end of the bar.

"How are you?" She squeezes both of my hands.

I take a deep breath. "Keeping busy and I'm not just talking about modeling."

"I've heard. I've even read some of your blog."

"Really?" I'm surprised and flattered.

"Yes, and I think what you are doing is very admirable."

"Well, thank you, Liya. That means a lot coming from you."

I tell her about the photo shoot and she seems excited. The more I explain the shoot the more interested she becomes.

"But I'm still working on the logistics with my dad and now a friend of mine who I hired to oversee the project with me."

"Only three of you?" She asks surprised. "Girl, you better use some of these connections you have. Why haven't you approached Clinique? They would be more than willing to help. It would be a perfect opportunity for them to take advantage of the free press and be involved in something charitable. You should think about it."

It makes perfect sense. I'm still the face of Clinique and they are by far the best company to ever work for. They've treated me like royalty from day one, and at our last meeting, they announced that since my involvement their sales have increased by sixty percent. My next call is to Clinique.

CHAPTER 44

Accentuate the Positive

Clinique executives are eager to meet with me. I kept stressing to them that this is an opportunity for Clinique to shine. After weeks of meetings and discussions, they agree to provide all makeup products in exchange for free advertisement on any and all press that surrounds the shoot. My idea is becoming a huge event with national implications for change. I leave Laylah a long voice message about the new developments and make sure I point out the financial benefits and national press not only for me, but for Clinique. I assure her that this will in no way hinder work. I'm ready to get started.

Although I have the makeup, I lack the artists. I call Dee-Dee. We haven't spoken or seen each other since my Perry Ellis shoot last fall.

"Hey, Dee-Dee."

"Hey, Lime. Girl, I've been meaning to call you ever since I heard about your blog. I know of too many women who are attacked physically because of their sexuality. You go, girl, and if there is anything I can do, let me know."

"Actually, there is."

"Okay."

"I'm photographing some of the women from the blog."

"You are? What for?"

"To try to bring some different national attention to violence against women. I want the world to see these women and what has been done to them."

"So where do I come in?"

"Clinique has agreed to supply all the makeup needs, but I still need makeup artists and hair stylists. Can you help with that?"

"Sure. When do you need me?"

"Sometime in the next couple of months. I will call you back soon. Thanks, Dee-Dee."

"No problem."

Spring is around the corner and Kevin has commitments from thirty-five women from as close as the north side of Chicago to as far away as the UK. Coordinating everyone's schedule proves to be a challenge, but Kevin makes it seem effortless. Because everyone has different commitments, we only have one month to complete the entire shoot. I have to go back and forth to Chicago, to meet with Kevin and my dad. We decide to begin the beginning of May.

Kevin arranges for each woman to be escorted from the airport to their hotel and to the photo shoot. The shoots are in the evening after business hours at the studio. Dad has everything set up and Kevin and Dee-Dee are cool as cucumbers; however, I'm a ball of nerves. The butterflies and I pace the studio every five minutes until Sandra arrives.

Kevin escorts her back to the studio. She is a slender woman with soft brown eyes that search the room for something recognizable. From where I'm standing in the corner of the room, her face looks normal, but as Kevin helps her to remove her jacket, she turns so he can remove it from her left arm and that's when I see what is left of an once defined jaw line, now hollow and sunken. The corner of the left side of her mouth appears sewn together to save what little is left. Dad and I make our way over to her.

"Sandra, this is Lime and Mr. Prince, her father." Kevin makes the introductions.

Sandra's mouth seems to ignore its closed position and smiles as wide as it can. Her brown eyes became wet.

"Hello, Mr. and Ms. Prince."

She places her hand over her mouth almost to apologize for how it looks.

I grab her hand away and squeeze it as I hug her.

"Thank you for coming, Sandra, and please call me Lime."

"And call me Malcolm," Dad says as he hugs her too.

Kevin also introduces Dee-Dee.

"Alright Sandra, you ready to rock-n-roll?"

Dee-Dee's energy changes the mood, as Sandra follows her to the changing room.

A half hour later, Sandra emerges with a new face and a stylish new hair style. Dee-Dee brought out all the natural hues that Sandra possesses. Her pinned up hair glistens under the lights. As Sandra sits on the black futon, with her eyes gazing upward and her neck, jaw, and face elongated toward the sky, dad snaps away. I watch over dad's shoulder, but after ten minutes something seems to be missing. Sandra is sitting there lifeless, just taking directions from my dad, Tiffany's photo shoot comes to mind. I remember how they placed their diamonds around my eyes to accentuate the dazzling colors of their diamonds. It hits me right then. I need to accentuate Sandra's jaw to bring out its beauty. I stop dad in the middle of shooting.

"Hold on a second, dad. Sandra, can you give us a minute?"

"Sure."

Kevin brings her some water while dad, Dee-Dee, and I talk.

"Something's missing. I want to try something that will really add a different twist to her scars."

I look around the room and notice a vase of four red roses, slightly limp, sitting in cloudy water on a desk.

"Can I use those roses?"

"Yeah, sure. Lona brings flowers into the studio from time to time to brighten it up, so this month she brought roses, but as you can see I'm terrible with keeping them alive."

I grab two of the roses and head toward Sandra. On the way, I notice a red, feather, boa-like scarf sticking out of Dee-Dee's coat. I pick it up and look at Dee-Dee. She gives me the nod of approval.

"Sandra, I want to try something different, if you don't mind."

"Like what?" She slurs.

"I want to accessorize."

After I remove the thorns, and cut down the stems a bit, I place both roses in Sandra's mouth between her teeth so that the stems crisscross each other and the roses make an X. Then, with Dee-Dee's help, we drape the red scarf around her neck. I take some of the petals from the other roses and throw them on her shoulders and in her hair. Dee-Dee adds a little bit more red blush and Sandra's face and jaw line have new life. Dad changes his film and begins snapping shot after shot. Sandra even begins doing some posing on her own. Kevin turns on some music and suddenly it's a photo shoot party.

For the next three weeks, we work as a creative team as the women arrive one by one and sometimes two by two. Dad and Dee-Dee with her staff know how to turn my visions into visual masterpieces. Where there are missing limbs, we replace them with beautiful orchids, more roses, tulips, and carnations in an array of colors. We adorn keloids, stab wounds, gunshot wounds, and burns with sparkling jewels, colorful sea shells, and shiny glitter. We clothe them with feathers, boas, Indian silk, iridescent fabrics, and love. Everything physically disfigured is altered with natural beauty.

There is only one more day before the photo shoot is over. I have to try AJ one more time, so I stop by her flat.

"AJ, we're almost done."

"Wow. How did it go?"

"Great. Emotional, but great. AJ, I don't want my dad to photograph you."

"Good, because I didn't want him to photograph me either."

"*I* want to photograph you."

"Why, Lime?" She sounds annoyed.

"Because it makes no sense not to." I give her a tearful smile.

"Don't give me that look."

I do it again and this time she melts.

AJ's shoot means more to me than the others, and I'm determined to handle her photo debut with extra care. We decide on elegant purple chiffon that covers one half of her unburned body and ties around her right hip. AJ stands tall as I adorn her body with the fabric exposing her burned neck, part of her breast, stomach, thigh, leg, and feet. She stands with her legs shoulder width apart, her face turned in the opposite direction of her burns, and both hands grasping her meaty hips. Her presence is Goliath which makes her burns, dusted with shimmering purple glitter, seem insignificant. I snap picture after picture, trying to freeze that moment in eternal time. AJ's boldness and presence give new meaning to Unpretty.

After AJ's shoot, I committed to another Erick Blak show in New York. As usual he requests me, minus another drastic change in my appearance. The theme this time is flesh tones. He left the colors for the accessories. Designs that match your skin tone might seem boring for any other show, but Erick makes it work. The show begins with dancers in natural colored body stockings. Their movements are fluid, and all the music selections throughout the evening are of natural sounds of waves hitting a shoreline, exotic birds, rainforests, marshes and swamps featuring frogs and crickets, and breezes with the sounds of children playing in the background. The finale scene is rainwear complete with realistic sounds of lightning bolts and thunderous rain. I feel privileged to be in a show that is so creatively done.

Since I am no longer blogging as much as before, I decide to stay for the after party this time, and I'm glad I do. It seems like every model, designer, and Hollywood superstar is in attendance. As Erick introduces me to his new model girlfriend who looks all of eighteen years old, I spot QT.

As usual, he is dressed in his signature green. He is sitting on a bar stool surrounded by two of the male models from the show. I excuse myself from Erick and his girlfriend, who are drooling all over each other, and walk over to QT. It has been a year since I've seen him, and something is different about him. His locs are down past his ears now, but he is thinner and his eyes and cheeks are sunken. Instead of his usual comical antics and loud greeting, he just waves the models away and with two fingers, summons me forward. We kiss on the cheek and find a place to sit.

"Ms. Lime, Ms. Lime. You still doing the damn thing and doing it well, I see."

"How are you, QT? It's been awhile." I rub his hand.

"Oh girl, me strong like bull. Been hearing about you, though." He lets out a couple of deep coughs.

"Yeah, what else is new? What have *you* heard?"

"Something about you leading the charge against violence against women and even taking a stance against the superficial world of modeling. Chile, I know you not about to bite the hand that feeds you."

"No, I'm not." I let out a deep sigh. "My best friend in life was attacked by an ex-boyfriend last year. He set her on fire." QT puts his hand over his heart and shakes his head in disbelief. "And through that experience I met other women, like her, who have also been attacked by some man, and I wanted to bring some national attention to their situation and try to prevent other woman from being attacked, that's all."

"Lord have mercy. The first time my baby sister's boyfriend hit her, I bit him." He clenches his teeth and growls. "So, I know what you mean."

"Yeah, I've been low key ever since."

"Me, too. After awhile all of these after parties are the same. I got models to train and performances to choreograph."

I want to ask QT about his health, but I don't want to pry, so I lie.

"Well, you look good." I grab his knee.

"No, I don't, but I'm alright, remember, strong like bull."

He tries to hold back more coughs with his dark green handkerchief, but they seem to burst out of his mouth. He grabs another drink off a tray held by a passing waiter. My phone rings in my purse. I look at the caller ID before I answer it. Instead of saying "International Call," it flashes "Asmeret." Since I haven't spoken to her in awhile, those same butterflies tell me it is about Grandmother Genet. I excuse myself from QT and head toward a quieter place on the terrace.

"Hello Asmeret." I try to remain calm.

"Hello, Lime. How are you?" Her words are low and deliberate.

"I'm fine. What's wrong?" Right not I'm not interested in pleasantries.

"Well, I'm not calling about Grandmother Genet."

I look up into the sky and close my eyes in gratitude.

"I'm calling about me." I hear her swallow. "The doctors want to perform a double mastectomy. They say it is the only—." She begins to cry.

"The only what?"

She regains her composure. "The only way to save my life."

I look up into the sky and close my eyes again. "Did you get a second opinion?"

"Yes, this is the third doctor."

"When do they want to perform the operation?"

"Right away. They're waiting on my permission."

I think about how fortunate she is to still be in a position to grant her permission.

"I just wanted to know what you thought about it."

I pause before I answer. She wants to know what *I* thought. Maybe this question would have been easier to answer if Asmeret and I were closer. I don't want her to die, but I'm not sure what she wants me to say. So, I just say the first thing that comes to my mind.

"I think you should do it."

I can't make it in time for the operation, but Nigel and I are there two days later. The walk and entrance to her hospital room is reminiscent of my days in the hospital with AJ. Aunt Miriam is in the room with her reading a book while Asmeret sleeps. Nigel waits in the waiting room. Aunt Miriam says the surgery went well and she is going to be fitted for prosthetic breasts soon. They were able to remove all the cancer. Aunt Miriam had been there since the early morning and wanted to run home and start dinner. She said Aunt Fenayte was coming by later. I promise to stay until she arrives.

I pull the chair closer to her hospital bed and sit down next to her. She isn't in as much distress as AJ. Her sleep is more peaceful, with fewer tubes and monitors and no oxygen mask; however, the flat white sheet that covers her chest only makes slight movements. Asmeret was never a busty woman, but aside from the bandages the sheet now lay perfectly flat. The awkward silence that surrounds us even now makes me uncomfortable. As I stand to pour myself some water from the pitcher on her tray, she opens her eyes and mumbles, "Lime," forces a half smile, and raises her hand for mine. I sit back down and hold her hand in mine until Aunt Fenayte arrives.

Nigel and I stay at my grandparent's home. I think Nigel has developed a slight crush on Asmeret and my aunts. He keeps telling me now he sees where I get my looks from. When he and I aren't at the hospital, we spend time at the café. When Asmeret is allowed to come home, the house is always full of relatives and family friends. One morning, Nigel agrees to help Uncle Tesfai with some painting, which leaves Asmeret and I all alone. As we eat our omelets and drink our tea, I tell her about my blog, the women, and the photo session. She is touched by their stories and by what

I have done for them. She shares with me that her ex-boyfriend in Spain was verbally abusive to her and in some countries abusing women is the norm, even in parts of Ethiopia. She seems to be in good spirits since the operation, but before the awkward silence joins our breakfast, I get an idea.

"Would you allow me to photograph you?" She looks perplexed. "I know you haven't been attacked by someone, but your body was attacked by cancer."

"What type of photo do you want to take?"

"I want to photograph you in a way that shows your decision to fight cancer. Not your face, your beauty in light of surgery."

"Oh, I don't know, Lime. I still have these compression bandages and drains and I have to get used to these plastic things first."

"No, I want to photograph natural beauty, not your prosthesis."

Her brow tells me that she's really confused.

"Let me show you what I mean."

She is in no position to go to a studio so I get creative with the space in my grandparent's home. When we are done eating, I call a local florist. I want flowers lots of flowers. Since I always travel with my own camera, I just have to make the light in the house and the natural light coming in from the windows work. I can tell she is still resistant, but she follows along. As I arrange the Ethiopian violets over the space that once occupied supple breasts, she looks away. The surgical scars are long but neat. As I touch her body, for the first time, I feel a closeness to her that I've never known before. I photograph her from the neck down with flowers replacing breasts and her hands cupping them. She is regal and the perfect model. When we are done, for the very first time in my life, we spend the rest of the evening, just being mum and daughter.

CHAPTER 45

Surprise

As soon as I arrive back in New York, I get busy organizing the photo exhibit. My dream is to have the exhibit travel across the country in every major city and rural town, giving women of violence center stage. What I don't have is a proper name for it. I consider Unpretty in honor of the blog that brought us all together, but after photographing all those amazing women, that name no longer fits. I need a name that defines the exhibit and gives it life. I think about New York and Faces, and how they made my modeling career come true, but this exhibit is about more than women's faces. It is about the woman on the inside that society refuses to see. That's it. I'll call the exhibit *Faceless*. I notify each woman in the show and they love the new name.

With the assistance of organizations, charitable donations, and even donations from fellow models like Tyra, Alek, Liya, Heidi, Gisele, and many others who commend my efforts, *Faceless* is getting bigger than I could have imagined. The show debuts on my twenty-seventh birthday, June 20, 2005, in New York at The Guggenheim Museum. I wanted a historic and prominent venue for a historic and prominent event. The crowd is so large that the line to get in curves around the block. The press camped out for two days to make sure they gained early access. Anyone who is anyone in the business is in attendance, and they are writing checks and making pledges left and right so that *Faceless* can achieve its goal. The guest list inside resembles the crowds at a runway show. I make sure that all thirty-five women who want to attend are there with their families, as well as AJ, Asmeret, dad, Lona, Nigel, his mum and sister, and Kevin.

The room inside is spacious and bright. Upon entrance, AJ's photo greets the visitors at the door. Each photo has a gold frame quote beside it from the woman in the photo. Their words describe their struggles, anger, joy, determination, and strength. AJ's quote, "I will dedicate my life prosecuting men who put their hands on us without *our* permission," sets the stage for the entire exhibit. Despite the size of the crowd, the mood inside on everyone's face is reflective and somber. People walk around in a daze, stopping at each photo to study it at length. As Lauryn Hill's raspy and earthy vocals sing *I Find it Hard to Say (Rebel)* float throughout the loud speakers, grown men are moved to tears. At the end of the evening, I say a few words to the visitors.

"First, I want to thank God and each of you for supporting this exhibit. We always hear about how things need to change. How violence against women needs to stop, but we never see the victims up close and personal. They are our mums, sisters, aunts, cousins, best friends, and it could be you. These courageous women want you to do more than look at their scars, but help to bring more awareness to their attacks. Help to protect them and other women and always remember that beauty means so much more than what the eye can see or what a photo can capture. I promise to make *Faceless* one of my life's missions—"

As I conclude my remarks, I notice a man in the crowd abruptly making his way toward the front of the audience. No one pays him any attention until they had to move out of his way for him to pass by. When he breaks through the crowd to the front, Pepper stands in my direct view. He's holding some envelopes similar to the one he sent me over a year ago. He stands there glaring at me, tapping the envelopes in the palm of his hand. I stop in the middle of my remarks and grab my stomach with my left hand and grip the podium with my right. I feel lightheaded. As the cameras flash, beads of sweat drip down my armpits and back. As the audience waits, I cough and begin again.

"So, remember what you've seen here. Thank you."

I had planned to say more, but Pepper's unannounced visit steals my thoughts.

Pepper looks around the room and walks towards the press. I follow him with my eyes while doing my best to not raise any more suspicions. Just as I finish posing for a few pictures, he spots Nigel, whispers something in his ear and hands him one of the envelopes. Nigel puts it in his suit pocket, gives Pepper a dap handshake, and meets me at the podium with some more yellow roses, but this time he presents them on bended knee. In his other hand, he holds out a red velvet box with a three-carat white diamond positioned inside.

"Lime, would you be the missing piece in my life for the rest of my life?" His voice is shaking.

The audience goes wild and the camera's flashes are blinding. I do my best to act elated in front of Nigel and the awaiting crowd, but all I can think about is reaching into Nigel's pocket, grabbing the envelope, and running like bloody hell.

"Yes."

I hug him close until I can feel the envelope inside his breast pocket. My dad and AJ approach us first and then Nigel's family. I keep searching the crowd for Pepper.

I lie and tell everyone I have to use the loo and will be right back. As I exit the stage, I do a frantic search for Pepper. I spot his bald head by the elevator. I pick up my pace bumping a few innocent bystanders along the way. I almost start running toward him when I see the small group inching toward the opening of the doors. Just then an older black woman in colorful African garments appears out of nowhere. Her eyes are glazed over and her movements are methodical. Without saying a single word, she pushes a copy of a magazine at me. Her timing for an autograph couldn't have been worse.

"I'm sorry, ma'am, but I need to get to someone before he—"

She flips it over to reveal the cover and backs away, never taking her eyes off me. It is a copy of *Newsweek* magazine, and on the cover is a frail looking African woman. As I look closer, I see the most horrific sight. The woman's lips are missing. The caption underneath makes my heart stop: *Tribal rebel and militia groups in the Republic of the Congo near the Rwandan border are finding more ways to mutilate women.* I look up but the mysterious woman disappeared just as quickly as she had appeared. The ding of the elevator doors closing snaps me back into panic mode.

I roll the magazine and grip it in my right hand as I dart for the nearest stairwell. It is four flights down to the main entrance. My adrenaline and I race down those stairs until the final stairwell, when we jump. With one hard swing of the door, I stand in the main entrance with my heart beating out of my chest. *Where is he?* I say through clenched teeth. Despite the number of people milling around, my eyes are in radar mode and I spot him getting into a cab on 5th Ave. I sprint, but the cab pulls off at the exact moment that I arrive.

"Wait…wait damnit."

I scream in the cab's direction. When it doesn't stop, I strike the tail end with the rolled up magazine as the exhaust fumes from the engine fill the street. Pepper never moves. His bald head never moves.

I stand there in the cab's empty space gasping for breath waiting for instructions on what to do next. No answer comes so tears haze my view.

The horn from the car behind forces me to turn around right into Nigel. The pained look on his face is more than I can take. I drop my head and bury it in the center of his chest. With Pepper's appearance tonight, my sordid past in the hands of my fiancé and the press, and the reality of African women being butchered at the hands of men, I know wedding plans will have to wait.

EPILOGUE

Six Months Later

The videotape was the most viewed sex tape on the internet since Paris Hilton and her then boyfriend Rick Salomon. Pepper enjoyed his "fifteen minutes" of fame doing no-name radio interviews and giving salacious sound bites to tabloid magazines. When his fifteen minutes were up, he was back to playing his drums in hole in the wall clubs.

Rohan faded into obscurity somewhere in the Netherlands after sending me an email a couple weeks after the tape was released. He told me that he tried to talk to Pepper about destroying the original tape and to back off so they could focus on making music and finally getting a record deal. According to Rohan, they argued a bit but Pepper called him a few days later and agreed to destroy it and to leave me alone. After the release of the tape, the press found Rohan and staked out his home, job, and even his family in Jamaica. He ended his email with another "saari," packed up his trumpet, and left the country.

Clinique cancelled my contract and Laylah almost followed suit, but not before she hired a top PR firm to put a different spin on the tape and me. Laylah didn't want to let me go until she exhausted all possible ways to capitalize on the scandal, because of course, Paris Hilton got her own reality show. She's still working on that.

The good news is that AJ and Scott started dating not too long after the exhibit. He has promised to never hurt her or to let her out of his sight.

As for my sweet Nigel, I don't know how much of the tape he watched or if he watched it at all, but everywhere he turned it was the topic of discussion. Then Hurricane Katrina came and flooded his childhood city and uprooted his family. He did his best to explain to me that he needed some time to think. That was four months ago. I guess he's still thinking. I too needed time to think and what better way than—

"Ladies and gentleman please return to your seats as the pilots have turned on the 'fasten your seatbelt' sign as we prepare for our descent into Kinshasa's N'djili Airport."

On a twenty hour flight to Democratic Republic of Congo.

If you are experiencing any of the following forms of abuse:

- **Physical**: hitting, punching, kicking, slapping, strangling, smothering, using or threatening to use weapons, shoving, interrupting your sleep, throwing things, destroying property, hurting or killing pets, and denying medical treatment.

- **Sexual**: physically forcing sex, making you feel fearful about saying no to sex, forcing sex with other partners, forcing you to participate in demeaning or degrading sexual acts, violence or name calling during sex, and denying contraception or protection from sexually transmitted diseases.

- **Emotional**: constant put downs or criticisms, name calling, "crazy making", acting superior, minimizing the abuse or blaming you for their behavior, threatening and making you feel fearful, isolating you from family and friends, excessive jealously, accusing you of having affairs, and watching where you go and who you talk to.

- **Financial**: giving you an allowance, not letting you have your own money, hiding family assets, running up debt, interfering with your job, and ruining your credit.

–www.nnedv.org

Please call National Domestic Violence Hotline
1-800-799-7233 (SAFE)
24/7

CPSIA information can be obtained at www.ICGtesting.com
Printed in the USA
LVOW11s2147201015

459108LV00001B/118/P